Hello Readers (both current and, hopefully, future!)

Austin Macauley Publishers are busy getting Judith Logan's third mystery novel ready for publishing. The trilogy follows the lives of Lloyd and Lacey, from the time the young siblings are sent to foster care, until and including their lives as adults. Judith advises that these books almost wrote themselves; she has swept away in a flood of emotion, empathy and love for her characters as their life stories rapidly unravelled.

Judith is currently working on another mystery novel, *The Regression of Molly Mclean*. The characters are unrelated to the previous books.

This third novel is dedicated to my husband, Bruce, who has proved yet again his love, patience, understanding and acceptance! I never planned on writing four books in such a short time – it just happened, and he never bats an eye when I continue to become engrossed in my writing!

I also dedicate this book to my adult children, Lori Bembridge and Ryan McLaughlin. Without their encouragement, there would never have been either a trilogy or a memoir.

Last, but definitely not least, I dedicate this book to all my family and friends who bought and read my stories and commented so favourably on each and every one. Bless all of you!

Judith Logan

SAFE IN THE ARMS OF LOVE?

Book III

AUSTIN MACAULEY PUBLISHERS

LONDON * CAMBRIDGE * NEW YORK * SHARJAH

A CIP catalogue record for this title is available from the British Library.

ISBN 9781398448049 (Paperback)
ISBN 9781398448056 (Hardback)
ISBN 9781398448063 (ePub e-book)

www.austinmacauley.com

First Published 2022
Austin Macauley Publishers Ltd®
1 Canada Square
Canary Wharf
London
E14 5AA

I wish to acknowledge any and all staff of Austin Macauley Publishers who may have worked on all three of my Lloyd and Lacey Trilogy. I would like to thank Adam Lake, publishing coordinator. He demonstrated endless patience and unwavering assistance for all my numerous questions. Thank you.

Table of Contents

Synopsis

Safe in the Arms of Love? is Book #3 in the stories of Lloyd and Lacey.

In Book #1, *Not Another Word!* Lacey and Lloyd Jordan are suddenly left on their own at the ages of 9 and 14. Their father is in prison for embezzlement; their mother deserts them. At three different times, three of their foster sisters disappear. Eventually, Lacey takes it upon herself to leave and try to find not only her missing foster sisters but her parents as well.

The story deals with two children coping as best they can in foster home after foster home.

In Book #2, *Shadows of the Missing* (Whatever Happened to Lloyd?) on a sudden impulse, with no plan and no idea of where to begin searching, Lloyd Jordan runs away from his fifth foster home in search of his three missing foster sisters and his parents.

This book tells the story of an impulsive young man overcoming adversity as he matures.

Book #3, *Safe in the Arms of Love?* tells the stories of Lloyd, Lacey and those who love them as they struggle to adjust, forgive and forget.

Hopefully you, dear readers, will find some surprises along the way, as you did when you read the first two books of this trilogy!

DISCLAIMER:

Safe in the Arms of Love? is a work of fiction. All of the characters, organisations, places and events portrayed in this novel are either products of the author's imagination or are used completely fictitiously.

NOTE TO READERS:

This story takes place in British Columbia and Alberta, Canada. Accordingly, Canadian spellings and units of measurement have been used.

List of Characters

(Alphabetical, in no particular order of appearance)
BELCOURT, Bernard ('Brutus')
BRONSON, Evelyn
CRYSTAL, Walter – Crown Prosecutor
DRAPER, Adam
FORD, Charlotte (aka Charley)
FORD, Mona Grace
GABLEHAUS, Fred
GABLEHAUS, Greg and Bethany
GRAY, Billy
GRESNER, Henry and Cora
HILL, Tony Thomas ('The Whistling Man', aka 'The Whistle Man')
JORDAN, Lloyd and Susanna
JORDAN, A.M.
JORDAN, Paul Martin
LABOUCAN, Lester and LABOUCAN, Emily
McGUIRE, Mickey ('The Drunk Bulbous Nosed Man')
McMASTER, Julie
SANCHEZ, Domingo
SANCHEZ, Jose
SANTONIO, Paulo – counsel for Brutus and for gang members of 'East Van Devils' and THE WARLORDS
SANTOS, Bill-Don
SILVERMAN, Jayson
SOMERS, Hilda
SUTTON, Lacey and Parker
TANNER, Justice G.P.
TURNER, Earl ('The Groper', aka 'The Grope')

WHITLEY, Dr – Surgeon on Call
WIDDIFIELD, Warren ('Bed #9 Man')
WILLIAMS, Justice J.M.
WILSON, Constable Curtis

Prologue

Book #2, *Shadows of the Missing (Whatever Happened to Lloyd?)* ended this way:

"Well, Lacey," Lloyd said, "now that we know the truth, we don't need to dream bad dreams any more. I think our mum would be the first to tell us that we have done pretty well, considering all the events in our lives."

"Agreed," Lacey said. She reached into a bag she had placed on the floor of the canoe and lifted out two beautiful yellow roses. Handing one to Lloyd, she said, "These are in memory of our beloved mama. Let's drop them into the water to honour her and to banish our dreams. It is time to get on with our lives."

Lloyd picked up his rose, dropped it gently into the water. Lacey did the same. "Rest in Peace, Mama," she said.

"Yes, Mum," Lloyd said. "Rest in Peace."

The shadows of the missing were no more. All of the friends and relatives had years of catching up to do. 'Now that everyone was reunited, each was safe in the arms of love!'

…OR WERE THEY?…

Book #3, *Safe in the Arms of Love?* is finished.

I now invite you to be a silent phantom on the wall of adventure. Please, join me as we follow yet again the lives of Braden Lloyd Jordan (known as Lloyd) and Lacey Colleen Jordan-Sutton.

Enjoy the ride!

Chapter 1
The Return of the Trumpeter Swans

Although Uncle Henry kept Lloyd busy learning the fine craft of furniture building, there was still plenty of time for Lloyd, Susanna, Lacey, and Parker (when he was not on duty) to spend time at the lake that they fondly remembered naming MOUNTAIN GOAT LAKE.

When Lloyd and Susanna first moved back to the beautiful log home that Uncle Henry had lovingly built himself, it was too early in the spring for the Trumpeter swans to have returned from their southern winter climes. As luck would have it, on the day they returned, Lloyd and Susanna, Uncle Henry and Cora, Lacey and Parker were all at the lake, enjoying an unusually warm and sunny afternoon.

"Look!" Lacey pointed. "Seven! Their number has grown to seven magnificent swans!"

Everyone stood in awe. The group never tired of watching the beautiful birds glide tranquilly on the mirror-like surface of the crystal clear, spring-fed lake. They never failed to offer a prayer of thanks for the safe return of the Trumpeters to the lake every year. To see the numbers grow from two to seven was truly a wonderful sight. Only one pair would nest in the reeds at Mountain Goat Lake; the others would leave in search of their own summer homes. It wouldn't be long before their preparations would be completed and they would be sitting on their nests, patiently awaiting their new offspring to hatch.

Cora said, "I think that the arrival of the swans while we are all together is a sign that we are in for much better times." Susanna and Lacey agreed. The men just rolled their eyes.

. . . .

While Lloyd threw himself wholeheartedly into his new occupational training, Susanna spent her time learning the computer-side of the handcrafted furniture business. With her newly acquired Bachelor of Commerce (Marketing Major) Degree, she and her father had agreed that she would take over the books and the marketing aspects of the expanding business venture.

Many hours were spent trying to come up with a catchy name. Suggestions ranged from 'The Furniture Guy', to 'The Trumpeters' Timeless Handcrafted Furniture', to 'From Forest to Home'.

Uncle Henry favoured 'The Furniture Guy'. "Too plain, too boring, too general," said the women.

Lloyd's favourite was 'The Trumpeters' Timeless Handcrafted Furniture'. Susanna thought (rightly) that it was too long for people to remember.

Lacey, Susanna and Cora were in favour of 'From Forest to Home'. More and more, people were being steadily drawn towards the need for environmental protection. The women all agreed that the name suggested that the magnificence of the trees would transform into the comfort and timeless beauty of the finished furniture. Recycling in a perfect way. Lasting pieces of usable art, to pass down from generation to generation.

Eventually, after hours and days of discussion, it was unanimously agreed that the business would be registered as 'TRUMPETERS' HANDCRAFTED FURNITURE' Directly below the registered name, a logo, carved inside the likeness of a Trumpeter Swan, would read: 'From Forest to Home'.

Uncle Henry took it upon himself to make an appointment with his lawyer to set up the company and register it with Corporate Registry.

To celebrate their unanimity, everyone gathered at Mountain Goat Lake for a celebratory wiener roast and canoe ride.

Lacey and Parker suggested that choosing a name was not their business, that the celebration should not include them. They were told in no uncertain terms that 'family was family' in all aspects of life; that they were not to bring the subject up again. Their suggestions were welcome in any and all things. Lacey grinned from ear to ear for the balance of the evening.

Despite their busy lives, Lloyd and his sister made a pact to meet at least once a month at the lake, just the two of them. So much had happened in the several preceding years, they agreed that all of the happenings could not be digested and dealt with in a very short time. They both concurred that, as much as their friends and family wanted to help, their experiences were such that only

Lloyd and Lacey could truly understand just how deeply they had been affected by all of the stressful events.

Whenever the pressures of the past threatened to overwhelm him, Lloyd would head for the lake, where he could reminisce undisturbed. As he watched the nesting Trumpeters, he would feel his equilibrium return, balancing the present with the past until he could begin to move forward once again.

When Lacey was threatened by ugly memories of her abusive foster homes, or by the extreme sadness that she felt because of Annie's death, she headed for the Mailbox, that secret place discovered by Lloyd while they were wards of the Child Welfare branch of the legal system.

Sometimes she would take Hilda with her; sometimes she went alone. Although she watched carefully each and every time, she never again saw the magnificent bull elk that both she and Hilda were convinced had contained the spirit of Stumpy as he lay dying.

Lacey would stretch out on her stomach on the large, flat rock that protruded over the edge of a ravine. She would cautiously peer over the edge, listening to the reassuring sounds of the babbling creek at the bottom.

Despite some sad memories, associated with long waits between mail, she was still able to find some peace in this secret place.

Chapter 2
Repercussions of Foster Care

Abandoned by their mother, coupled with what the children perceived as a major betrayal by their father, Lloyd and Lacey were placed in a number of foster homes. At the tender ages of 14 and nearly 10, every single time it appeared that they might become complacent, their eyes were rudely jerked open.

The shortage of caregivers, together with the increasing number of children in need of foster care, accelerated the search to increase the number of foster care providers. Sadly, this was often to the detriment of many, many foster children. Intensive screening of potential foster parents suffered because of the desperate need for foster homes. Cursory interviews with prospective foster parents became common. Follow-up visits by over-extended Child Care workers were spaced further and further apart.

With the exception of a couple of placements, the Jordan siblings, along with their foster brothers and sisters, suffered many forms of abuse. This abuse ranged from sexual, physical, and mental, to confinement, withholding necessaries, and child labour.

Some foster children, who survived inappropriate actions by foster parents, grew up with severe psychological and behavioural problems, often requiring years of therapy. Some of these children turned to gangs, mistakenly believing that the gang would offer protection against further abuse.

Running away from an abusive home was common. Sad to say, running away was not an effective answer. Too many runaways slipped through cracks in the system. Instead of finding love and acceptance, they learned to be tough, outwardly uncaring individuals, often bullying those whom they perceived to be even weaker than they were. Whatever compassion and love they might have once felt was buried under a thick and foggy layer of lack of self-esteem.

Children in the care of an abusive foster parent were often made to believe that there was no point in pursuing a better life, because they were not worth loving or receiving help of any sort. They were told, time and time again, that nobody wanted them, that they were so terrible that nobody could possibly love them.

Unfortunately, it has been this way for a very long time and will probably continue for an equally long period of time.

It breaks my heart.

Chapter 3
The Further Education of Lloyd

Time passed swiftly. In late spring, Lloyd travelled to the City of Edmonton for his first six-week round of classes geared towards completing his carpentry skills. He studied harder than at any previous time in his life.

Although he missed Susanna terribly, he didn't go home at all during the weeks he was in school. It was expensive. Uncle Henry paid the entire costs, including motel charges. Although Lloyd protested that he could pay his own way, Uncle Henry wouldn't hear of it. Consequently, Lloyd didn't want to disappoint him. It provided even more incentive for him to study and learn. When his classes were over and exams written, Lloyd had earned the highest marks in every one of his classes.

At the end of the six weeks, a very proud Susanna was waiting at the airport to pick him up.

During the hour and a half drive home, Lloyd enjoyed listening to her incessant chatter; it meant he didn't have to talk much. Talking was definitely not one of his finer skills. Neither was listening. Fortunately for him, Susanna didn't ask him any questions that were not rhetorical!

As if reading her husband's mind, Susanna pulled off the highway and turned onto the road leading to Mountain Goat Lake. She parked on the gravel, close to the water's edge and turned towards Lloyd. He was sound asleep!

She quietly exited the vehicle. By the time Lloyd opened his eyes, she had set a picnic lunch out on the old wooden picnic table that wobbled slightly on the rocky beach. A bottle of white grape juice chilled in a cooler filled with ice. Taped to the cooler was a 'Welcome Home' card. A bouquet of flowers completed Susanna's ministrations.

Yawning widely, Lloyd climbed out, walked over to his wife and put both arms around her. "I've missed you, Susanna," he mumbled into her hair. He breathed in deeply, enjoying the softness. Her hair smelled like coconut. "I don't tell you enough how much I love you, how much you mean to me." He squeezed her tightly. He was uncomfortable with overt displays of emotion. It always caused a curious lump to form at the back of his throat. It was something he was working towards changing.

"Hmm," Susanna purred. "Maybe you should go away more often?" Laughing, she grabbed him by the hand. "Let's eat. I'm starving!"

When lunch was over and the site was tidied up, she said, "Come on, let's go for a canoe ride!"

"Nah, better not, Suz," he said, "I've been away for six whole weeks. I should get some work done."

"Dad and Cora are still in Arizona. He said to tell you to take it easy and stay out of the shop today. The workshop will still be there tomorrow. He also said to tell you he is looking forward to hearing all about your classes."

"Okay, but let's be quiet so we don't disturb the swans. I wonder if they have completed their clutch yet. Have you checked the nest, at all?"

Susanna said, "I'm pretty sure they are done their egg laying. I counted three eggs in the nest the other day. If that's the last of them, in about six weeks, we should have cygnets paddling around the lake. That is always my favourite time of the year, when the eggs have hatched."

"Mine too," Lloyd said. He held the canoe steady as Susanna climbed in. Once she was securely seated, he pushed off from the shore and climbed in himself.

With a single push of his oar, Lloyd felt his rigid shoulder muscles endeavouring to release, to fall into an easy rhythm as Lloyd paddled. The knots in his stomach cramped painfully as they strained to loosen. He hadn't realised how stressful the past six weeks had been until the minute he began to paddle the canoe. In fact, he didn't realise that ever since he and Lacey were left on their own, his entire body's muscles, tendons, and nerves, believed that 'normal' for them was to be strung as taut as a tightrope, aching as painfully as if they carried the entire weight of a circus tightrope walker, balanced on a rope high under the dome of the Big Top. Often his jaw remained so stiff that his cheeks became numb. Only then would Lloyd become aware of the pain in his face. He would loosen his jaw and move it around until he could once again feel his cheeks, rubbing them briskly until the pain in his face would ease.

Stopping a respectful distance away, Lloyd and Susanna sat quietly watching the pen (female) sitting on her nest. The cob (male) was not far away. He would soon relieve his mate, take his turn sitting on the eggs.

After several minutes, Susanna said softly, "Let's paddle to the island, Lloyd. The sun is so lovely and warm today. I think we should sit on the beach and you can fill me in on 'The Big Smoke'."

Lloyd looked puzzled. Laughing, Susanna asked him, "You haven't heard Edmonton referred to by that name before?"

"Well, if I have, I've forgotten," he replied. "Anyway, sure, let's go to the island. We should have brought that bottle of white grape juice with us."

Susanna tapped Lloyd on his shoulder. He half turned. She clutched a half-full bottle in her hand. Lloyd chuckled. "Should have known. You're not just another hat rack, wife; you are always a jump ahead of me." Their carefree laughter drifted behind canoe, causing the swans to ruffle their feathers contentedly.

Reaching the ancient wooden jetty on the backside of the small island, he grabbed the edge. Once Susanna was out and steadying the craft, Lloyd got out and dragged the canoe up on to the shore. Staring ruefully at the dilapidated jetty he thought, not for the first time, that he really needed to rebuild the rotting structure before it completely disintegrated.

He stood in the peaceful quiet on the island's shore, eyes closed, breathing deeply. When he finally turned and stepped away from the canoe, he stared at Susanna, his mouth wide open! His wife, his beautiful, extroverted wife of only a few months stood completely starkers on the beach. She had spread a blanket on the ground and now was giggling uncontrollably at the sight of her husband's face. Wildly, Lloyd glanced around. Still giggling, Susanna said, "Lloyd, we are on the backside of the island, completely out of sight of any human being. We may be in full view of the birds and the bees, maybe even the deer and any other of God's creatures that may inhabit this quiet little island, but they sure won't care what we are doing." She finally managed to stop laughing and stood in silence, waiting for Lloyd to approach. Handing him his glass of juice, she whispered, "Welcome home, my love, welcome home."

Two hours later, Lloyd awoke. Susanna was still naked, snuggled up next to him, snoring softly. Watching his wife lying there, so completely relaxed and totally unconcerned about anything, he thought to himself that he should learn to be more spontaneous, less concerned about everyone else's perception of him.

He knew that wasn't in his nature. He did admit to himself, though, that this afternoon had been a ton of fun!

He grabbed his clothes from the edge of the blanket and hastily dressed. He turned around to find Susanna's sleepy eyes watching him. He knelt down beside her. "Time to go home, Suz," he said. "You make a great welcoming committee!" Leaning over, he gently kissed her lips before jumping off the blanket, scattering sand everywhere and shouting, "Last one to the canoe has to swim home!" Knowing full well it was too cold to swim in the chilly lake, Susanna nevertheless got up and dressed while Lloyd folded the blanket and placed it in the canoe beside the empty juice bottle and plastic glasses.

Later that night, Lloyd lay in their bed. He was wide awake as he waited for his wife to finish her lengthy, mysterious female rituals as she got ready for bed. He had previously claimed that she had 106 items on her bathroom vanity.

At last, Susanna crawled into bed beside him. "Well, Mr Jordan, I believe you found out today that you are being educated in more ways than one." She smiled as she kissed him goodnight. "Happy to see you home again, Lloyd. I missed you something awful." Patting him on the leg, she rolled over and fell instantly to sleep.

. . . .

Although deeply immersed in learning the exacting woodworking skills that Uncle Henry was painstakingly teaching him, Lloyd's mind was never far from the impending trials of Domingo, Brutus, and Paul. As the dates for trial drew nearer, Lloyd called Sergeant Gablehaus in East Vancouver. The sergeant was happy to hear from Lloyd, to find out how things were going. He was delighted Lloyd was loving the trade he had chosen, or, as Lloyd put it, "The trade that has chosen me."

Because of the number of charges against each of the accused, the trials were expected to be lengthy. Three full days had been reserved for each of the accused, each trial within days of the previous trial. As a witness, this would save travel time and expenses for Lloyd. He would stay in Vancouver rather than travelling from Alberta to Vancouver on three separate occasions. An uncomfortable flyer, Lloyd was happy not to be winging back and forth more than once.

Sergeant Greg Gablehaus suggested to Lloyd that perhaps Mona Grace would rent her spare bedroom to him for the week or 10 days that he was likely to be in East Van.

"That sounds like a great idea," Lloyd said. "I'll give her a call."

They chatted for a few more minutes. Just before disconnecting, the sergeant asked Lloyd to come to the detachment the afternoon before the first trial, so that they could once again review the statements and Lloyd could be briefed regarding trial procedures.

"Sounds fine," Lloyd said. "I'll see you then."

Checking his watch, Lloyd dialled Mona Grace's office number. An automated voice message advised that she was with a client. He left his name and number. It was only a few minutes before his phone rang.

"Hey, Lloyd! How's it going? It's really good to hear from you."

"It's going great, Mona Grace. I love learning the carpentry business from Uncle Henry, and my first six weeks of school went very well."

"So happy to hear that, Lloyd, although I really miss you as a roommate. How's that beautiful new wife?"

"She's great, Mona Grace; she sends her love."

He changed the topic. "How are things going between you and Charley? I imagine you two are spending a lot of time together. After all, you have years of catching up to do."

There was an awkward silence on the line before she responded. "Oh, things are going pretty well, I think, Lloyd, considering there is a lot of water yet to pass under the bridge. I would say things are going okay."

Lloyd asked her what Charley was doing now.

"She got a job in the office at UBC. Just as a file clerk for now, but when an opening comes up for something else in the office, she can apply. She's living with a couple other girls in an apartment close to the university. She's really busy learning her new job. She wants to prove to her employers, and to herself, that she will become excellent at what she is doing. Oh, yes, and she has a part-time job at Starbucks three nights a week. She is trying to save money, because she, of course, never earned anything while she was held captive, and she was a high-school student when she ran away. She has never really had a chance to earn anything for herself."

"I can certainly understand that, Mona Grace," Lloyd commented. Although he detected from her tone of voice that perhaps things weren't all that rosy, he didn't let on.

Once again, he smoothly changed the topic. "Actually, Mona Grace, I'm wondering if there is any way I can rent your spare room? Just for 10 days. Just while the trials are on," he hastened to add.

This time, there was an even more awkward, even longer silence. Finally, just when Lloyd was getting really uncomfortable, she said, "Of course, you can stay with me. You don't have to pay me anything either. Just come. I'll be happy for the company."

Lloyd told her that would be great, but he would only stay there if she would accept some payment. He told her that he would be reimbursed for expenses incurred by him as a witness. Hearing that, she told him that she would charge him whatever amount the government paid for private accommodations. That settled, she told him to let her know when he would be arriving so she could pick him up at the airport.

After chatting for a few minutes more, Mona Grace apologised for having to run, but she had a client.

Later, in the living room of her little house, Mona Grace sat in her favourite chair, contemplatively staring into space. Some time passed. The sky outside faded from dusk and then to darkness. Lit by the streetlight, eerie shadows flickered in through the open drapes and onto Mona Grace's sombre face. Suddenly realising how dark it had become, she sat straight up and mentally gave herself a shake before going into the kitchen to turn on the light and prepare herself something for supper.

. . . .

When Lloyd and Susanna moved back to Alberta, Uncle Henry had presented Lloyd with a gift, a wood-burning set, which consisted of an adjustable soldering iron pen, 15 wood-burning tips, 16 soldering tips, 2 stencils, a converter, a stand, and a carrying bag. Uncle Henry had called it a 'pyrography kit'. He told Lloyd that he would find it extremely useful as a design aid in the custom furniture-building business. He told him that a lot of their customers wanted something personal carved into the furniture so that, years later, it could be identified as a family heirloom.

Never one to sit idle for long, Lloyd had set up a small table on the front veranda of the house. A fairly thick piece of lumber had been cut into a square slightly smaller than the tabletop. Lloyd had carefully drawn and then traced on the lumber, several different sketched outlines of a Trumpeter swan that he wanted to choose from, to use as a logo under the name of the business. His plan was to burn the different sketches and then have the rest of the family help him choose the perfect symbol.

Since receiving the gift, Lloyd had spent quite a bit of time on his project. He found it a most relaxing way to unwind at the end of the day. Often Susanna would curl up in one of the comfortable veranda chairs and read, while Lloyd was busy with his new tools.

After his perplexing phone conversation with Mona Grace, Lloyd sat at the small table. He was unable to figure out just what the problem was with his former landlady and friend.

Charley, now? Lloyd completely understood that Charley was bound to have some emotional problems. She had more on her plate than any young woman her age should have. He just hoped she would be willing to seek help rather than try to fight her emotional battle scars all alone. Perhaps he might find some time to have a visit with her while he was in British Columbia. Maybe Mona Grace would invite her to come for supper, and they could somehow come up with a way to help one another.

He picked up his wood-burning pen, exchanged the tip he had chosen for a slightly larger one and then continued outlining a Trumpeter swan.

. . . .

It was roughly a two-hour drive from the log house to the Fort St John, British Columbia airport. Uncle Henry and Susanna got up early and drove Lloyd to catch his plane.

The Arrivals and Departures board in the terminal indicated that the flight to Vancouver was on time.

"No sense you hanging around," Lloyd said to Uncle Henry and Susanna. "The plane's on time. I'll just go straight through Security and by that time, they'll be boarding. I'll keep in touch and let you know what's going on. As soon as I know when they are through with my testimony in each of the trials, I should be able to tell you when I'll be coming home."

"Thanks for the ride, Uncle Henry." Lloyd shook his hand before turning to Susanna.

She launched herself at Lloyd, nearly knocking him flat on his butt, caring not a whit about the people milling around her. Kissing him soundly and loudly on the mouth, she said in a very resounding voice, "You behave in that rotten big city, husband, you hear me?"

Extremely conscious of the snickers and grins surrounding them, Lloyd turned beet red and murmured softly, "I will, wife, I will. Now, I've got to go." He gave her a chaste little peck on her cheek before escaping into the anonymity of the Security waiting area.

He did turn, just before he went through the scanner and waved briefly. He found a spot to sit, feeling grateful that he didn't know anyone waiting to board the same plane.

As he waited, he thought to himself that he definitely had a lot more to learn about human behaviour and not caring about appearances in public! He would sure have to work hard to change that part of his makeup. Secretly, though he would never in a million years admit it out loud, he loved it when Susanna publicly displayed her affection, even though, on another level, it discomforted him. He had always had a proclivity to blush, which made it impossible to pretend that he wasn't embarrassed.

The attendant announced that they were now boarding the plane for the approximately one-hour flight to Vancouver. Lloyd waited patiently until passengers requiring assistance had boarded. He then showed his boarding pass to the attendant and headed out onto the tarmac to board the WestJet aircraft.

As promised, Mona Grace met him at the airport. His suitcase was the first one off the plane and on to the carousel, and so they were able to exit the terminal fairly quickly.

On the drive to Mona Grace's house, she said little. When Lloyd asked her if something was wrong, she insisted that she was fine, that she was just tired. She'd had an exhausting day. Lloyd didn't believe her protestations for a minute, but he let them go.

He asked if he could take her out for supper later. She said that she had everything prepared. When they got home, they could have a visit. Supper wouldn't take long to cook when the time came. Lloyd opened his mouth to ask if Charley was coming, thought better of it and closed his mouth before the words could escape.

As they approached Mona Grace's house, Lloyd saw that little had changed since he lived there. The tiny yard was mowed, trimmed, and weeded. Perky, colourful flowers appeared to nod in the breeze, welcoming him back.

Glancing sideways at his former landlady, he observed that, as they approached her house, she seemed to let out her breath with a sigh. 'Relief? From what?' Lloyd wondered silently to himself.

Once they went into the house, it was a different Mona Grace that took off her coat. Laughing, excited, she hugged Lloyd. Talking non-stop, she set out a plate of cold meats, crackers, and cheese. Mindful of the fact that Lloyd didn't drink alcohol, she handed him a Coke. "You must be hungry," she said. "I know they don't serve a meal on the plane anymore. Sit down, help yourself. I'll be right back. Make yourself at home." She turned and went into her bedroom, closing the door firmly behind her.

Fifteen minutes later, Lloyd was still sitting at the table, the plate of snacks untouched. Mona Grace finally came out of her room, looking guiltily at Lloyd. "Sorry," she muttered, "work call."

"No problem," Lloyd muttered back. "I waited for you."

"Well, then," Mona Grace said in a pseudo-cheery tone. "Snack away!"

After much chin-wagging, the two friends had caught up on the happenings in their lives, in the year since Lloyd and Susanna had moved back to Alberta.

Lloyd finally asked Mona Grace if Charley was going to be able to come over for a visit while Lloyd was in town. Mona Grace, with an odd look on her face, said no, she was sorry, but Charley had to work. She didn't get a day off for the next couple of weeks. She was taking extra shifts at the Starbucks; she couldn't afford to turn any shift down.

"I see," Lloyd said. "That's too bad. I would have loved to have seen her. Maybe next time."

After a late supper, before retiring for the night, Mona Grace handed Lloyd his old house key.

"Might as well make yourself at home, just like old times," she said. "Come and go as you please. I know the trials will take up a lot of your time, so we'll catch up when we can, okay?"

"Of course," Lloyd said reassuringly. "Thanks for supper, Mona Grace. Go ahead and use the bathroom first. I'm going to call Susanna on my cell. Sleep well. Good night."

Lloyd waited until he heard the shower running before calling Susanna. She answered the phone on the first ring. "Lloyd! I've been waiting for your call. How was your flight? How's Mona Grace? Did you see Charley? Are you going to see Charley? Fill me in! I'm going crazy here." She finally paused for breath.

Lloyd answered what questions he could, ending with, "I haven't seen Charley, and I doubt that I'm going to."

"Something strange is going on here, Suz. Mona Grace is very secretive, skirting around any of my inquiries regarding Charley. And she appeared to be nervous and uncomfortable in the extreme, when we arrived at her house. It was as if she was expecting someone, and when they didn't show, she was relieved. Oh, well, it's none of my business, I guess. She certainly doesn't want to talk about it."

"I've decided just to let things ride, at least for a while. Mona Grace and I are close enough friends that if she wants to talk to me, she will."

Lloyd deftly steered the conversation back to Susanna. "How are you doing, wife? Miss me yet?" He was much more talkative over the phone than he was at home with Uncle Henry, Cora, and who-knows-who else, around. He had no trouble at all whispering sweet nothings into the telephone. Fortunately, he had a wife who understood his reticence; although she silently promised herself that she would cure him of his bashfulness, one way or another, and she would make it fun along the way!

After he and Susanna had hung up and he was finished in the bathroom, Lloyd lay awake in the darkness. Suddenly, the impending trials were upon him. They were real. Lloyd wasn't too worried about being a witness in the trials against Domingo and Brutus. He, understandably, though, had very mixed feelings about testifying against his own father. Although Lloyd had pretty much disowned Paul as his 'real' father, it still felt somewhat odd, definitely wrong, that a son should have to testify against his own dad. With thoughts swirling in his head and butterflies the size of moths hammering his sore stomach, Lloyd finally managed to fall fitfully asleep.

After restlessly tossing and turning far into the night, Lloyd was exhausted. He slept late the next morning. He didn't have to see Sergeant Gablehaus until the afternoon. By the time the ringing of the phone woke him, it was already eleven o'clock. Mona Grace was long gone to the shelter. Lloyd let the phone ring. He didn't feel he should answer it. Whoever was calling would either leave a message or call back.

Looking out the front room window, he noted it was a clear and sunny day. Lloyd decided to take a short run before he showered and went to the detachment. He ran straight to Oppenheimer Park, thinking he might run into someone he knew. He did not. Disappointed, he ran back to shower and change for his meeting with Sergeant Greg Gablehaus.

On his way back, he came upon a vendor selling flowers. On impulse, he stopped and bought a bunch of the most colourful ones, to give to Mona Grace. Not knowing whether she had any flower vases, he had the vendor arrange the bouquet in a tall, bright yellow, glass vase. Arriving back at the house, he set the arrangement in the middle of the kitchen table with a card, that simply said: 'This sunny floral arrangement reminds me of you. Thanks for letting me stay here.'

On a separate piece of paper, he wrote Mona Grace a brief note. It said: 'I'm going out for supper and might be late. Don't cook anything for me and don't wait up. See you tomorrow.'

Lloyd didn't put his name on either the card or the note. She would know it was from him. After all, who else could it be from?

He grabbed his ever-present backpack and headed out the door. Glancing at his watch, he hurried towards the police detachment and his meeting with Sergeant Gablehaus.

The sergeant was waiting for him. Lloyd shook his hand vigorously, genuinely happy to see Greg once again.

They spent the next couple of hours reviewing statements, going over Lloyd's testimony, and familiarising him with the procedures and protocol to be followed in the Supreme Court of British Columbia. Sergeant Gablehaus told Lloyd that he had hoped to hear that at least some of the charges had been settled out of court, but so far, there was only silence from the offices of the crown prosecutors and defence counsel for the three accused.

"Lloyd, I know that I told you my wife wanted to have you for supper this evening, and you agreed to come, but she woke up this morning with a ferocious migraine. She apologises profusely, but she is not well enough for company. Perhaps one evening before you leave would be better. But please allow me to take you out for an early supper. My wife will welcome a few more hours to rest, and I won't be banging around in the kitchen." He looked at Lloyd questioningly, awaiting an answer.

"Sure, an early supper would be fine with me," Lloyd replied. "With Domingo's trial tomorrow, I can use an early turn in. I didn't sleep all that well last night."

"Great! Do you like Thai food? There's a great little neighbourhood Thai restaurant not far from here."

"I like any type of food, sir, except cottage cheese, and yogurt. Thai food will be just fine."

Sergeant Gablehaus grinned. "Let's go, then. My car is in the back."

The two men spent an enjoyable couple of hours talking, about a lot of things. The sergeant dropped Lloyd off at Oppenheimer Park because he wanted to walk off some of his dinner. Lloyd thanked Greg for the pleasant meal and for the informative afternoon. He told him that he was prepared for the trials and wasn't nervous, thanks to Sergeant Gablehaus' excellent tutelage.

Walking through the park, Lloyd spied his old friend whom he had nicknamed 'the Whistler'. He walked over to the man who was busy picking up trash from around his sleeping site under a park bench and depositing it into a large trashcan close by.

"Hello! How are you doing? You're looking great," Lloyd greeted the homeless man.

"Well, well, I know you, I know you!" the Whistler said. "How are you doing, how are you doing?" Lloyd reached out to shake the man's hand, but the Whistler self-consciously put his hands behind his back. "Too dirty, too dirty," he repeated to Lloyd. "Good to see you, good to see you."

"You, too," Lloyd responded. "You're looking very well." Although his homeless friend appeared happy, he began looking anxiously around, started to pace. Recognising his impending anxiety, Lloyd quickly started to walk away. He turned and waved. "Was nice to see you again, sir," he called. "I hope to see you again soon."

The Whistler waved weakly at Lloyd and called 'Goodbye, goodbye' before crawling into his sleeping bag under the park bench. He covered his head, blocking his view of anything outside his sleeping bag, shutting out the dangers of the night.

Lloyd continued walking through the park. He did not see anyone else he recognised, although there were many homeless people lying on the ground throughout the park, bundled in dirty sleeping bags, or covered with old blankets, or newspapers. Throughout the park, as full darkness rapidly approached, gentle snores, and not-so-gentle snores, could be heard.

When Lloyd arrived at Mona Grace's house, he barely noticed a large, dark car leaving the area. It was too dark to see the colour of the car or to get a look at the driver. In any event, Lloyd wasn't looking for anything or anyone specifically. He just happened to catch an instantaneous glimpse of it as it passed by. He paid it little notice.

When he unlocked the back door and entered the kitchen, the entire house was in darkness. Even though it was early, he assumed Mona Grace was either still at work or had already gone to bed. He reached for the light switch.

"Please, don't turn on the light, Lloyd. It's too bright." The disembodied voice came from the dark, in the general area of the living room. Lloyd let his hand drop from the switch. He walked over and turned on the hall light instead.

Mona Grace was curled up in her easy chair, completely covered with an Afghan. She held tightly to the cover. The only part of her that Lloyd could see were her dark eyes shining in the dim light. Moisture threatened to spill over her bottom eyelids and surge down her cheeks at any moment.

Lloyd sat down across from his friend and reached towards her. "What's going on, Mona Grace? You know you can talk to me. Why don't you want the light on?"

She did not reach out; she simply clutched the Afghan more tightly around her body.

Deciding to leave her be for a few minutes, Lloyd stood up. "Want some tea?"

She said meekly, "Yes, please."

Mona Grace was trembling visibly; Lloyd suggested that she come and sit at the kitchen table to drink her tea. Rather than wait to hear a negative response, he went into the kitchen and prepared the pot of tea.

As soon as he placed the cups and the teapot on the table, he heard an audible sigh. Mona Grace got slowly and painfully up out of her chair and dragged herself the short distance into the kitchen, her Afghan trailing partly on the floor behind her.

Sitting down at the table, she winced before she said quietly, "Okay, Lloyd, you can turn on the light now. Just be prepared."

He walked over and flipped on the light switch that was located on the wall to the left of the stove. Turning around, he caught, in his peripheral vision, a glimpse of the flowers he had bought. The vase was smashed to bits; the flowers were mangled and drooping over the edge of the countertop. His note was crumpled and torn. It lay forlornly on the floor, amidst the pieces of the shattered vase. Water from the flower vase damply stained the front of the bottom cupboard. There was blood in the sink.

Turning slowly, he walked over to the table and sat down beside Mona Grace. Saying nothing, he simply looked at her and waited. After a few minutes, she gently removed the Afghan from her face. Now the tears began to leak from her red and swollen eyes.

Her nose was bleeding slightly, but it must have bled profusely earlier, because her face was covered in drying blood. Noticing that she had something clutched tightly in one hand, Lloyd reached over and slowly unfolded her fingers one by one. Two teeth. She had held on to them so tightly that there were tooth marks embedded in her hand.

Looking at her sadly, Lloyd asked the question, even though he was pretty sure he knew the answer. "Who did this, Mona Grace, and do you know why?"

"It doesn't matter, Lloyd. I asked for it."

Lloyd leaped to his feet, shouting at the top of his voice, "WHAT! For crying out loud, Mona Grace, what kind of counsellor are you anyway? I don't believe for a second that you asked to be beaten. You don't believe it either. It's the shock talking, not you." He got a paper towel from the holder on the counter and then sat down again. He reached over and gently removed the teeth from her hand with the paper towel, not wanting to contaminate anything before the police arrived.

"What time did you call the police?" he asked.

"I didn't."

Lloyd couldn't keep the disgust from showing as he said, "What do you mean? You didn't call the police?"

"I couldn't. He said if I called the police, he would send someone to kill me next time, rather than just teach me a lesson. He also said that he might not kill me but would kill Charley instead."

"Who said that?"

No response. Lloyd paid careful attention to the phantom image that floated through the shadowy recesses of his brain. He struggled to recall any details about the vehicle that drove by him when he got home a short time ago. He gasped as the light finally dawned. "Domingo? Oh, my God, Mona Grace, Domingo did this to you! Why?"

Holding his mouth shut with his right hand, Lloyd breathed deeply, thinking before he spoke, before he said something he could not take back.

Mona Grace sat shivering. She couldn't stop. The hardest thing she had to do for a very long time was to talk to Lloyd about the events that occurred earlier in the evening. Her hands shook so hard that she was unable to hold her teacup. Lloyd reached over and steadied her hands so she could drink. He then sat back and waited.

"I'll wait all night if I have to, Mona Grace," he said. "I'm going to wait you out. And, despite the fact that I yelled at you a few minutes ago, I'm your friend. You know that. There is nothing you can tell me that I will judge you for. So, take your time, but I'm not going anywhere until you tell me what happened."

Mona Grace believed him. Rather than prolong the agony, she stood up and removed the Afghan. It had been wrapped so tightly around her that it was all tangled up. She struggled, trying to take painful, deep breaths around either cracked or broken ribs, as she attempted to remove the wrap. Just as Lloyd stood up to help her, it fell free. It took all of Lloyd's concentration and strength to avoid gasping.

There was, of course, her bloody nose and her two missing teeth. In addition, she had the beginnings of a horrific shiner around her left eye. Finger marks stood out starkly against her skin. Both her arms were turning black. Her fingernails were torn. Some of her fingers were bleeding from her efforts to try to fend off Domingo's heinous attack. Her shirt was ripped. Through the gaping fabric Lloyd could clearly discern a boot print embedded into Mona Grace's stomach. There were several deep scratches on her cheeks, possibly from glass shards when the flower vase smashed. Several bleeding bald spots on her scalp evidenced that she had been dragged by her hair.

"I need to take you to the hospital, Mona Grace. You probably have internal injuries."

"No!" she shouted, forgetting her excruciatingly painful ribs for a second. Fighting for breath, she continued. "I can't Lloyd; he'll go after Charley! I don't care if he comes after me, but he can't harm my daughter. I just found her, Lloyd, you know that!" Whimpering with pain, both physical and mental, she stared pleadingly at Lloyd, begged him. "No hospital, I'll be fine. I just need to lay down. If you get me a couple of Extra Strength Tylenol out of the medicine cabinet in the bathroom, I'll be okay."

Shaking his head, Lloyd nevertheless did as she asked. He helped her to her room. Out of the linen closet in the hallway, he picked up two more pillows, placed them gently behind Mona Grace. The elevation helped her breathing. She lay back, puffing, eyes closed, too exhausted to be distraught any more.

"Mona Grace, nice try by closing your eyes, but you haven't told me why Domingo beat you. I'm still waiting."

He pulled a chair in from the kitchen, plopped his body awkwardly onto the chair, folded his arms across his chest. He waited.

In a quiet monotone, Mona Grace spoke. "I got home about a half an hour, maybe 45 minutes before you did, Lloyd. I went into the kitchen, saw your beautiful flowers and read your note. I'd had a crappy day at work, and I can't tell you how much your thoughtfulness improved my day."

"I had just finished reading your note when the doorbell rang. I hollered for whoever was at the door to come on in; the door was unlocked. I had left it unlocked because I had groceries in the car and needed to bring them in. Stupid of me, I know, but I've never had a problem in the daytime here. Besides, most of the homeless people are very protective of the residents of what they consider 'their neighbourhood'. That's why I wasn't the least bit concerned."

"I was just setting your note back down on the table. Before I could look up, Domingo grabbed me by the hair and shoved my face down on the table, HARD! I think he broke my nose. It bled a lot. He spoke in a calm and quiet but deadly tone of voice. He wanted to know who the flowers were from, who the note was from. When I told him they were from you, that you were staying here while you visited with friends in East Van – I didn't think I should tell him you were here as a witness. Maybe he knows; maybe he doesn't, but if he didn't know it already, I wasn't going to be the one to tell him. Anyhow, he didn't believe me."

Mona Grace stopped talking so she could catch her breath. She repeated, "He didn't believe me." She continued shakily, "He was positively apoplectic as he started swinging at me with both fists. I tried to back away from him; he shoved me into the corner of the kitchen counter – I'm pretty sure that's when my ribs either cracked or broke. I heard them. Between the blood pouring out of my nose, and my damaged ribs, I couldn't take a breath or speak, not even to ask Domingo to stop. I fell once, and he kicked me. He had his heavy motorcycle boots on. He was so enraged; I really was convinced he was going to kill me. He picked up the flower vase and aimed it at my head. Lucky for me, he was so angry that his throw was wild. He missed. Although I tried to duck, most of his blows landed. He punched me in the mouth. That's when my two teeth came out."

Lloyd had to ask. "Mona Grace, were you seeing him again?"

A crater-deep blush burned its way right through all the bruising on her face. She said nothing. Watching her, Lloyd was afraid if he made her speak, she would choke on her own words.

"Never mind, it's none of my business, Mona Grace," Lloyd said.

Mona Grace was crying silently. "Yes," she whispered.

It took every ounce of self-control and common sense he possessed for Lloyd to make no comment or not display outwardly what he was thinking.

"Has Charley met him?"

"Yes."

"Did you tell her he's her father?"

"Of course not."

"Domingo knows, though, right? That Charley's his daughter."

No response.

"Mona Grace?"

"He knows, but he doesn't acknowledge it."

"So, he doesn't spend any time with her, quality time or otherwise, right?"

Mona Grace just nodded.

"I'm guessing that Charley knows deep down that Domingo is her father. She doesn't like him, and that's why she isn't coming to see you. Did she give you an ultimatum, Domingo or her?"

By this time, Mona Grace's tears had reached the speed of a spring creek run-off. She cried so hard she got the hiccups. "Y-y-yesss," she choked.

"And, you chose Domingo," Lloyd said flatly, trying not to judge. "Do you know why you made that choice, Mona Grace?"

She shrugged her shoulders.

"Come on now," Lloyd said, trying unsuccessfully to control the exasperation in his tone. "You have to have some idea why you picked the head of a criminal gang, a so-called 'man' who ordered you to have an abortion, a man who left you in the lurch when you wouldn't comply with his direct order."

When Mona Grace didn't answer, Lloyd went on, "Mona Grace, for God's sake, give me something, anything! Just make me understand!"

Subdued, she whispered, "I owed him."

"You owed him what? Your two teeth? Your broken ribs? Your life? Come on, woman, pretend you are the excellent counsellor that I know you to be. Put yourself in your client's place. What would you tell that poor, abused, non-functioning soul?"

Lloyd could tell by looking at her that she was close to breaking down completely. He had to stop, at least for tonight.

He went into the kitchen and got a bag of peas out of the freezer in the top of the fridge.

"Here," he said gently, "put this on your face; it'll help with the swelling. Try and get some sleep. If you're no better in the morning, I'm taking you to the hospital."

"You have to be in court."

Lloyd moaned. "Crap! That's right. Well, after court, I'll check on you. If you aren't better by then, we're off to the hospital. There'll be no arguing."

"Okay, boss," Mona Grace said.

"Call me if you need anything tonight, Mona Grace. It doesn't matter if I'm asleep or what time it is. Just holler." When she hesitated, started to protest, Lloyd brooked no nonsense from her. He simply said, "I'm your friend – remember that!"

"I will," she said and closed her eyes.

The next morning, Lloyd was definitely feeling his lack of sleep the past few nights. Nevertheless, he got up before his alarm and shut it off so it wouldn't awaken his friend. He had a quick shower.

Once dressed in the new dress clothes that he had bought to wear when he proposed to Susanna, he quietly went to the kitchen, made himself a slice of toast while the coffee machine slowly dripped out a cup of coffee into his travel mug.

Before he left for court, Lloyd wrote a brief note to Mona Grace, suggesting she have a hot soak in the tub with two cups of Epsom salts added to help her sore muscles. He told her he would see her after court. He then signed his name – in extra-large, bold letters!

The Vancouver Supreme Court on Smithe Street in downtown Vancouver was, Lloyd estimated, probably at least 1/2 to 3/4 of an hour of brisk walk. He debated briefly whether or not to walk it but decided that he would probably be better off appearing in court calm, cool, and collected, not sweating and red in the face. A taxicab drove slowly by. Lloyd flagged the driver, who pulled over and stopped. As the cab driver drove him to the courthouse, Lloyd clung to his trusty backpack like a toddler clutches a favourite teddy bear. He thought that if he was going to look as professional as he would like to (from time to time), he really should purchase either a briefcase or a portfolio to carry, instead of the backpack.

A second 'Excuse me, sir?' from the driver's seat jerked Lloyd back to the here and now. "We are here," the driver repeated, his accent strong. "The building of the courts."

"Ah, yes, thank you." Lloyd fumbled inside the infamous backpack for his wallet. He asked for a receipt and then exited the cab.

He stared at the mass of concrete and glass in front of him. Before he could even begin to wonder where he should be going, Sergeant Gablehaus was standing beside him. They stood in line in front of the scanner, awaiting Lloyd's turn. When he set his backpack on the conveyor belt, nothing beeped. Lloyd was asked to remove his belt and anything metal that he might have in his pockets, including coins, before he walked through the scanner. No beeping.

Sergeant Gablehaus had entered via another entrance, thanks to the security card he carried with him at all times. Touching Lloyd's elbow, he whispered, "Follow me. Say nothing to the reporters." Lloyd looked around, trying to see how many reporters might be standing in the hallway. It was easy to spot them milling around this area. *However*, Lloyd thought silently, *inside the courtroom it'll be a different story.*

"Remember, as I told you earlier, you may very well be asked to leave the room until it is time for you to testify. You can sit in the courtroom unless or until Justice Tanner asks you to leave, if indeed he does. Again, if you are asked to wait in the hallway, do not speak to anyone, especially any reporters." Pointing at two available chairs, he said, "Let's sit here."

Right on the dot of ten o'clock, the court clerk rose, looked out at the spectators and droned, "All rise." A stern looking man, dressed in the black robe denoting that the man was a justice of the Supreme Court of British Columbia, entered the courtroom through a rear door. As he headed to the bench, the clerk droned again in a bored-sounding voice, this time stating the court, date, and time that court was beginning. She ended with, "Justice G.P. Tanner presiding. You may be seated."

Shuffling some papers on her desk, she called out, "In the matter of case #1234-4321-2017, Domingo Sanchez."

Domingo and his lawyer stood up. The crown prosecutor rose and addressed Justice Tanner. "My lord, the crown asks that the charges against the accused, Domingo Sanchez, be stayed."

Justice Tanner peered over his reading glasses at Domingo and his lawyer. In a dry voice, he noted, "I assume that Mr Sanchez and his counsel have no objections?"

"No, my lord," mumbled Domingo. "Thank you."

Lloyd turned to Sergeant Gablehaus, stricken. "What the heck just happened?"

Sergeant Gablehaus replied glumly, "The crown decided that they didn't have enough evidence to proceed to trial against Domingo. The man is the worst. I call his type a 'triple S criminal' – slippery, sleazy, smart. He is the leader of the 'East Van Devils', but he, himself, has never been convicted of anything. He has his henchmen do all his dirty work. He never soiled his own hands, at least as far as being arrested and charged with a crime. The slippery bastard has successfully avoided tangling with the law up until now."

"The crown's office has one year during which time, they can re-lay the charges. If they find enough evidence, they will do so. More often than not, though, when the year is up, the file is closed."

Lloyd turned ashen.

"Are you okay, Lloyd?" Greg asked.

Knowing full well that Mona Grace would be horrified, Lloyd decided, on the spot, that the matter was too serious not to tell Sergeant Gablehaus about it. He quickly recounted all of the details of the assault against Mona Grace.

"They must be able to arrest that creep. Can't you charge him with aggravated assault or something?"

"He'll go after her again, and this time he'll kill her – or he will go after Charley! He told Mona Grace that's what he would do!" Lloyd sounded frantic.

The sergeant stared sternly at Lloyd. "If you had called me last night, we could have arrested him and asked that the court hold him without bail pending proceedings. If Mona Grace doesn't want him charged, she won't be any use as a witness. Without a witness, the man would likely walk."

"I think, right now, the best thing is for us to go and talk with Mona Grace, see if we can convince her that charging Domingo is the safest thing for her right now and for her daughter."

Lloyd sounded terrified; nevertheless, he managed to choke out, "Certainly, sir, let's go."

Sergeant Gablehaus looked sympathetically at Lloyd. "Lloyd, don't you think it's time you called me Greg?"

Lloyd looked at Greg Gablehaus like he had just sprouted a devil's horn in the middle of his forehead. He didn't think that what he called the sergeant had anything to do with the matters at hand. *In fact*, he thought, *what a strange time to bring that up!*

He was far too worked up over Mona Grace's plight to be able to recognise that his friend was just trying to loosen Lloyd up a little, that he was worried, because Lloyd was strung out to the point that he could have a stroke if he didn't try to unwind just a touch.

The sergeant stood up and said, "I'm going to quickly call the detachment and tell them where I am. Wait here for me; I won't be long. Then we should go. It'll probably be at least an hour before the papers are prepared and Domingo will be released. Let's see what progress we can make with Mona Grace before then, shall we?"

Sergeant Gablehaus walked several paces away from Lloyd. When he was sure he was not within hearing distance, he phoned his office. He explained that Domingo Sanchez would be released, probably within the hour. He ordered that an unmarked police car with two officers be dispatched to follow Domingo when he left the courthouse.

"Tell them to tail Domingo but surreptitiously. If he goes to Mona Grace Ford's house" – here he gave the street address of her house to the dispatcher – "I will be there with a civilian and will most certainly need backup. Tell them that under no circumstances are they to either lose Domingo or get close enough for him to make them, to scare him off."

"I'm almost positive that the very first place he will head will be to the address I just gave you. If that is the case, tell the officers to be prepared for anything. That man is dangerous." He finished off his conversation and returned to where Lloyd was waiting.

"All right, Lloyd, let's go and check on Mona Grace. No, not that car. We're taking an unmarked vehicle. We certainly don't want Domingo to drive up, spot a trap and leave. Hop in."

When they reached the street where Mona Grace lived, Sergeant Gablehaus parked at the far end of the block, on the opposite side of the street from her house. Even though Domingo wouldn't have been released yet, they scrutinised the area carefully before they got out of the car, just in case.

Even though Lloyd had a key to the house, he didn't feel right about using it while Mona Grace was home. Rather than have her panic at the sound of the doorbell, not knowing who was at the door, he used the key but called out loudly as they entered, "Hey, Mona Grace, it's me! Sergeant Gablehaus is with me. Come on into the kitchen, and we'll fill you in on the court proceedings."

"I'll be right there, Lloyd," she called out weakly from her bedroom. "Can you make some coffee, please?"

"Sure. Take your time; I know you're sore. We're not going anywhere at the moment."

The coffee was nearly ready by the time she walked slowly and painfully into the kitchen.

Despite having thought he had seen everything during his career, Greg Gablehaus was shocked and appalled at Mona Grace's appearance. Lloyd had tried to describe her injuries to the sergeant, but even Lloyd wasn't prepared for the sight of Mona Grace in the daylight.

Despite applying the bag of frozen peas on her face the night before, the ice hadn't reduced the swelling at all. Some of the punches that had pummelled her face had split both her top and lower lips in several places. Swollen and painful, a few of the cuts had broken open and bled again, not allowing scabs to form. She was walking at a snail's pace, leaning heavily on a cane, in obvious agony.

"Sorry that Lloyd brought you to see me looking like this, sir," Mona Grace said. At the same time, she shot Lloyd the evil eye.

Lloyd said, "Don't bother shooting me the evil eye, Miss Mona Grace Ford. I told you I was going to check on you after court, and here I am. Also, when we tell you what happened in court today, you are going to be grateful to the sergeant and me that we came here."

"Did you eat anything today at all?"

Mona Grace looked at Lloyd, tried to smile sarcastically, failed miserably. "I can't open my mouth enough to put food in it, Lloyd. I was too sore to eat. So, nope, I didn't eat today."

"Are you hungry at all?"

"A little," she said.

Lloyd opened the cupboard in search of soup. "Plain chicken broth, beef broth or tomato?" he queried. "We can soak some crackers in it and then you can just swallow, not chew."

"Some of that chicken broth that says 'no salt added' would probably work. Anything else would probably sting like hell, because of the salt."

Mona Grace turned to Greg. Mumbling slowly and carefully around the pain, she said, "Seeing as Lloyd is intent on fussing over me whether I want him to or not, I guess you will have to fill me in on the day's events."

As Greg Gablehaus explained what had transpired in court, she blanched, shook as hard as a wet dog coming out of a creek. 'Oh', was all she could squeak out.

The sergeant reached over and took Mona Grace's hand gently. He explained that, despite being the leader of the 'East Van Devils', Domingo had no criminal record.

"He has always had someone else to do the dirty work for him; never once has he been caught doing anything the least bit crooked."

Sergeant Greg looked directly into Mona Grace's red and watery eyes. "Lloyd told me that Domingo threatened to harm Charley if you don't do what he says. Mona Grace, you have dealt with troubled clients your entire career. You've counselled criminals when court has ordered counselling. 'You know' that when these guys make a threat, they rarely fail to carry it through to the end."

"What can I do?" she whispered to the sergeant. "I have to do something. I can't spend every day terrified that Domingo will hurt my daughter. How can I protect her? I need to protect her!"

Mona Grace looked towards Lloyd. "Give me some idea of what I can do," she pleaded. "I promise, I'll do it."

Lloyd set a cup of soup in front of her and handed her a small spoon and a straw. "If you don't want to try the crackers soaked in broth, try the straw," he said. "I left the crackers out." He then sat down and turned towards Greg and waited for him to speak.

The sergeant looked at his watch. It had been exactly an hour. Domingo could be on his way, or alternatively, he could still be sitting at the courthouse, waiting for the papers.

"Here's our plan, Mona Grace," Greg said. "I have two police officers in an unmarked car standing by. As soon as they see Domingo leave the building, they have orders to follow him. I am pretty positive that he will head here first, and the officers have orders to back us up. When he shows up, answer the door, invite him in. Sit with him at the table. Don't say anything to him, just stare at him."

Alarmed, Mona Grace interrupted, "He'll go ballistic! He'll hit me again!"

Once more, the sergeant reached for her hand. "After Lloyd told me what happened to you, I had a colleague speak to the matter in court, stressing the urgency and the impending danger to you and to your daughter.

The justice has issued a temporary restraining order. Domingo is not allowed to come within a kilometre of your house, your office at the shelter, or within 500 metres of you, personally. I realise that Domingo Sanchez is not a man who obeys the law, but with the restraining order in place, if he breaks even one of the terms, he will be arrested and charged with a breach. With a restraining order, if it is breached, charges will usually follow rapidly. Once he is picked up and charged with the assault on you and served with a copy of the order, we will have to speak with the justice again to get the restraining order amended so that it will no longer be temporary."

Mona Grace desolately responded, "You and I both know about the effectiveness of restraining orders, Greg, or should I say, the ineffectiveness. They aren't worth the powder to blow them off the face of the planet. The only time they do any good is if they are issued against a person who wouldn't cause trouble anyway. Domingo doesn't give a crap about a piece of paper, and you know it!"

"Mona Grace, think. Lloyd will be here, I will be here, and there will be two armed officers here, one at the front door, one at the back. We will not let him hurt you any further. I want him to get aggravated. As soon as he tries to hurt you again, he will be arrested and thrown in gaol. We will request that he be held without bail pending further court proceedings. He will be charged with aggravated assault. Given the severity of your injuries, I can't imagine any justice in the courts denying our request that he be held without bail."

"You will, of course, have to appear as a witness. You will have to identify Domingo as the man who so viciously attacked you. You will also have to come to the detachment so we can have photographs taken of all of your injuries."

"I know it is really frightening, Mona Grace, but it is time that scum like Domingo get off the streets, pay for their atrocious crimes."

"We've been trying for a very long time to shut down the East Van Devils. It should be a lot easier with their leader in prison."

"One thing, once you let him in, leave the front door and the back door unlocked so that the officers can come in if need be without breaking down a door."

"During the time that Domingo is waiting for his trial, we will have a car parked in front of your house and in front of Charley's place, all day and all night. You will both be safe."

"What might be even better would be if Charley comes and stays with you. That way, we can cut down on manpower. Also, there is safety in numbers. Think about it; you don't have to decide immediately."

"You're a very strong woman, Mona Grace; you've endured many things growing up in East Van. Are you ready to do this one important, vital thing?"

She nodded. "Let's do this."

The sergeant's cell phone rang. He listened, hurriedly hung up.

"Domingo's on his way. The officers have followed him to the end of this street. Remember, Mona Grace, you are safe; you just have to help us catch him. We need to arrest him, for your safety, as well as for your daughter's safety."

He turned towards Lloyd.

"Lloyd, get in the bedroom. Stay out of sight, and do not try anything! Leave this to the people who are trained. Understand?"

Lloyd nodded, mute.

Sergeant Gablehaus repeated, "Understand? I need a vocal response!"

"Yes, sir, I understand," Lloyd said quietly. "I'll do as you say."

"Ready?" Sergeant Gablehaus asked Mona Grace.

"Yes, sir."

Lloyd and Greg headed for the bedroom. No sooner had they gone in and partially closed the door, when the doorbell rang.

Mona Grace called out in a feeble voice, "Who is it?"

"Oh, for Christ's sake, MG, who the fuck else were you expecting? Let me in, NOW!" Domingo rattled the door. Mona Grace tried to hurry, but she couldn't move quickly.

"I'm coming, Domingo, hold your horses!" She thought to herself, *nothing like pissing him off before he even gets invited in*!

"I ain't got all day, MG!"

Reaching the door, she took as deep a breath as she could manage with her injured ribs, then opened the door.

Domingo was hyper; impatient but excited at the same time. He pushed by her, causing her to gasp in pain. "Any coffee?" he asked her. Before she could answer, he was in the kitchen, pouring his own.

Mona Grace limped painfully to the table, winced as she tried to sit.

"For God's sake, Mona Grace, quit wimping around. You've had worse than that!"

She looked at him. "What happened in court today? Something good for you, obviously, you're out!" Remembering that Sergeant Gablehaus had told her not to say anything, just sit quietly, she shut her mouth.

"Yeah, I'm out. They had nothin' on me so couldn't keep me. Told ya that would happen!"

Mona Grace sat, saying not another word, just stared at Domingo, speechless.

"What the fuck, MG! Cat got your tongue or what? You should be happy for me."

She said nothing, just kept staring.

"What the hell is wrong with you, woman?" He stared back at her, becoming more aggravated by the minute.

"Mouth hurts, ribs hurt." She shut up again.

Domingo said, "Come on, woman, let's go into the bedroom and celebrate my release!" He turned and headed towards her bedroom.

She just sat at the table and stared after him, astonished.

By the time he reached the bedroom door, he already had his shirt off.

Suddenly realising that Mona Grace was not behind him, he whirled around on his heel. Between clenched teeth, he ordered, "MG, get your sorry ass into this bedroom. Now!"

Although she was visibly shaking, Mona Grace managed to sit without saying another word.

Suddenly, with a loud roar, Domingo left the bedroom, both hands curled into fists.

"Get out of that chair," he screamed at her. Reaching for her hair, he grabbed a solid handful and pulled. Mona Grace screamed at the top of her voice.

The front door and back door opened simultaneously and the two backup officers reached the kitchen at the same time as Sergeant Gablehaus. It took all three policemen to cuff the raging bull that was Domingo Sanchez. It took all three men to get him into the unmarked police car.

One of the backup officers began to read him his rights. "Domingo Sanchez, you are under arrest for aggravated assault on Mona Grace Ford…" He continued until he had read him his rights in their entirety.

Mona Grace was still sitting at the table when Greg came back into the house. "Help me," she whispered, "Lloyd, please, help me to the bathroom. I'm going to be sick!"

While they waited for Mona Grace to come out of the bathroom, Sergeant Gablehaus said to Lloyd, "She needs medical attention. We'll take her to the hospital when she comes out."

Lloyd asked, "What's going to happen with Domingo?"

"He'll be in gaol overnight and appear in front of a judge in the morning. We are requesting that he be held without bail. I'm hoping that Mona Grace will be in good enough physical shape to appear in court so the judge can have a first-hand look at her visible injuries. We'll have pictures taken at the hospital of all of her injuries. If they admit her, then we will use the photos in our request to have bail denied for Domingo."

Lloyd said, "I think while we are waiting for Mona Grace, I should call Charley and tell her to meet us at the hospital."

"Good thinking, Lloyd," Sergeant Gablehaus said. "You do that."

Lloyd said, "I'll be quick. I want to come to the hospital with you. I'll stay with Mona Grace until the doctor sees her and find out what's going on."

"When is Brutus's trial again? All this action has my head off in la-la land somewhere."

Greg said, "Not until tomorrow afternoon. You can spend time with Mona Grace. Now, go phone Charley!"

Lloyd quickly found Charley's cell phone number on his address list and called that number. Charley answered on the third ring, just as Lloyd was about to hang up.

"Hey, Lloyd, what's up?" she answered.

Lloyd quickly filled her in about the assault, about her mother's injuries and told her that they were going to be taking Mona Grace to St Paul's hospital in just a couple of minutes.

"Let me know how she's doing, Lloyd. I'm not coming. She made her own bed; she can lay in it, as the old saying goes."

Lloyd was quiet for about 10 seconds, then he let her have it. "Charley, I can't believe you won't come to the hospital and see how your mother is doing.

She is badly injured, to the point that there is a boot print imbedded into her stomach. For heaven's sake, Charley, this is not the time to judge her!"

"Do you need a ride? Sergeant Gablehaus said he would pick you up and take you to the hospital."

Another 10 seconds of silence, this time from Charley.

"You're right, Lloyd," she said. "I can get there on my own. Thank the sergeant for me, though, please. I'll see you there."

Mona Grace was standing in the kitchen doorway. Well, standing was maybe being a little too generous. She was doubled over in spite of her damaged ribcage, clutching her stomach, and gasping in pain.

Greg Gablehaus asked, "Would it be easier if I called for an ambulance rather than drive you to the hospital myself?"

"No, please," she whispered. "I can handle the car ride. Let's just go. You'll probably have to help me, though."

Lloyd pushed his way into the kitchen and lifted Mona Grace into his arms. "Get the door please, sir?" he requested.

Once Mona Grace was settled into the front seat of the car, Greg looked over at his passenger. Her face was a sickly white, but what concerned him more was the blue tinge around her lips and fingers. He turned on the lights and the siren and sped off towards St Paul's. He radioed ahead, requesting a stretcher be ready at the emergency entrance. "Ten minutes out," he relayed.

When they arrived, a medical team was waiting. "Are you with her?" one attendant barked at Lloyd.

"I am," said Lloyd.

"Do you have her health care papers?"

Mona Grace overheard the question. Weakly she waved her right arm, the required papers clutched in her blue-tinged fingers. "Here!" she called weakly.

The barking attendant looked at Lloyd and quickly pointed out the ER waiting room. "Wait there and someone will come and find you when they know anything."

"Thank you," Lloyd managed to say. "I'll wait there."

Too worked up to sit, Lloyd paced back and forth in the small waiting area. When he began to feel claustrophobic, he went outside and paced for several minutes more.

Even though he knew it was too soon for a report on Mona Grace's condition, he went back into the waiting area and continued to pace. Afraid that someone would come looking for him and not find him, Lloyd didn't go outside again.

He looked at his watch. It was 1:45 pm. They had been at the hospital for a mere 15 minutes. It seemed like hours. *Where the heck is Charley*, he thought to himself. *She should be here by now*. He sat down and rested his head in his hands. He was worried. Mona Grace looked so terrible, and she was in so much pain. He refused to think about why she had hooked up with that evil man again, especially after all these years.

Where was Charley? Why wasn't she here? Lloyd looked at his watch once again. Only 10 minutes had passed since the last time he checked. He leaned back in the chair, closed his eyes, opened them again because all he could see was Mona Grace and her injuries. He leaned back once more and tried shutting his eyes. He must have briefly dozed, because a poke on his right shoulder had him jerking upright in the chair.

Charley stood in front of him. "Hey, Lloyd, I made it."

Lloyd stood up and hugged Charley tightly. "Thank God you've come, Charley. Thank you, thank you. I need your company."

"Have you heard anything yet?" she asked.

"No, but it's pretty early. By the time they check over all her injuries, and there are many, they'll likely have to x-ray her. I'm hoping we'll hear something soon, though."

He looked over at Charley. She seemed pretty composed about the whole matter. *Maybe she's in a bit of shock*, he thought. *At least she's here*!

"Hey, Charley, want a coffee or something? I'll just run down to the cafeteria quickly. You stay here in case they come looking for me."

"Thanks, Lloyd. No coffee, but I could use a Coke."

"Be right back," Lloyd said. He took off running down the hall towards the elevator.

He was back in less than 10 minutes. "Any word?" he asked anxiously, handing over her can of Coke with shaking hands.

"Nope."

They sat in silence, waiting. The minutes ticked by, turning into a half hour. Just before the hour was up, a nurse dressed in green scrubs approached. "Are you Lloyd?" she asked.

Lloyd stood up quickly. "Yes, ma'am, I'm Lloyd. This is my sister, Charley."

"Come with me," she said. "We are just waiting for the doctor to come in and speak with all of you. Ms Ford asked that the two of you come in and wait with her. She wants you both there when the doctor comes."

They followed the woman through a set of double doors and down to the far end of a large area. Individual beds were curtained off from the people walking by. Mona Grace was in the last cubicle.

When she saw both Lloyd and Charley anxiously standing at the foot of her bed, she patted both sides of her mattress. There was a plastic chair on each side. "Thank you for coming, both of you," she said quietly. "Please, sit and wait with me. They hope the doctor won't be long."

Charley was staring at her mother with her mouth hanging open. Large tears pooled in her eyes but refused to fall. "Oh, Mum!" she whispered. "You look terrible!"

Mona tried a miserable smile. She patted Charley on the hand. "Thanks, kid," she said. Her voice was raspy and sounded very painful.

She closed her eyes and appeared to doze, so Lloyd and Charley just sat quietly, hoping she would be able to rest until the doctor came in.

It was about a 20-minute wait. A tall, thin man wearing disposable booties, a mask hung around his neck, and a stethoscope dangling behind the mask entered the cubicle, followed by the nurse.

He looked at Lloyd and then at Charley. "I'm Dr Whitley. I'm the surgeon on call today. Are you family?"

Before Lloyd could say he was not family, Mona Grace croaked out, "They are, Dr Whitley. They are my family."

"Okay, then, you can both stay and hear what I have to say, if Mona Grace wants you both in here."

"I do," said Mona Grace. "Is everything intact? Nothing's broken, I hope?"

Clearing his throat uncomfortably, the doctor kept his gaze on the chart. Finally, he looked up and said, "You are a very lucky lady, Ms Ford, despite the fact that your jawbone is cracked, you are missing two teeth, you have three broken ribs, a dislocated shoulder, a broken finger, and a fractured left foot."

"I want to keep you in hospital at least for another day or two, under observation. I didn't detect any further internal injuries, but we need to keep a close eye on you, nonetheless."

"We usually don't tape up ribs any more. We find they heal just as well, and often better, than if they are taped. In your case, though, I was concerned that they might move and puncture something vital, so that is why they are taped so tightly."

"I have immobilised your cracked jaw with bandages that wrap around your head and underneath your chin. The crack is not too severe, so the immobilisation should be enough. If not, you may be looking at surgery sometime down the road, but at this early juncture, I doubt it."

"I had to pin your dislocated shoulder to keep it in place. Your arm is secured to the side of your body with bandages. Once the bandages are removed, you will need to wear a sling. How long will depend on how fast it heals."

"Your fractured left foot has been casted. Once I am sure it is healing well, we will replace the plaster cast with a boot.

"I splinted your broken finger. I see no reason why it shouldn't heal nicely.

"So, despite all those injuries, I still say you are a very lucky woman. Whoever did this to you very nearly killed you."

The doctor paused. Mona Grace watched his Adam's apple work in his throat, up and down, up and down.

Finally, he spoke again, softly and compassionately. He said, "Ms Ford, I am very sorry, but we were unable to save the baby."

. . . .

Mona Grace stared uncomprehendingly at the doctor. "Say that again?" she whispered. "Please, what did you just say?"

"I said, Ms Ford, I am so very sorry, but we were unable to save the baby. The injuries from the kicks to your stomach were too deep, too extensive. I am so sorry."

Mona Grace turned to Charley. "Charley, baby, did I hear him correctly?"

Charley let out a long, drawn out, strangled cry. Stuffing her fist into her mouth to try to stop the noise, the moaning continued. Eyes wide, Charley backed away from the bed, turned tail and ran from the room.

"Lloyd, go after her."

Lloyd glanced wildly around. Both the doctor and the nurse, ostensibly to let the sad news sink in, had left the cubicle.

"I'm okay, Lloyd. Go! Go be with Charley. When she settles, bring her back in here. We need to have a family meeting, and by 'family', you are included. Now go!"

The nurse was nearby. Lloyd waved at her and then pointed towards Mona Grace. The nurse nodded and started towards Mona Grace's bedside.

Lloyd ran down the hall towards the elevator. The doors were closing when he reached it, but he reached out his arm and stopped them.

Charley was standing inside. When she saw Lloyd, she resolutely turned her back to him. She said nothing.

When the elevator reached the main floor, he grabbed Charley by the arm and, despite her protests, marched her outside, away from the building towards a park bench near the small area of lawn and carefully tended flowerbeds. Fortunately, no one else was hanging around within earshot, although Lloyd was so worked up, he couldn't have cared less if there was.

Not too gently, Lloyd pushed Charley down onto the bench. When she went to get up, he said tersely, "Sit! Stay! Listen to me!"

"You're not the boss of me, Lloyd," she said defiantly. "What makes you think you are?"

Irritated beyond measure, Lloyd answered her, "Of course, I'm not your boss, Charley, but right now, you are acting like a spoiled, petulant brat and somebody needs to tell you a few things. Since I'm the only person available at the moment? Well, lucky me!"

Charley stared straight ahead, failing to notice the beauty of the small area where they sat. She felt like she was stuck rolling around inside a huge thundercloud, with no way to escape before lightning struck.

Lloyd sat patiently, arms crossed, waiting until she showed some sign that she was paying attention. It took a while, but finally, she put both her legs up on the bench. Knees bent, she rested her head on her knees and looked over at Lloyd, interested in what he had to say, in spite of herself.

"You already know, Charley, you found out the hard way, that the world is full of creepy people, people who are always ready to play the role of bully, or big shot, or abusers of some sort. Heck, Charley, you lived that first-hand. That guy cut off your thumb for pity's sake!"

She interrupted, "Yes, but I didn't have anything more to do with him after we were rescued from that awful trailer. My so-called intelligent mother jumped from the frying pan straight back into the fire!"

"Mona Grace, is screwing around, AGAIN, with the same guy who dumped her back in the not-so-good old days, just as soon as he found out Mona Grace was pregnant with me! A guy who nearly beat her to death! Are you telling me

52

I'm supposed to condone her behaviour? Because, Lloyd, I can't do that! Mona Grace is my mother. I want good things for her, not abusive things."

"No, you don't have to condone her behaviour, Charley, but you want to know what I think? I think, no, I KNOW that Mona Grace needs support and love more than ever right now. Our job is not to judge her; our job is to support her. We don't have to like what she's doing, but she's an adult. She's free to do whatever, whenever, and with whomever, she chooses. We don't have the right to abandon her for her choices, no matter how much we disagree or how ill-founded those choices are."

"If she had died, and she nearly did, you wouldn't have had a chance to say goodbye. You wouldn't have had a chance to hear her side of the story. You might well shrug your shoulders, Charley, but think about it. You would have missed out and felt awful about it for the rest of your life. You already missed having her as a mother for so many years! So many years that she agonised over you, about where you were, were you in a good foster home, were you happy? Do you really want to walk away when you have just reconnected with your mother? Do you really?"

"I think Mona Grace will tell you that it is okay for you to be upset with her, to tell her what you think about her and Domingo. Heck, I'm pretty sure she is thinking the same thing! I can't believe for a single second that she was happy with Domingo. I'll bet you dollars to donuts that if she could change the past, she would never have fallen in love with such a loser. I think she hates herself for her weakness."

"Don't judge her, Charley. She judges herself enough for everybody. I think she'll tell you that herself, if you give her half a chance."

"What she won't tell you, though, is that you should run away. Nothing gets solved by running away. Again, Charley, you found that out the hard way. You ran away and ended up captured and held captive for years. What did that solve? Not a thing, right?"

Charley's face looked as if a light bulb had suddenly turned on. She looked over at Lloyd and quietly, brokenly said, "But Lloyd, a baby! Didn't she learn her lesson when she became pregnant with me? I don't understand; I just don't understand."

Lloyd put his arm around the confused young woman. "Well, Charley, I think the best thing is to go back and see Mona Grace. Sit with your mother and ask her. I know she will answer any of your questions, if she even knows the answers herself."

Charley muttered, "Sure glad she wasn't counselling me! She must have been a crappy one."

Lloyd said, "Absolutely not! She was, and is, an excellent counsellor, Charley. That makes her present situation even sadder. Life got in the way and she fell off the rails. She's going to need a fair bit of help and counselling herself, but she'll bounce back. Your mother is the strongest woman I know. Not many have the strength and the courage to give up their three-year-old babies so that those babies could have a better life than their mothers could give them."

"And remember, Domingo is going to go to prison, hopefully for a long, long time."

Lloyd stood up, held his hand out towards Charley. She grasped it, sighed. Turning to face Lloyd, she said, "Okey-dokey, Foster Brother, o' wise one; let's go talk with Mona Grace!"

. . . .

The next morning, Lloyd woke up exhausted and bleary-eyed from all of the events that occurred the previous day.

The doctor had reiterated that he wanted to keep Mona Grace in hospital for at least the next few days. He was very concerned about internal bleeding and wanted to keep a close eye on her.

Lloyd had waited until they moved her to a regular ward before he left to go back to Mona Grace's house. Mona Grace smiled at Lloyd when he stood up and announced that he was leaving. She reached out her hand and held his, as tightly as her injuries permitted.

"It's been quite a day, hasn't it? You go home and get your rest. You have Brutus's trial tomorrow. That's enough to deal with in one day without being totally exhausted when you testify. Let me know what happens."

"Thank you, Lloyd, for everything. Good luck."

Charley opted to stay with her mother. The nurses were so helpful. They brought a folding cot in so that Charley could stay overnight. She was happy to stay. She and Mona Grace had a lot to talk about and with her mother feeling so poorly, staying overnight gave more time for Mona Grace to rest, in between bouts of serious conversation.

Back at the house, Lloyd checked, double-checked, and then triple-checked all the doors and windows. He wouldn't put it past Domingo to come back to the house on the pretext of picking up the few belongings of his that were still there. In actuality, Lloyd figured that it would be to cause further harm to Mona Grace and to trash her home!

Lloyd made himself a bowl of soup. He wasn't hungry, but he knew he should eat. He sat at the kitchen table and forced the hot liquid down his throat, all the while reviewing the events of the day in his mind. One good thing, at least, had come out of the mess. Charley and Mona Grace were mending fences.

Not sure that he would be able to sleep, he nonetheless got ready for bed. His head barely hit the pillow before he was sound asleep, too soundly asleep to even dream about the upcoming trial of Bernard ('Brutus') Belcourt, the 'Tattoo Man'.

The next morning, he awoke just before the radio alarm came on. For a second, he didn't remember where he was, but only for a second. NOW he was nervous about testifying!

Just as he came out of the bathroom, the phone rang. Lloyd, thinking it might be Charley, phoning to let him know how Mona Grace was doing, answered without first checking the screen to see who was calling.

"Hello?" he spoke anxiously into the phone. Too late – the call display read 'Unknown Caller'. Nervously, Lloyd repeated himself, "Hello?" Only heavy breathing on the other end.

Before Lloyd could disconnect the call, a deep, menacing voice said, "Whoever you are, get the hell out of Mona Grace's house and don't come back! You could be killed."

With a sudden burst of bravado (or more likely a sudden burst of foolhardiness!), Lloyd said, "Uttering threats? I know, whoever you are, that you are phoning for Domingo Sanchez. You tell him that if he is dumb enough to violate the conditions of a judge's restraining order, to go ahead and keep up the harassment! I'm pretty sure getting someone else to do his dirty work would still constitute a breach in the eyes of the court. Now, whoever you are, I would suggest you think about that. Are you certain that Domingo would stick up for you? Never! Absolutely not! You would be the fool who would pay for the harassment charges, because your beloved boss would turn on you in a split second!"

"Have a nice day," he continued in the sweetest tone of voice he could spit out. Despite a feeling of impending doom, after disconnecting the call, he whistled edgily as he dressed for court.

Outside the courthouse, Sergeant Greg Gablehaus was waiting. Lloyd approached him. Falsely cheerful, trying to convince himself that there was nothing to be nervous about, he greeted his friend, "Morning, Greg! Beautiful day for a trial, isn't it?"

Cutting right to the chase, Greg asked Lloyd, "Do you want to sit in on Domingo's first appearance this morning regarding the assault against Mona Grace?"

"Can a fish swim?" Lloyd rhetorically asked. "Is there time before Brutus's trial begins?"

"Yup. There are several docket matters being held in the trial courtroom this morning because the docket court judge called in sick. It was too short notice to call in another judge. The justice hearing Brutus's trial volunteered to hear the docket matters first."

Lloyd quickly got into the line-up and then went through the security scanner. He walked with Sergeant Gablehaus down the hall and up the stairs to a courtroom on the second floor.

Lloyd chose two seats at the back of the room, hoping not to be noticed by Domingo. He took the second seat in from the aisle; Greg took the aisle seat.

They had barely seated themselves before the clerk stood up, making the usual announcements, followed by, "All rise. The Honourable Justice J.M. Williams presiding."

A rotund justice, dressed in his black robes, sporting a decent-looking, but still obvious, toupee, sat down. He adjusted his round, gold metal reading glasses, looked down at his docket, then held out his hand to the clerk, who hurriedly slapped some papers into his outstretched hand.

The clerk droned, "You may be seated." She then called out, "Domingo Sanchez."

The guard standing beside the door leading back to the cells area, bowed to the justice, opened the door and waited for a second guard to escort the prisoner into the dock.

Domingo sat down.

"Stand up," barked the clerk.

Domingo made quite a show of insolently and slowly rising. With an arrogant look on his face, he slouched and glared at everyone in the courtroom, including the justice.

"Stand up straight, sir, and listen to me!" Justice Williams' eyes were frosty as he glowered over the top of his readers. For the moment, the justice said nothing; he simply sat back in his chair and let Domingo finish his little show.

Finally, the justice leaned forward. "Are you quite finished, Mr Sanchez?"

"Yeah," Domingo responded.

Justice Williams repeated, even more sternly, "Are you quite finished, MR SANCHEZ?"

The guard leaned over his prisoner and whispered something in his ear.

Domingo straightened up, looked at the justice. "Yes, Your Worship."

Justice Williams handed the file back to the clerk, instructing, "Madam Clerk, would you please read the charges?"

After hearing the numerous charges read aloud, the justice asked Domingo if he had anything to say for himself. Domingo refused to speak but sported a menacing demeanour, which visibly irritated the justice.

Justice Williams said, "Well, Mr Sanchez, you don't have to speak, but you do have to listen to me."

"The charges against you are extremely serious. You nearly killed the woman you allegedly assaulted, and yet you stand before me with an arrogant grin on your face, clearly not bothered in the least by that fact."

"I'm not sure what to make of you, Mr Sanchez, but I certainly know what to do with you!" He sat up straighter in his chair high up on the bench and stared down at Domingo.

"This matter is adjourned for one week. Domingo Sanchez, stand up! You are to appear in court next Tuesday, at 9:00 am for plea. In the meantime, because of the seriousness of your charges, you are to remain in custody pending that appearance."

Domingo's lawyer stood up. "Can we have a bail application now, Your Worship? It will only take a couple of minutes."

"Certainly not! Take it to the Hearing Office, counsel. You know the procedure, quit trying to buck the system. In the meantime, I have ordered that Mr Sanchez remains in custody. Guard, get him out of here."

Domingo swaggered towards the door leading to cells, raising a middle finger towards the bench as he left. Justice Williams wisely chose to ignore the profane gesture.

Several more docket matters were heard. Justice Williams then called a brief recess. "When we reconvene, we will commence with the trial of Bernard Belcourt."

The clerk intoned, "All rise. Court is adjourned for 15 minutes."

Exactly 15 minutes later, the justices' entry door into the courtroom opened.

The clerk quickly stood and announced, "All rise." Once the justice was seated, the clerk droned, "Court is now resumed. You may be seated." After calling Bernard Belcourt's name, she handed the court file up to Justice Williams.

The guard standing near Brutus whispered to him, "Stand up and answer any questions politely."

Brutus stood, his cuffed hands held waist high.

The justice looked down at the large, completely tattooed figure standing in the prisoners' dock.

"Are you Bernard Belcourt?" he asked.

"Yes, sir, but I go by Brutus."

Justice Williams asked Brutus if he had counsel. Brutus pointed to a rather sleazy looking character with longish, gooped-up hair, dressed in an expensive but rather tacky, khaki-coloured suit.

"Are you counsel for Mr Belcourt?"

"Yes, Your Worship. My name is Paulo Santonio, counsel for Bernard Belcourt."

From the prosecution's side of the courtroom, a tall, slim man, dressed in a perfectly tailored navy-blue suit stood up. He had short salt and pepper hair and dark-framed eyeglasses. He appeared to be in his mid-50s.

"Good morning, Your Worship. I represent the prosecution. My name is Walter Crystal."

"Your Worship, I believe that crown and defence have reached an agreement regarding the charges against Mr Belcourt. We have prepared an Agreed Statement of Facts for your perusal."

"May I approach the bench, Your Worship?"

"Just stay where you are, Mr Crystal; Madam Clerk will take the document from you."

The clerk walked over and took the document from the prosecutor. She handed it up to the justice, who flipped through it quickly. He then announced, "This document appears to be rather lengthy. I am going to adjourn in order to peruse it more carefully. Madam Clerk, I will call you when I am ready to reconvene." He rose from his chair and prepared to leave the courtroom. The clerk stood up, saying, "All rise. Court is adjourned briefly."

Thirty minutes later, the justice re-entered the courtroom.

"Stand up, Mr Belcourt, I have some questions for you," Justice Williams said.

Slowly, slovenly, Brutus rose from his seat.

The justice began, "Mr Belcourt, I have read the Agreed Statement of Facts very carefully. You were charged with a lot of offences, the most serious of which was manslaughter. Defence counsel and the prosecutor agree that in exchange for your guilty plea to the manslaughter charge, wherein you have been charged with the killing of Ms Shelby Sidor, all other charges with regard to this incident will be dropped. Is this your understanding?"

"Yes, it is my understanding," Brutus responded.

Justice Williams turned his attention to the prosecutor. "Mr Crystal, is there a medical report that either connects the beating of Ms Sidor to her death or establishes that there is no connection between the beating and the death?"

Walter Crystal spoke, "Yes, Your Worship, there is a medical report."

The justice said, "No medical report was attached to the Agreed Statement of Facts. It is important that I examine that report."

Turning his head towards defence counsel, the justice asked, "Is there any reason why I should not examine the report?"

Defence counsel responded, "You certainly may see the report, Your Worship, but I would argue that it does not establish a direct connection between the beating and the death."

Justice Williams turned back to the prosecutor. "Mr Crystal, do you have any comment?"

"No, Your Worship, no comment."

The justice addressed both counsels. "It is my intention to enter this medical report as Exhibit 1 to the Agreed Statement of Facts."

Turning to Paulo Santonio, Justice Williams asked, "Do you have any argument with respect to that?"

Paulo Santonio said, "I have no objection to the medical report being entered as evidence." He repeated himself, saying, "Although I do submit that the report does not prove a connection between the beating and the death of Ms Sidor beyond a reasonable doubt. That doubt relates to the existence of other medical conditions, as disclosed in the report."

Justice Williams turned to the prosecutor and asked, "Do you have any reply to defence counsel's comments?"

Mr Crystal responded, "I have no argument."

"Madam Clerk," the justice said, "please enter this medical report as Exhibit 1 to the Agreed Statement of Facts."

Justice Williams continued, "The proposed sentence in the Agreed Statement of Facts does not match the egregious behaviour of Mr Belcourt and his connection to the death of Ms Sidor."

"Crown and Defence have agreed to a term of imprisonment of 18 months, followed by two years' probation. Mr Belcourt, stand up! Do you have anything you wish to say before I impose sentence?"

Brutus looked angrily at the justice. "Yes, I have something to say. I didn't beat that woman to death. Paul Jordan wanted to learn about collections. Him and me were just making collections. Paul went nuts and started beating on the old lady when she would not pay. When I realised how bad he was beating her, I pulled him off and shoved him out the door of the trailer. When we left, I saw her laying on the floor, but I can tell you for a fact, that she was definitely alive."

The justice stared at Brutus. "Thank you, Mr Belcourt. Because you were acting in concert with Mr Jordan, you are equally guilty of the manslaughter charge."

"I hereby impose a sentence of five years' imprisonment, with no possibility of parole."

"Bailiff, please remove Mr Belcourt from the courtroom."

As Brutus was led from out of the prisoners' dock, he was heard shouting all the way back to cells, "This is bullshit! I didn't do nothing."

"Next matter," Justice Williams held out his hand for the next file.

Lloyd and Sergeant Gablehaus got up to leave. They had just reached the courtroom door when they heard the clerk call out, "Paul Martin Jordan."

Stunned, Lloyd and Greg looked at each other, then immediately slipped quietly back into their vacated seats.

"What's going on?" Lloyd whispered worriedly to the sergeant.

Greg Gablehaus shrugged his shoulders. "Don't know. Listen!" he said.

Paul stood at counsel table. Paulo Santonio was the same lawyer who had represented Domingo. He stood by Paul Jordan's side.

Greg turned to Lloyd and whispered in his ear, "That sleazy jerk is counsel for the 'East Van Devils'. As well, he represents anyone associated with the gang who requires legal assistance. Bugger is getting rich off the proceeds of crime!"

The crown prosecutor stood and addressed the court, "Your Worship, all charges against Paul Martin Jordan are stayed."

Justice Williams looked down at Paul, stating simply, "Mr Jordan, you are free to go."

. . . .

Chapter 4
Lacey and Parker

Lacey and Parker were working hard at solidifying their marriage, but it was definitely a difficult endeavour, an uphill battle.

Lacey still resented all the time that Parker spent at work. She was convinced that he was a workaholic, and it was definitely not part of his R.C.M.P. career to work himself into an early grave.

Parker, on the other hand, still resented that Lacey had taken off for British Columbia in search of her missing foster sisters, leaving only a note behind. She was untrained and had no backup should things have gone terribly wrong. When Parker tried to discuss it with her, she just said, "Parker, it's water under the bridge. All's well that ended well. Can't you just concentrate on the future?"

It was a never-ending circle, each blaming the other, yet each wanting to forget about the past and deal with their future.

Not too long after Lacey arrived on their doorstep, Hilda and Stumpy Somers had applied for and become permanent guardians of Lacey. Their home was Lacey's sixth foster home. It took adjusting on the parts of all three of them, but Lacey quickly grew to love her guardians. When Stumpy died, both Hilda and Lacey suffered terribly and clung to each other for support.

Hilda's health was failing. Now in a wheelchair, she was unable to live alone at the farm. Despite protests from both Lacey and Parker, Hilda was adamant. She would move into the seniors' home. She would not live with Lacey and Parker. She had all her affairs in order.

Lacey was the sole beneficiary in Hilda's will. She asked Lacey and Parker if they would move to the farm. Hilda was moving into the seniors' home. It was not far from the small town where Parker was stationed. This was a win-win situation for all three people. Hilda could still visit at the farm and, Lacey and Parker had a new home, one they could call their own.

. . . .

Late one morning, after a particularly acrimonious disagreement, Lacey looked at Parker and said, "I'm going to visit with Lloyd and Susanna. I need to get out of here for a bit. It's your day off – want to come with me?"

Parker looked ruefully at Lacey and quietly said, "I'd like to, Lace, I really would, but I've got some paperwork to catch up on. I'd better not."

"Whatever!" Lacey retorted. She grabbed her jacket and purse and left, slamming the door hard behind her, so disappointed and frustrated that teardrops pooled in her eyes.

Fiercely determined to have a pleasant day despite Parker's absence, Lacey applied a rather heavy foot as she drove towards Lloyd and Susanna's place. Suddenly, she heard the abrupt sound of a siren being flicked on and off rapidly. Glancing in her rear-view mirror, she immediately pulled over, thinking 'CRAP!'

Lacey didn't know the young constable who approached the driver's side. He politely asked for her licence, registration, and pink insurance card. Fumbling in her purse, she removed her driver's licence and handed it to the policeman. She then reached into the glove compartment and withdrew the registration and insurance documents.

Checking his nametag, Lacey spoke, "Sorry, Constable Curtis Wilson, I guess I wasn't paying attention to my speed. I'll set my cruise control and be more careful."

She remembered that Parker had once told her that should she ever be stopped for any traffic infraction, whether or not she felt it was unjustified, she should just quietly take the ticket and pay it. She now stared straight ahead, not looking at the young cop. Lacey implored, "Please, just give me my ticket and I'll be on my way."

There was no response from the young constable except for the strange look on his face.

"What's wrong?" Lacey asked.

"Well, ma'am, you see, it's this way. Your husband is my boss. I'm not sure what to do. I'd like to let you off with a warning, but I really don't know if I should do that. If you can wait a minute, I'll call the detachment."

"No, don't do that!" Lacey exclaimed. "The proper thing for you to do is write me out a ticket and let me get going."

If she wasn't still so upset with Parker, she might have felt sorry for the embarrassed young rookie. As it was, she was impatient and annoyed; she just wanted to get the damn ticket and be on her way.

Finally, after what seemed like forever, young Constable Wilson used his own discretion and wrote out a ticket for 10 kilometres over the posted speed limit (even though she had been going 30 over!). He then handed her the ticket, tipped his hat and mumbled, "You take care now, ma'am. Drive carefully. Have a nice day."

As she turned off of the main highway, on impulse, Lacey turned onto the side road approaching Mountain Goat Lake. She needed to do some thinking and calm down before her visit with her brother and her sister-in-law.

The lake lay calm and serene before her. The glassy surface of the water sparkled in the sunshine, as if to say, 'lighten up, Lacey girl, be calm, like me!' The water was so clear that the shoreline was reflected in the shimmering surface.

Lacey instinctively turned her head towards the area where the Trumpeters had built their nest. She was delighted to see both adults swimming with three fuzzy little cygnets paddling in between their parents, trying mightily to keep up.

Lacey watched the swan family for a long time. She could feel the tension easing from between her shoulder blades as she admired the beautiful birds. She couldn't help but envy the co-operation that the two adult swans employed. From the very beginning – each adult taking a turn sitting on the nest – all the way through to swimming with the cygnets, the parent swans shared responsibilities equally. It was obvious that they enjoyed raising their family together, that they enjoyed spending quality time together.

Lacey recognised that perhaps it was unfair to analogise her situation with that of a family of Trumpeter swans, but it was the best she could come up with at the present time.

Finally, she stood up, stretched, and returned to her vehicle. Much calmer, Lacey was now prepared to drive up the hill to Lloyd and Susanna's beautiful log home.

She was determined not to whine or talk about Parker in a negative manner. It wouldn't be fair to put Lloyd and Susanna in the middle of her tottering marriage. Lacey knew that. She and her husband would just have to sort things out on their own, without any help from family.

Although she hadn't phoned to say she was coming, Lloyd and Susanna were happy to see her. Instinctively noticing that Lacey was feeling despondent, they knew not to ask her why Parker wasn't with her.

After sitting on the veranda for a short time, Lloyd excused himself. He had an order he had just completed, a beautiful headboard for a king-sized bed. It was going to be picked up at 1 pm, and he wanted to ensure that everything was in order before the delivery truck arrived.

"See you at supper, Lacey? You can stay, can you not?"

"Sure," Lacey said quietly, unable to hide most of the bitterness in her voice. "Parker is working."

Lloyd headed for his workshop with a cheery wave of his hand.

Lacey couldn't help herself. She was jealous of Lloyd and Susanna's relationship. They never seemed to argue, and they both looked excessively happy. Too bad they couldn't pass on some of that excess, Lacey thought to herself.

She turned to Susanna. "I'm sorry I didn't call to see if it was all right for me to come visit," she said to her sister-in-law. "It was kind of a spur-of-the-minute decision."

Susanna said, "Don't be silly. Lacey, you know you are welcome here any time, whether you phone first or not."

"I'm baking bread and cinnamon buns, and they need some attention. Come on in to the kitchen and we can visit while I punch the dough down. Come to think of it" – she glanced sharply at Lacey – "you might want to punch the dough down yourself. It's a great way to work off any frustration or discontent."

Despite herself, Lacey grinned. "Thanks, Susanna! I really need to punch that dough. Let me just go and wash my hands first."

Susanna waited until Lacey was up to her elbows in bread dough before she quietly asked, "So, Lacey, what's up?"

All of Lacey's good intentions evaporated like a spoonful of sugar in a cup of hot coffee. Burning tears dribbled crookedly out of her eyes and down her cheeks, threatening to drop off the bottom of her chin and fall into the bread dough. She quickly backed away from the table and gestured for Susanna to complete the kneading. She grabbed a Kleenex from the box on top of the fridge, sat down on a kitchen chair, and tried to regain some semblance of composure.

Susanna wisely kept her counsel to herself. She just continued punching the dough as she waited for Lacey to calm down and tell her what was going on.

It took a while. Susanna finished with the dough, covered the bowl with a tea towel, washed her hands, grabbed two cans of Coke out of the fridge, and then gently pushed Lacey in the direction of the veranda at the front of the house. Taking a seat, she watched her sister-in-law pace back and forth on the veranda. Back and forth, to and fro.

Lacey could neither calm down nor stop the tears from raining down her face. Sobbing bitterly, she talked as she walked. Susanna listened. She said nothing, just let Lacey vent.

So much had gone on in her young life. Lacey moaned and then enumerated some of what had occurred. She and Lloyd had been abandoned by their mother after their father went to prison for embezzling funds from his employer. A series of foster homes; the disappearance of three of their foster sisters, at separate times; her marriage to Parker Sutton at the tender age of 16; the capture of the people who had held her foster sisters hostage. The mystery of the missing girls had come about mostly because of Lacey's courageous (but foolhardy) steps towards solving the mystery.

Susanna had, of course, heard Lloyd's version of things. His story was pretty much the same as Lacey's. The subtle differences did not matter. What did matter, though, was Lacey's feeling of despair. Susanna continued to sit quietly and listen to her sister-in-law.

Lacey still paced and vented. Now, back in small town Alberta with her husband, how was she supposed to carry on? There was no excitement, only constant bickering with Parker. He was a workaholic, going in to the R.C.M.P. detachment seven days of every week and most evenings. He didn't want her to find a job because they were going to be moving to the farm, and he said that would keep her busy enough. He said if she wasn't content looking after the farm, then they should consider starting a family!

"Susanna!" Lacey wailed. "I love kids, and I do want a family, but it would be like being a single parent. Parker isn't even around enough to spend a little time with me. How is he going to find time to be a father, to spend quality time with me and the kids? He's more married to his profession than he is to me!"

Susanna interrupted Lacey's lament.

"Do you love Parker, Lacey?" Susanna asked bluntly.

Lacey stopped her ranting and pacing and glared at Susanna. "What kind of question is that?" she asked. "I love Parker – more than anything. It's just that he makes me so mad! When I was staying in Hope, I had a full-time job at the grocery store, a job that I loved, by the way, and I helped solve the mystery of my missing foster sisters."

"I'm lonely, and I'm bored, Susanna. Why can't Parker see that?"

"Have you told him how you are feeling, Lacey?"

Lacey was bitter. "And just when would I do that, Susanna? He's never around! Besides, he should see that for himself."

Unbeknownst to Lacey, Lloyd had heard some of her diatribe. He couldn't avoid it. Lacey was practically screaming. He came out of his shop and walked over to the veranda and up the steps.

He watched his sister wallowing in self-pity for a few minutes before he spoke up. "Lacey, sit down!" His voice was firm. She heard the 'no nonsense allowed' command in his unspoken demeanour. She plopped herself down, folded her arms across her chest and pouted like a two-year-old as she waited for Lloyd to continue.

"First of all, Lacey," Lloyd began, "tell me what you think of Parker's idea of starting a family."

"I want kids," Lacey said agreeably.

Lloyd said, "I didn't ask you if you wanted kids; I asked you what you think of Parker's idea to start a family."

"I think that it's just another thing that Parker feels he needs to control. If he says it's time to start a family, well then, that's that," Lacey said petulantly.

Lloyd was getting mighty irritated. He held his breath and silently counted to 10 before he said, "Lacey, think back to the foster homes we stayed in. Do you think it was a good idea for the biological parents of those kids to have had them, only to give them up or have them taken away?"

"For God's sake, girl, something as earth-changing as having children has to be a joint decision. If it isn't, one or the other of you will end up being a single parent, either raising the children alone or…" He left that thought dangling while he breathed deeply, trying to suppress his irritation with his sister.

Susanna asked, "Lacey, have you considered going to counselling?"

"Parker would never go," Lacey grumbled.

"Have you asked him about it, Lacey?"

Completely vexed, Lacey snapped, "No, Susanna, I have not. I briefly thought that maybe I should go by myself, but you know what, I'm not dumb. I can figure things out for myself!"

Wryly, Lloyd said, "Oh, yeah, Little Sister, and how's that going for you?"

Embarrassed, Lacey hung her head. "Not so good, Lloyd. Not so good."

Taking a large swallow of her Coke, she looked at her only brother. "Lloyd, how is it that you and Susanna get along so well? You never seem to argue or fight; you are so well suited. I can't help but envy you both."

Susanna reached over and held Lacey's hand while Lloyd tried to explain.

"Well, little sis, there isn't a marriage in this world where couples never disagree. If they tell you that, they are either lying or they don't care a fig about each other."

"Susanna and I don't agree all the time. Heck, we probably don't agree half the time. But we are both in accord on one important thing. We communicate. We talk things out until we are able to reach a mutually agreeable outcome. Sometimes things go my way, other times they go Susanna's. Sometimes we figure it out in minutes, other times we figure it out after days go by, after a cooling off period."

"In the short time we have been married, we have been blessed to have Uncle Henry and Cora to go to for advice. Uncle Henry says that once married, if a guy ever had a selfish thought in his body, he better stomp on it really quickly; same for the gal. There is no room in a good marriage for selfishness, self-pity or rigidity. I'm not saying that everything has to be totally agreed to by both partners. You just have to pick your battles. Ask yourself, 'is this really so important to me that I cannot reach some kind of compromise?'"

"These questions may hurt, Lacey, but they need to be asked. Are you selfish? Prone to self-pity? Are you so rigid in your beliefs that you can't listen to what Parker has to say, with an open mind to the possibility that you might end up changing your opinion? Have you ever picked a good time to talk? By that I mean really talk deeply with Parker? Talk at a time when he wasn't exhausted after just working all night or all day, at a time when he had a relatively stress-free day so that he had some energy to try to work things out? Have you ever asked if he would spend some quality time with you on his day off, time when you two could have a heart-to-heart discussion about problems in your marriage? Maybe in a place with no distractions, such as Mountain Goat Lake. Heck, have you ever even told him how lonely you feel?"

Lacey listened, not with just her ears but also with her heart. Smirking, she said, "That's more than one question, Big Brother!" She paused for a moment, absorbing all the questions Lloyd had aimed at her. "But seriously," she asked, "it's really that simple?"

"HELL, NO!" Lloyd and Susanna yelled in unison.

Susanna took over. "Marriage is often referred to as a 50/50 union. It's more like 150/150. It's constant work, constantly trying to put yourself in your spouse's shoes when it comes to matters that you are having difficulty bending to. It's not easy, but then, anything worthwhile is worth working hard for." She stared intently at Lacey. "Do you understand? I know the math doesn't compute, 150/150, but my point is, there is no such thing as a 100% division of labour in a good marriage, in any marriage really. People who believe that their marriage chores will be split right down the middle are in for a sad surprise."

"How do you and Lloyd split things, Susanna?" Lacey asked.

Susanna glanced over at Lloyd. They both laughed.

"We have 'pink jobs' and 'blue jobs'. Regardless of the 'colour', we each do whatever needs to be done," Lloyd said.

"What do you mean, 'pink jobs' and 'blue jobs'?" Lacey looked at Susanna for an answer.

Her sister-in-law grinned again. "Well, for instance, repairing nicks and scratches around the house – filling chips and touch-up painting, that's a 'blue job' in our house, In other words, Lloyd's job. Household chores such as washing floors, laundry, and gardening, that's a 'pink job' in our house. In other words, my job. In reality, it's just a fun way of divvying up daily living requirements. There's no such thing as 'blue' or 'pink'. Whatever needs to be done, gets done, often with both of us working together to lighten the load."

Susanna leaned back in her chair, scrutinising Lacey as she struggled to put everything she had just been told in perspective.

They had been so deep in discussion that they neither saw nor heard the vehicle that had approached some time before. They all jumped when Parker climbed the steps to the veranda.

"Hey, Parker!" Lloyd held out his hand to shake his brother-in-law's. "How long have you been here?"

"Long enough," Parker said. Walking over to his wife, he put his hand on Lacey's shoulder. "After you left, Lace, I got to thinking. It's my day off, what the heck am I doing? I have a beautiful wife whom I love dearly but I spend no time at all with. The detachment can survive without me for one day."

Parker looked over at his in-laws and quietly asked, "Am I interrupting anything, arriving unannounced as I have?"

"ABSOLUTELY NOT!" Once again, Lloyd and Susanna spoke in unison, almost as if they could read one another's thoughts. The sombre mood lightened considerably as everyone chuckled.

Lacey couldn't let go of Parker's hand. The lump lodged in her throat was too big for her to speak.

Parker looked at her. "You're so right. It's time we started communicating, Lace. We'll figure out the best way to do that, beginning perhaps with some counselling sessions to help us form a plan to get established. What do you think about that?"

Lacey squeezed his hand even harder, nodding her head in agreement.

She stood up. "Sounds great, Parker."

She was quiet for a minute before she continued, "Just for now, though, let's enjoy a beautiful sunny day with Lloyd and Susanna. There has to be some fun as well as hard work in a successful marriage. Let's start with the fun!"

"Hey, everyone," she called out, "I forgot to tell you – the Trumpeters are now parents. The little ones were swimming when I stopped at the lake on my way here. Let's grab the canoes and go have a look."

Laughing, Lloyd glanced over at Parker. "Race you to the shed!" He took off before the last words were even out of his mouth.

Susanna suggested to Lacey, "Let's let the guys go ahead. You and I can make up a picnic for supper. It is such a beautiful day. We can meet them at the lake when we are ready."

She called loudly to Lloyd, "Lacey and I will wait for the delivery truck to pick up the headboard and then come down to the lake!" Lloyd hollered back, "Thanks, Suz!"

Lacey gave a thumbs-up to Susanna and then walked to the storage shed and kissed Parker on the tip of his nose. "Later, 'gator."

Parker gave his wife a pat on the butt before he turned and helped Lloyd fasten the canoes to the top of the vehicle.

Later, standing on the veranda before heading home, Lloyd asked Parker when they would be moving to the farm. Parker said, "On my next day off. Let's see…" Checking his ever-present pocket-sized calendar, he said, "Two weeks from Saturday."

Lloyd responded, "Perfect! Uncle Henry and Cora will be back from Arizona by then. How about we all show up at your place about eight o'clock Saturday morning and get the move done?"

"Great!" Parker replied. "See you then. Thanks again for a super day."

He turned to Lacey and said, "You go first. I'll be just behind you but far enough behind to keep out of your dust."

Lloyd and Susanna stood arm-in-arm, waving as the pair headed off down the hill.

"Positive day, hey, my love?" he whispered to Susanna. She smiled dreamily at her attentive husband. "Only one thing left to make it perfect."

"Oh?" Lloyd said, grinning lewdly. "And what might that be?"

Laughing, Susanna raced into the house and down the hall towards their bedroom. Just before he caught her, she turned around and ran upstairs. "You'll have to catch me to find out!"

. . . .

Moving day dawned crisp but clear. Puffy, lazy clouds dangled in the sky. With not a breath of wind to chase them, the clouds peeked in Lacey and Parker's bedroom window. Bright yellow sunlight flirted with the couple in the bed as if to say, 'Come on, you lazybones! It's moving day!'

When the alarm rang at 7 am, Lacey opened her eyes, yawned, and stretched. Leaning on her elbows, she watched Parker as he slept soundly, through the ringing.

There had been no magic elixir the past two and a half weeks, but they were both definitely trying to communicate, not only their feelings but their thoughts and ideas. It was getting easier every day. They both were happy with the move to the small farm that Stumpy and Hilda had worked so hard to keep in shape. Lacey was willing to try staying at home, not looking for a job, at least until they had the house unpacked and set up the way they wanted it to be. Parker had told her that if she was willing to go that far, he would be willing to further discuss Lacey finding a job, once they were settled in the beautiful old farmhouse.

Lacey left Parker to sleep a bit longer. Although he had been on day shift the day before, he had been called out on an emergency in the middle of the night. She quietly shut off the radio and then went into the bathroom to shower. Dressing quickly, she went to the kitchen and began making pancakes and sausages for breakfast. Her brother and Susanna and Uncle Henry and Cora would arrive any minute now. She made coffee and set the table for six people.

At 7:30, she called Parker. "Hey, lazybones, it's time to get up! Uncle Henry and the moving crew will be here any minute. I've got breakfast cooking!"

A loud, exaggerated, extremely fake moan came from the bedroom, but she heard Parker get right up and head for the shower. Lacey quickly went into the bedroom and made the bed before everyone arrived.

Parker and the crew entered the kitchen simultaneously, right on the button of 8 am. Lacey hugged Uncle Henry and Cora, welcoming them back from their winter sojourn to Arizona. They all dug in hungrily to the excellent breakfast Lacey had prepared.

Uncle Henry pushed back from the table with a phony groan. "Oh, no! I'm too full to pack now. Count me out, Miss Lacey, just count me out!"

Lacey laughed. "It's okay, Uncle; I've already packed everything except our breakfast dishes. You just need to load all the boxes onto your truck. Then, when we get to the farm, you just have to unload those boxes. Each box is marked with a black marker indicating which room to put the box in. With all six of us helping each other, we'll be done in no time."

Parker grinned and pointed at his wife. "Little Miss Efficiency, hard at work!" he said. "I didn't even have to crack the whip."

"Tee-hee!" snorted Lacey. "Lucky for you, I'd say!"

While the men were carrying out the boxes Susanna helped Lacey clean up the kitchen, putting each dish into a moving box once they were dried. Lacey had already marked the box 'KITCHEN'.

"Sounds like things are going better in this household?" Susanna questioned her sister-in-law.

"So far, so great," Lacey said. "You were right, though, it's not easy. We have to remind ourselves constantly that it is a full-time job but worth the effort. You know, Susanna? It truly is worth the effort. It's getting easier every day. Thanks so much for all of your excellent suggestions."

Within the hour, Uncle Henry's truck was fully loaded and ready to roll. Parker took a last look around to be sure nothing was missed. Lacey was a good housekeeper, so she, Susanna, and Cora said they would only have to do one last quick clean-up and then they would head straight out to the farm.

"Well," Lloyd said, "can you stop and pick up some pizza before you come? We'll be pretty darn hungry by the time you ladies get there."

"Already on our list," Cora sweetly replied. "We'll be at the farm by noon."

At 11:30, the ladies were on the road, four large pizzas safely stored on the seat in the back, next to Lacey.

About two kilometres away from the driveway leading up to the farmhouse, Susanna, who was driving, screamed as a large black car headed straight for them, driving down the wrong side of the road. At the last second, the driver swerved, avoiding a collision. He did not stop; he just sped away, laughing maniacally!

Susanna slammed on her brakes, stopped the car in the middle of the driving lane. Her teeth chattered and her hands shook.

"What?" Lacey had been dozing in the back seat. "What's happening?"

Speechless, Susanna and Cora both pointed to the ditch. Uncle Henry's truck lay tipped over on its roof, the wheels still spinning, the engine still running.

Lacey directed Susanna to drive into the ditch and stop behind the truck. As she leaped out of the car, she was already dialling 9-1-1. Cora took the phone from Lacey's trembling hands. As she spoke with the operator, Cora pointed towards the truck. "Go!" she mouthed silently.

Susanna and Lacey walked around the truck, then pulled on the driver's door. They had to wait a minute for Cora to get off the phone because they needed her assistance. It took all three women to finally yank the door open.

Uncle Henry was dangling from his seat belt, upside down. He was conscious but dazed. His forehead was bleeding profusely where his head had hit the steering wheel. "I'm okay," he said to Cora. "Stop fussing! Check on Lloyd and Parker."

Parker was sprawled awkwardly across the front of the cab, seat belt digging in to his chest, upside down except for his right leg. His leg was trapped between the door and some smashed-in parts of the truck that had landed inside the cab and settled firmly against the passenger's seat. Shattered glass from the broken windshield littered the dash, the seats, the hair, and clothing, of both Henry and Parker. Blood was leaking slowly through Parker's jeans.

"I'm all right," he said, gritting his teeth against the pain. "I just can't move my leg; it's stuck! Call for help and see how Lloyd is doing."

The three women raced once again to the driver's side of the truck.

Lloyd had been sitting behind Henry. He too was upside down, his seat belt tight against his chest. He had smashed his head against the side window. The back window had blown inward from the force of the accident. Other than some pretty severe bleeding on the top of his head and two swollen, blackened eyes, he was conscious and alert. Afraid to move him, Lacey told him to just stay still; the ambulance was on its way.

"What happened?" she asked.

Lloyd's white face looked as if it had been washed in flour. "Black BMW with B.C. plates. I got a quick, but clear, look at the driver. Lacey, it was Domingo. I'd bet my last dollar on it."

Susanna looked at Parker, terrified. "Parker, did you see him too?"

"Yes. The driver sure looked like a poster of Domingo we received yesterday at the detachment."

Lacey gasped. "Why was there a poster? I thought Lloyd said he was in jail pending a court appearance! Why didn't you say something, Parker?"

"Because I had no reason to suspect he would come to Alberta. He's the leader of the East Van Devils. Everyone thought he would hole up in B.C. somewhere, hide out within his gang. Nobody even remotely considered that he might come to Alberta. Nobody."

"Domingo purposely came at us, forcing Uncle Henry to take the ditch at highway speed. There was a large boulder and deep ruts in the ditch. We hit that boulder. Before Uncle Henry could bring the truck to a stop, it tipped right over onto its roof. We're lucky to be alive."

Lacey brought Parker back on topic. "You haven't said what Domingo is doing out of gaol. What is he doing out?"

"Apparently, they were transferring him from the courthouse to a Sheriffs' transport van. The justice had ordered that his handcuffs and shackles be removed, because Domingo had promised the justice that he wouldn't cause any problems!"

"Stupid, stupid, stupid! That justice needs to retire! How could he have been so naïve as to believe a man like Domingo? That justice has been on the bench for years! I just don't get it!"

"Just as the deputy was opening the back door of the van, which was parked in a special area inside the parkade, Domingo hit him with both fists, right on the guy's left temple and then again to the back of his head. He shoved him into the back of the van. He also managed to grab the deputy's gun. Domingo then locked the doors and threw away the key."

"Domingo was so quiet, so quick that the driver of the transport van didn't even realise what was going on until it was too late; he was locked inside the van with his injured partner."

Horrified, Susanna's voice trembled as she said, "He drove right at me too! He swerved at the last possible second. He was laughing like a crazy person as he roared on by!"

"Parker," Lacey asked in a deceptively calm tone. "Domingo? How would he even know where to find us? We're sitting ducks! Somebody must have posted a very high bail for him to be out. I don't know anybody with that kind of money, do you?"

"Sure," Lloyd interrupted, "the East Van Devils. If they don't have the cash, they certainly have access to that much money. The WARLORDS have that kind of dough. They also control the East Van Devils. Now, if they have put up Domingo's bail, they will have even more control over them."

"I think I should give Greg Gablehaus a call, give him a heads up."

Susanna said firmly, "Yes, give him a call but not until AFTER you are checked out at the hospital!"

In the distance, they heard approaching sirens. It was only a couple of minutes after that, the flashing red and blue lights of a police cruiser came roaring into view, followed by an ambulance, sirens screaming, followed by a fire truck, its deep-toned siren growling.

The EMTs, with the assistance of the firemen, carefully supported their necks with cervical collars before they removed Henry and Lloyd from the overturned truck and laid them on stretchers.

"Whew!" Uncle Henry joked feebly. "We were getting mighty dizzy hanging upside down like opossums!"

It took quite a bit longer to extricate Parker from the front passenger's area. The firemen pulled out the Jaws of Life and needed to remove the entire door before Parker could be freed. An EMT quickly put a tourniquet above the deep gash on his leg before Parker was transferred to the waiting ambulance.

Just before the ambulance pulled out to turn around and head back to town, Fred Gablehaus approached Parker.

"Just thought you would like to know, Parker, they caught up to Domingo Sanchez a couple minutes ago, going 150 kilometres an hour in that black BMW of his. Thought they might have to let him go rather than chase him, but he suddenly pulled over. One of the officers drew his gun, approached the car and opened the door. Sanchez leaped out like an enraged bull in a Mexican bullfighting ring!"

"He put up quite a fight with the police, but with assistance from the firemen, he is now in custody. He is in handcuffs and in shackles and under armed guard. We are going to meet the Vancouver guys half way and turn him over to them. He sure is an evil dude."

"You take care now. Get that leg looked after and don't worry about the detachment. I've got it covered."

"Thanks, Fred," Parker said quietly, "thanks for the update. We'll all be able to settle down some now."

"Oh, another thing, Parker. I'm going to be talking to my brother Greg today about this. Just thought you'd like to know." He gave a small wave and headed back to his police car.

Lacey was so relieved that Domingo was in custody once again, that she started to cry. Parker grabbed both of her hands, holding on for dear life. "Guess moving day will have to wait a bit, huh?"

Henry Greshner wasn't sure if it was divine intervention or just plain old dumb luck, but none of the men suffered serious enough injuries that they had to remain in hospital.

The most severe injury was Parker's leg – it required 30-some stitches. The doctor on call told him that if he swore, he would stay off his leg for a couple of days and then come back to get it checked, he could go home with the rest of the group. Lacey didn't wait for Parker to answer; she told the doctor that he would stay seated or lying down with his leg up if she had to tie it up!

One benefit of living in such a small community was that the local insurance adjuster was able to come out and assess the accident scene that very day. Once he completed his work, he gave them the go-ahead to move the boxes both from the back of the truck and those that lay scattered in the ditch, to the farm. He also called the local towing company, who said they would be able to flip the upside-down truck and haul it to the garage first thing the next morning.

The women took control. Cora would have made a good drill sergeant. She barked at the men to get to the farmhouse and rest while the women moved the crates. Uncle Henry voiced his concern that someone would hurt themselves lifting those heavy boxes. Susanna assured him that if the box was too heavy for the three women to lift, they would empty it right in the ditch and transport the contents in manageable numbers.

Henry was, understandably, worried about the damages to his truck. Lacey suggested that he and Cora, and Lloyd and Susanna, spend the night. That way, they would be available in the morning when the tow truck arrived. Fred Gablehaus had said he would be out to the farm the next morning as well, to tidy up any missing details about the accident.

Hilda, before moving to the seniors' home, had surprised Lacey and Parker by hiring three cleaning ladies to clean the house from stem to stern. All four bedrooms and bathrooms were as sparkling as if they were brand new. Every kitchen appliance shone brightly. There wasn't so much as a single dust bunny anywhere. Everyone agreed that staying overnight was a good idea.

Suddenly remembering the large pizzas, Lacey made a salad while Susanna turned on the oven to reheat the pizzas. Everyone ate hungrily, and when they finished, there wasn't so much as a crumb left.

Once supper was over, the men were ordered to do absolutely nothing while the women headed back to the accident site to load the boxes from the truck and the ditch into both cars and bring them back to the house.

Cora worked as hard as Lacey and Susanna. Although there were a few boxes that they had to unpack because they were too heavy for the women to lift, by 9 pm everything had been removed from the truck and the ditch and transported back to the house. Each marked box sat in the appropriate room, ready to be unpacked the next day.

By 9:30 pm, the only sound in the farmhouse was an occasional snore or groan from one or another of the men as they tried to turn over, sore and aching muscles vehemently protesting the slightest movement.

. . . .

One morning a few weeks after the 'accident', Parker went back to work. A telephone message slip showed that Sergeant Gablehaus had called this morning and asked that Parker return his call.

They played telephone tag for an hour. When Parker and Greg were finally able to connect, Greg Gablehaus gave Parker some very disturbing news. Domingo had made his first court appearance the day before. He had plead 'Not Guilty' to the charges involving the assault on Mona Grace. A different justice took his pleas. Despite an application by the crown to hold him without bail, Domingo was released on $500,000.00 cash bail. It had been paid by the WARLORDS.

"Parker, I'm pretty sure that Domingo will be constantly shadowed by members of the WARLORDS. With the amount of cash they have just posted to bail Domingo out, the gang is not going to risk him breaching his bail conditions."

"I tried to reach Lloyd. There was no answer at his place. I'm thinking it might be a good idea if Lloyd and Susanna were to ask Mona Grace and Charley to come for a visit, just until Domingo's trial. We will protect Mona Grace when she comes back to East Van to testify against Domingo. The justice expedited the date for the trial, but unfortunately, it is still two months away. There was no earlier trial date available."

Parker said that he knew that Lloyd and Susanna had gone to Edmonton. A building supply company was going out of business and all of the company's assets were being auctioned today. They planned on returning home the next day.

"In the meantime," Parker told Sergeant Gablehaus, "I will try and get hold of them. It will very likely be an uphill battle to get Mona Grace to leave her house and her job for such a lengthy period of time and even more difficult to convince Charley that she needs to come with her mother. I am sure that Lloyd will give convincing her his best shot. If Mona Grace will listen to anyone, she will listen to Lloyd."

Greg advised that Domingo had been served with a copy of the information with respect to a dangerous driving charge arising out of the 'accident' in Alberta. He had plead guilty to the charge and was fined $1,500.00.

"Disgusting!" was Parker's only response to that unwelcome news.

The two men agreed to keep in touch and then hung up.

By lunchtime, Parker's leg was throbbing painfully, and he advised the receptionist that he was going home for the day.

Immediately after supper, Parker called Lloyd.

"Sorry to interrupt your trip, Lloyd," Parker began. "How was the auction?"

"It was just fine. I'm having a whole lot of lumber being delivered next week. The best part? I got all of it, including delivery, for about 25¢ on the dollar. Susanna and I are celebrating by attending dinner and a play at the Mayfield Dinner Theater."

Parker said, "Now I'm even more sorry to interrupt."

"No problem, buddy, what's up?"

Parker explained why he was calling, emphasising the danger both Mona Grace and Charley were in with Domingo out on the street.

"Lloyd, do you think you can convince them that they would be safer if they came and stayed, either with you and Susanna, or with Lacey and me until it is time to go back to Vancouver for the trial?"

Lloyd thought for a minute before he replied, "It'll be like pulling hens' teeth, but I'll give it my best sales pitch, Parker."

"We'll be home by mid-afternoon tomorrow. As soon as we get home, I'll try and get in touch with Mona Grace. I'll let you know how I make out."

Parker returned to the living room, sat down next to Lacey and held her hand. A feeling of impending disaster permeated his thoughts for the rest of the evening. Not wanting to worry Lacey unduly, he just supplied her with the barest details of his conversations with both Greg Gablehaus and Lloyd, omitting that the WARLORDS had posted Domingo's bail in the sum of a half million dollars. He figured that was more information than she needed to handle at the moment.

Susanna called Lacey as soon as they returned from the city, telling her she could only speak for a minute, because Lloyd needed to get hold of Mona Grace.

Lacey suggested that Susanna and Lloyd come for supper. Then they could tell them all about their trip to Edmonton. After that, Lloyd could fill them in on Mona Grace's reaction to the suggestion that she and Charley come and hide out until it was time for Domingo's trial.

Checking first with Lloyd, Susanna readily agreed that they would come to the farm in time for supper.

Spring was definitely in the air. The evening air was warm and inviting. Parker informed his wife that he would barbeque steak, potatoes, and corn for supper. Parker nursed a beer; Lloyd sipped on a Coke. The girls were in the kitchen making a salad. The guys used this opportunity to talk about the danger that Mona Grace and Charley were in.

"Any luck convincing Mona Grace?" Parker asked.

Lloyd gritted his teeth and shook his head dejectedly. "I talked my head off for an entire hour, but I couldn't convince her. She says she can't miss any more work. I told her she wouldn't need that job if she was dead! She says that Domingo won't hurt her again. When I asked her how she could be so sure about that, she said he promised her! I said, if she wouldn't listen to reason, would she please try and convince Charley that she would be safer in Alberta. Mona Grace said that Domingo has no reason to harm Charley."

"Finally, I shouted at her. I couldn't help myself. I told her that the danger was not so much from Domingo as from the WARLORDS. I told her that the gang would stop at nothing to ensure that Domingo didn't breach his bail. The gang would be out their half million dollars if Domingo breached even the smallest term of his release. I told her she was in far more danger from the WARLORDS than she ever would be from Domingo."

Parker asked, "What was her response to that?"

Lloyd grunted. "She said she was born and raised in East Van; she knew how to take care of herself!"

"Now what?" Parker asked.

"I called Greg Gablehaus and filled him in. He said they will do what they can to keep Mona Grace and Charley under their radar, but they are so short-handed they can't promise much."

"Susanna called Charley and told her what's going on, hoping Charley can convince Mona Grace of the urgency and danger of this whole mess."

Parker asked, "What was her response?"

Lloyd said, "She's as stubborn as her mother. Susanna couldn't get it through Charley's thick head either that there is a genuine risk of harm if they stay in Vancouver. Charley said that if her mother thought it was okay to stay, then Charley was fine with that."

"I'll keep the pressure on. I'll keep trying, Parker. It's all I can do."

Seated at the dining room table, Lacey and Parker listened to the details of Lloyd and Susanna's successful and entertaining trip to Edmonton. When dessert was served, Lloyd reached over and picked up his wife's hand, kissed it tenderly and said, "You tell them, Suz."

Lacey stared at them. "Tell us what?"

With the biggest grin on his face since before they were abandoned by their parents at ages 9 and 13, Lloyd squeezed Susanna's hand.

Her eyes practically sparking with excitement, Susanna announced, "We're pregnant!"

Lacey jumped up so quickly that she knocked her chair over. Hugging both Susanna and Lloyd at the same time, tears of joy trickled down her cheeks. "I'm going to be an auntie! Parker, you're going to be an uncle! Congratulations! We are so excited for you!"

Chapter 5
Mona Grace and Charley

After Lacey and Parker left for home, Lloyd and Susanna sat on the front veranda, enjoying the fading of the day.

A few stars had already begun to twinkle in the darkening sky when Lloyd announced to Susanna that he had already begun fashioning a cradle for the little one. He asked if she would like to see it and perhaps give him some input into its design. Susanna kissed him thoroughly before she replied, "I trust you implicitly, husband, and I would rather be surprised and amazed by your expertise. Don't show me until it is completed, okay?"

"By the way, Lloyd," she asked, "have you let Mona Grace and Charley know our news?"

"I'm just about to give them a call," he said. "Want to tell them yourself?"

Susanna stretched and yawned loudly. "No, Lloyd, you should do it. I'm exhausted, and I'll head off to get ready for bed while you speak with your friends. While you're at it, maybe try once more to convince them to get out of Vancouver and stay with us for a while, just until it's safe."

"Yeah, r-i-i-i-i-ght!" Lloyd drawled sardonically. "It's not going to happen." Seeing the look on Susanna's face, he quickly added, "But of course, I will try again to convince them. Just don't hold your breath!"

Susanna gave Lloyd a hug before she handed him the phone. As she opened the front door, Lloyd was already dialling Mona Grace's number.

The phone rang four times before Mona Grace answered it. She yelled into the receiver as loudly as she could, "Dang it, Lloyd! I told you I am not going anywhere and neither is Charley! No one is going to bother us. Why won't you just give up?"

Lloyd chuckled quietly before he spoke. "Well, Miss Mona Grace, you see, it's this way. I'm actually calling about something totally different." He waited for at least a minute before Mona Grace spoke rather cautiously.

"You are?" she queried.

"Yup!" Lloyd said gleefully. "It's not always all about you, my friend; it's not always all about you."

Exasperated, she wailed into the phone, "Well then, why are you calling me? Quit being so doggone mysterious and tell me why you're calling. Is everything okay? Is someone sick or hurt?"

Detecting a tone of voice that was bordering on panic, Lloyd took pity on her. "Relax, Mona Grace! I've got good news, no, not good news, GREAT news!" He hastened to correct himself, then paused once again, listening for Mona Grace's groan of frustration.

"WELL?" she screamed at him. "Are you going to tell me or just jack around for the rest of this call?"

"Now, now," Lloyd admonished with feigned disappointment while trying to speak loudly over her ranting. "Is that any way to talk to a new father-to-be?"

She didn't hear him; she continued to yell. Suddenly, the line was so silent that Lloyd wondered if perhaps the connection had been lost.

"What did you just say to me, Lloyd?" Mona Grace asked. "I didn't hear what you said."

"Well," Lloyd said in a very serious manner, "perhaps if you were to close your mouth for a second or two, you might have heard what I said."

A deep sigh, followed by a heart-rending moan, followed by an irritated mutter, reached Lloyd's ear. Silence finally prevailed as she waited for him to repeat what he had said.

"I asked you, my dear friend, Mona Grace Ford, if that was any way to talk to a new father-to-be!"

This time, Lloyd had to wince and cover his ears as she let out an eardrum-piercing scream. When she settled down, he grinned to himself, thinking that this was the only time he had been able to put one over on his friend.

After several more minutes of chitchat, Lloyd said he really had to hang up and call Charley and let her in on the good news. Mona Grace told him that Charley had exams the next day and was studying with a friend. She asked Lloyd if he and Susanna would mind if Mona Grace told Charley his good news the next time she spoke with her.

"We don't mind," Lloyd said simply.

Changing gears abruptly, he continued, speaking swiftly before Mona Grace could interrupt. "Mona Grace, this is big news for Susanna and me. We are so delighted about this new baby. The last thing we need, though, is to have to worry about you and Charley. Make no mistake about it; we will worry ourselves sick if you don't get out of Vancouver. Please, come and stay with us, just until Domingo is in prison. It's the only way you'll be safe."

"We are safe, Lloyd," Mona Grace said firmly. "I've told you dozens of times, Domingo won't hurt either Charley or me. I know him, and I know for a fact that he won't hurt either of us. So, Lloyd, thanks for all your concern, but we aren't coming."

Before she could disconnect, Lloyd hastily called out, "Wait, wait please, Mona Grace. Maybe you're right, maybe Domingo won't hurt either of you, but what about the rest of the East Van Devils? Or, more importantly and even more dangerously, what about the WARLORDS? They'll stop at nothing. If Domingo breaches his bail conditions, and make no mistake about it, he 'will'. Do you think there is any possibility that they won't come after anyone they feel might be close to Domingo? That major gang has more money than they know what to do with, but they're no fools. No gang, no matter how small and insignificant, no matter how big and powerful is willing to lose a half million dollars' bail. Make no mistake, the WARLORDS will do whatever it takes to get that money back. If it means holding somebody close to Domingo hostage until the trial is over and they get that money back, they'll do it!" He finally stopped his discourse, mostly because he ran out of breath.

"Lloyd, listen to me. I'll make a deal with you. When Charley's exams are over, she and I will meet with Sergeant Gablehaus to discuss how we can remain safe. I promise you, that if anything untoward happens, we will head directly to Greg's and do whatever he instructs us to do."

"In the meantime, you just be happy and take care of that beautiful young mother-to-be. Maybe when university classes are over, Charley and I will come for a short visit."

"Thanks for caring, Lloyd, I know you are speaking out of love for Charley and me, but as I have told you so many times, we're big girls; we can take care of ourselves!"

"Now, keep in touch. Love ya, Lloyd. We'll be careful." She blew a soft kiss into the phone and hung up.

A short time later, Lloyd lay in bed beside his wife. Watching Susanna sleeping peacefully while she rested her hand on the miniscule bump that was their developing child, Lloyd wished he was as certain as Mona Grace that everything would be all right. He had done his best to convince her that she needed to leave Vancouver in order to be safe, but it was now completely out of his hands. He rolled over and tried to sleep. The early hours of dawn were streaking through the dust motes in front of the bedroom window before he finally dozed, dreaming of new-born babies and aging gangsters.

Late the following afternoon, Lloyd was sanding the baby's cradle. Truly a work of art; he was building a family heirloom, knowing that their new baby would be the first of many generations to grow up, use the cradle and then pass it on and to appreciate its beauty and sentimental value.

As comforted as he found himself while working on this labour of love, something insistently niggled at the back of his mind as he worked. He knew he was being paranoid, but he couldn't help feeling that something was wrong. He shook his head, told himself he was being ridiculous. If something was wrong with either Mona Grace or Charley, someone would have contacted him. If not him, then that someone would have called Sergeant Gablehaus.

After a couple of hours, he could stand it no more. Picking up his cell phone, he hit the speed dial button. Charley's phone rang – and rang – and rang. Her cheery voicemail clicked on. "Hey, there! You've reached Charley. Sorry I can't answer my phone right now, but if you leave your name and number, I'll get back to you – I promise!"

Lloyd disconnected the call. He took several deep breaths before chastising himself. He thought, *don't be a dope, Lloyd. You just spoke with Mona Grace this afternoon! She told you Charley had exams to write. Charley's either still in class or at the library studying. You know how conscientious a student she is. Try her again in a day or two. Don't disturb her school routine!*

When he heard Susanna calling him in for supper, he started walking towards the house, hitting the speed dial for Mona Grace's cell number. As had happened with Charley's phone, Mona Grace's cell rang – and rang – and rang – until her voicemail picked up. He hung up without leaving a message but immediately dialled her office number. This time he got a message. "You have reached the office number for Mona Grace Ford. I'm with a client, so I am sorry, but I cannot take your call right now. Please leave your name and number, and I will call you back as soon as I am able. Thanks for calling!"

Susanna sensed something was up when Lloyd sat down at the table. He stirred his food aimlessly with his fork but ate nothing. Normally a big eater, this was so unlike Lloyd. Susanna asked quietly, "Is something wrong with the food, Lloyd?"

Her husband looked up but appeared not to see her. "Huh? What? What did you ask me, Suz? I'm sorry, I didn't get that."

"I asked you if anything was wrong with your food. You've pretty much stirred it into a mushy mess, and you are a million miles away."

Lloyd ran his hands through his thick hair. His jaw clenched as he spoke to his wife. "I'm sorry, Susanna. There's nothing wrong with the food. I'm worried, is all. I can't help it. I have a deep sense that something is very wrong. I can't get an answer either on Charley's cell phone or on Mona Grace's cell either. I even tried Mona Grace's office number. Something is not right. I can feel it!"

Susanna said calmly, "Lloyd, you just spoke to Mona Grace this afternoon. Did she sound like anything was wrong?"

"No, she sounded fine. In fact, she sounded better than fine. Stupid but fine."

Susanna said, "That's not a very nice thing to say, Lloyd. Mona Grace is far from stupid. If she had any concerns, you would likely be the first one she would call."

Lloyd sat up straighter in his chair. "Susanna! You're a genius. I would not be the first one she or Charley would call. We agreed that she would call Greg Gablehaus if something wasn't right. Why didn't I think of that myself? Thanks, Suz!"

Lloyd pushed his chair away from the table, reaching for his cell phone lying on the kitchen counter behind him. In a great hurry, he carelessly hit the wrong speed dial button. He hung up and carefully connected with Sergeant Gablehaus' cell phone.

Greg answered on the first ring. "Sergeant Gablehaus here, how can I help you?"

"Greg! Thank God you picked up! It's Lloyd. You'll think I'm crazy, but I have a terrible premonition. I spoke with Mona Grace this afternoon. I just tried to call Charley, then I tried Mona Grace's cell, and then her office number. I'm getting no answer anywhere, only voicemails. Something is wrong, Greg, I just know it!"

Greg Gablehaus interjected, "Whoa, whoa, slow down there, Lloyd. Let me ask you a couple of questions. Firstly, how did she sound when you spoke with Mona Grace earlier?"

"Fine, she sounded fine."

"Well then, why do you think something is wrong now? You only spoke with her this afternoon. What could possibly have occurred since then to cause your panic?"

"I don't know, Greg, I only know that something is not right!" The fright Lloyd was experiencing reverberated loud and clear through the phone lines.

Greg Gablehaus asked Lloyd, "How did your conversation with Mona Grace this afternoon go?"

Lloyd fought hard to regain some sort of control. Taking a huge breath in, he let it out slowly before speaking. "She told me that Charley was writing exams and so she wasn't available until after exams. She said that perhaps they would come here for a short visit once the exams were completed. She also said that she and Charley would come and see you to discuss a safety plan."

Greg asked Lloyd, "Did you honestly expect that Mona Grace would hang up the phone and then she and Charley would come and see me immediately? You did say Charley was writing exams, remember?"

Lloyd was beginning to feel like an idiot. "I'm sorry to have bothered you, Greg. I guess I am a lot more spooked by the Domingo thing than I thought! I'll try to settle down and not overreact again."

"It's not bothering me, Lloyd," Greg said, "although I'm kind of concerned about your state of mind at the moment. We are really trying to look out for Mona Grace and Charley as best we can, you know."

"Yes, I know," Lloyd said morosely.

Suddenly, he sat straight up in his chair. His panic dissipated, to be replaced by a feeling of total excitement, utter joy. "I almost forgot to tell you, Greg," Lloyd said happily, "and this is terrific news! Susanna and I are expecting a baby, isn't that something?"

"That sure is, Lloyd! Best news I've had in a long time. Tell Susanna congrats from me."

"Now, you take care. If anything transpires, I'll be sure to be in touch. Just enjoy your good night sleeps while you can. Once that little one arrives, your sleeping days are over, my friend. Take care and don't worry. If you want to call me, I assure you it won't be a bother. Talk soon, Lloyd. Have a good night."

Susanna looked over at Lloyd, her eyebrows raised. "Everything's fine, right?"

Lloyd reached over and squeezed Susanna's hand. "Sure it is, Suz. I'm just an over-anxious numbskull! The police will be watching out for Mona Grace and Charley. I can't do anything for them this far away, so I'll just have to relax and leave the protecting to Greg and his shift."

Susanna asked, "And you, Lloyd, how are you doing now? Has your panic subsided?"

"I'm fine, Suz, don't worry about me. Like I said, I'm just a numbskull."

Susanna grinned widely. "Yup, I agree with you, Lloyd, but get this – you're MY numbskull, and I wouldn't have it any other way!" She added, "And, don't you forget it, mister!"

That made Lloyd feel a great deal better. He went back to his shop after supper and worked some more on the cradle. Later, he lay on his side, watching his beautiful wife snoring softly. Gently, he lifted a stray lock of hair away from her face before he rolled over and fell sound asleep.

. . . .

A few days later, Lacey called and invited Lloyd and Susanna to come for supper on Saturday night.

"You haven't been to our place since we got unpacked and settled in, Susanna; we'd really like you to come. In fact, why don't you plan on staying overnight rather than driving home in the dark? Parker actually has the entire weekend off!"

Susanna reached over and pulled on Lloyd's shirt as he walked by her on his way out to the shop. "Want to go to Lacey and Parker's on Saturday for supper and sleep over?"

"Why not?" Lloyd said. "We haven't been there for a while. Sounds good to me. Tell Parker we'll bring a big jug of iced tea…and some herbal tea for you, my chubby one!" he hastened to add, giving his blossoming spouse a quick peck on the cheek. Susanna pushed him playfully out of her way before she returned to speaking with Lacey.

It was decided between the two women that Susanna and Lloyd would pick up Hilda, her overnight bag, and her wheelchair, from the nursing home at ten o'clock. That way, they would arrive at the farm early. Weather permitting, the five of them would take a light picnic lunch and eat it on the flat rock close to the Mailbox. Hopefully, they would spot some wildlife along the scenic way.

Saturday morning, promptly at 10, Lloyd ran up the walk and in to the nursing home.

Hilda Somers was already sitting and waiting in her wheelchair, coat on, purse in hand. The nurse at the desk waited while Lloyd signed Hilda out for the weekend before she whispered, "She's been dressed and sitting there since seven o'clock! We finally brought her breakfast to her and she ate it at the door!" Lloyd smiled broadly at the nurse, then turned to Hilda and grabbed hold of the chair handles. The doors opened automatically, and Lloyd raced her madly down the sidewalk towards his vehicle, whooping and hollering all the way. Hilda was laughing too hard to tell him to be careful. They both arrived at Lloyd's vehicle, out of breath. Susanna took a surprised look at the two so-called adults, before joining in their contagious laughter.

The day held the promise of fresh air and sunshine. When they reached the farm, the yard had already been aerated and raked, the flowerbeds dug up and ready for planting. Wheeling Hilda around to the back, they noted that the garden had been rototilled and was ready to receive the vegetable seed offerings that Lacey would no doubt be planting in the near future.

In response to her unspoken plea, Lloyd wheeled her around the entire farmyard, pausing so she could look at all of the buildings. He worried that she would become unbearably sad, looking at her former home where she and her husband Stumpy had resided for so many years.

"Hilda, is all this reminiscing making you sad?" Lloyd asked her.

"Goodness no!" she replied. "I think it's wonderful how Lacey and Parker have taken over the farm and already made it their own. I couldn't be happier. And those two are so generous with their time! One of them always picks me up to come for Sunday supper, with never a complaint or a grumble between them. Why wouldn't I be happy?"

She reached out and took Lloyd's hand. "Thanks for caring, Lloyd. Oh! Look! Here comes Susanna. She is such a beautiful person, in both body and soul, Lloyd. You are a very lucky man."

"And don't I know it!" Lloyd beamed.

Susanna reached for the wheelchair and started wheeling Hilda towards the house before Lloyd could protest. His plaintive, "Hey, you two – you're ganging up on me! Susanna! That's too heavy for you to push!" Lloyd's whine echoed behind them.

"What? Does your dear husband think you are made of glass or something? What's his problem anyway – you look plenty fit to me." Hilda stared back quizzically as Lloyd hurried towards them. When he reached the spot where they waited, he was slightly out of breath.

"Did you tell her, Suz?" he wheezed.

"Without you? Hardly!" she replied.

"Tell me what?" Hilda said. Suddenly bright lights burst forth from the depths of her faded, aging eyes. "Oh! Susanna my dear child, are you in the family way?"

"What – oh, if you mean are we pregnant, the answer is yes! Isn't that wonderful, Hilda? Won't it be nice to have a baby in the family?"

Hilda positively beamed. "You're rootin'-tootin' right about that young woman! Congratulations and all my love and best wishes."

"Good thing I can still knit. I'll get right on that when I get back to the lodge. What colours would you like the baby's sweaters to be? Do you know the sex yet? Oh, never mind, I'll figure something out and surprise you."

"Do Lacey and Parker know? Oh, silly me, of course they do!"

"Well, well, this family has a great deal to be excited about. Let's go in; they must be wondering what in the world we are doing out here."

"Oh, my good heavens, I haven't been this excited since Lacey became our own child!"

Once she finally ran out of steam, Lloyd and Susanna both leaned over at the same time and hugged the fragile, but still feisty, old lady, a wise and loving woman whom they had come to love as completely as if she was their grandmother by blood instead of by choice.

Before they could reach the back door to the farmhouse, it opened. Lacey and Parker came out, each carrying one handle of a large picnic basket. They staggered down the steps and put the basket in the back of a fancy new quad. Parker then ran back into the house and appeared again, carrying a cooler filled with various drinks – Coke, ginger ale, and thermos bottles filled with hot coffee and iced tea.

Parker came over and wheeled Hilda over to the front passenger's side and helped her onto the front seat.

The last items to be squeezed into the back of the Rhino were four folding lawn chairs and the folding wheelchair.

"This is quite the contraption, isn't it?" Hilda said, "Are you sure you can drive this thing, Parker, without dumping an old lady on her butt?"

"Piece of cake, Hilda," Parker laughed. "Although I have to admit, it does make me feel kind of lazy. Lacey and I just figured that it would be more comfortable for you to ride in than having one of us hump you over rocks and ruts in your wheelchair whenever we wanted to go for a walk or a picnic."

Susanna piped up, "Which one of us has to walk, Parker? I only see four seats."

A padded rectangle in the box, closest to the back passengers' seats, stretched across the width of the quad. Parker deftly flipped a lever on the side of the box. The rectangle folded forward, revealing two jump seats but still left room at the very back for the picnic basket, the cooler of drinks, the wheelchair, and the folding lawn chairs.

"Wow!" was Lloyd's only comment.

Lacy leaned forward and tapped Hilda on the shoulder, asking her loudly, "Isn't this a fine way to travel, Hilda? We'll be at the Mailbox much more quickly now. It will give us more time to spend on our picnic, without carrying so much stuff with us that we are played out before we get home."

Hilda grinned. "Well, kind of reminds me of a modern 'Flint-Mobile' – like Fred and Wilma rode in on the Flintstones TV show. Remember that? Of course, those cave men and women would certainly have stronger legs than this modern generation, what with them peddling with their legs and feet and all."

"Well, it was just a television show," Lacey commented, "and a cartoon program at that! Our mama wouldn't let us watch it very much unless she watched it with us so she could comment on some of it. She thought it was a very sexist program – Fred and Barney were always ordering Wilma and Betty around, treating them like servants. Lloyd and I didn't think of it that way. Being kids, I guess, we had a totally different take on the show, but our mama was being extra cautious, I think."

Everyone thoroughly enjoyed the trip through the countryside, basked in the unusually warm and sunny day.

Overhead, a pair of Trumpeter swans flew by, their gigantic wings and heavy bodies appearing weightless, floating calmly through the clear blue sky.

When they reached the spot where Lacey and Hilda had seen the mystic bull elk (that they both were convinced was the spirit of Stumpy, appearing to the women just before he passed away), Hilda asked Parker if he would mind stopping for a minute. He immediately pulled over and went around to assist Hilda as she climbed out of the quad. With Parker supporting one side of her and Lacey the other, the three of them stood at the edge of the cultivated farm field, each silently dwelling on his or her own separate thoughts and memories of their beloved Stumpy.

After several minutes, Hilda indicated that she was ready to continue on.

"Next stop, the Mailbox!" called Lacey from the back where she was gamely trying to sit comfortably on the two small jump seats. "I'll flip a coin to see who rides back here on these butt-pinchers on our way home?"

It seemed like no time at all when the vehicle deposited its passengers and cargo beside the flat rock overhanging the deep ravine. Spring weather and snow melt had filled the creek bed and the water made a relaxing gurgle and whoosh as the freshet passed rapidly beneath the overhanging flat rock.

Leaving the women to lay out the lunch, Lloyd motioned for Parker to follow him. "Just going to check the Mailbox, Susanna," he called. "Be back in a flash."

Puzzled that Lloyd would want to check the Mailbox, which hadn't seen any use in a long time, Parker nevertheless followed his friend. "What's up, Lloyd?" he queried. "There can't be anything in that Mailbox. Its usefulness is past."

"Just a hunch, Parker. Also, I wanted to talk to you without the women hearing what I have to say. It'll just upset them."

Parker stopped and looked Lloyd right in the eye. "What's up? You are acting weird, even for you." He sportively punched Lloyd on his shoulder, dancing around him like a boxer sparring with a partner to warm up before a big fight. Suddenly realising that Lloyd wasn't participating in the fun, Parker stopped, sat down on the bare ground and waited. When Lloyd remained silent, he patted the ground beside him. "Have a seat, Lloyd. Tell me, buddy, what's troubling you."

With a painfully deep sigh lodged too far down his windpipe to escape, Lloyd told Parker about his conversations with Mona Grace and Sergeant Greg Gablehaus, told him about his further attempts on the same day to contact Mona Grace and Charley. He left nothing out, even though he felt like a fool for voicing his concerns when he really had nothing to base them on.

Parker sat silently for a couple of minutes after Lloyd stopped talking. Finally, he asked, "Lloyd, just exactly what are you afraid of? Domingo is out on bail, yes, but do you honestly think that he would jeopardise his own life by breaching even one of those bail conditions? When the organisation that you owed for posting your half a million-dollar bail was the largest, ugliest, and most evil gang organisation in Western Canada – the WARLORDS? Somehow that just doesn't fly with me. I honestly can't see anything happening – at least before Domingo's assault trial is finished and his bail money is released back to the WARLORDS."

Lloyd stared pensively into the distance. "When you put it that way, my head knows that you're probably right, Parker." He paused. Defiantly, he suddenly burst forth, "But Parker, my heart is burdened with a deep-seated fear, almost a phobia. I just know that something bad is going to happen before this is over. Domingo is not the type of man to care about rules, regulations, threats, or anything else. He acts without thinking, I tell you. He acts without any fear of consequences. He has always, up until this point, evaded the law. He thinks he's invincible. He is the head of an East Vancouver gang, for heaven's sake! Heck, he doesn't even have a record, so I suppose if I were him, I'd feel invincible too!"

Lloyd felt nauseated. He leaned over, his head in his hands. He remained that way until he got himself under control. He then slowly raised his head and, ashamed of his outburst, apologised to Parker.

"No problem, Lloyd. I understand how much this has upset you. You are worried for Mona Grace, for Charley, and everyone else close to you. But Lloyd, you have to keep the faith. Greg and his team are going to be religious in their efforts to protect those two women. It is less than two months until Domingo's trial. Things will work out, buddy; they will. Now, come on, I see Lacey waving a dish towel at us – lunch must be ready."

Parker stood up, stretched, then hollered, "Race you back!" He took off before he even finished announcing the race, but Lloyd managed to beat him by a nose. He felt like a winner, even though he was breathing so hard from the run he had to bend over and wait to catch his breath.

The small group enjoyed a leisurely lunch. When they were finally finished eating, there was not a scrap of food or drink left.

Moaning contentedly, Parker stretched out on the blanket and closed his eyes. A couple of minutes later, a dish towel snapped dangerously close to his ear. He opened his eyes and smiled up at Lacey. "What's up, woman?" he drawled. Suddenly, he was wide awake. He stood up and put his arms around his wife. "Listen up, everybody," Parker said, "we've got something to announce!"

Lacey was shuddering with excitement. Parker stood behind her and rested his chin on the top of her head.

"What's going on?" Hilda asked.

Lloyd and Susanna echoed her question, "Yeah, what's going on?"

"Well, you see, it's like this," Lacey was definitely enjoying prolonging their curiosity. "My little niece or nephew is going to have a little cousin to play with!"

Dead silence among the group, then shouts of excitement and happiness echoed throughout the countryside. Gone were the feelings of sluggishness from overeating a fabulous picnic lunch. Gone were any feelings of impending problems or doom. The news that a second baby would be born within weeks of the first birth created a feeling of such happiness. What a wonderful bit of news to end their relaxing excursion to the countryside!

Susanna then announced that seeing as she and Lacey had prepared the lunch, perhaps the men should clean up and reload the Rhino while the two women went for a healthy walk. When the men half-heartedly tried to veto that plan, Susanna said, "Exercise is compulsory for pregnant women. We need to have our daily walk before our little bundles (and here she patted her barely protruding belly contentedly) are born. We are starting right now!" With that, she and Lacey walked away from the rest of the group, towards the Mailbox.

As they approached the tree, Lacey couldn't help herself. "I know there won't be anything in this old stump," she said to her sister-in-law, "but for old times' sake, I'm going to do a sweep regardless." She knelt down and reached her arm into the dark, cave-like interior.

"That's funny," she said a minute later. "Susanna, can you reach inside and tell me if it feels like there is a piece of something lodged in a crack near the back of this Mailbox? If you think so, be very careful. It will be old and probably crumble."

Susanna immediately knelt down beside Lacey and swept her arm around the space. Suddenly, she exclaimed, "You're right! I feel it, Lace, there is definitely something in there!"

Frowning intensely, she carefully tried to work the object loose without damaging it. After several minutes, she pulled her arm out. "Voila!" she announced. "It appears to be an envelope with something scribbled on it."

Lacey stood up, helped Susanna to her feet. "Let's not open it here, Suz," she said. "Let's take it back to the rock and open it with everyone around."

"Sure, not a problem, Lacey," Suzanna said in a puzzled tone, "but you realise, don't you, that it probably is just some little kid playing around. He or she put it in an obviously hollow tree stump, kind of a 'message in a bottle' if you will."

"Just humour me, Susanna, please." Lacey's face was so stern, stoic really, that Susanna quickly told Lacey that she didn't have a problem taking the item back to the guys where it could be opened with everyone present.

They quickly walked back to the picnic site. The fellows had the Rhino loaded and ready to return home. Lloyd was assisting Hilda, getting her settled in the front passenger's seat. Once he had fastened her seatbelt, he turned around. He had been about to joke that they needed to flip a coin to see who was stuck riding in the jump seats when the women's faces stopped him cold.

"What is it?" Lloyd asked. He looked right at Lacey. She was clutching a grubby looking envelope close to her chest.

Lloyd walked over to his sister. Gently, he pried her fingers open. "Let me see it, Little Sister."

"It's probably nothing," Susanna said. She then reiterated her theory about a child putting a 'message in a bottle' or, in this case, a 'message in a tree stump'. No one was listening. They were concentrating on watching the envelope. There wasn't a sound as Lloyd handed it to Parker.

"You open it please, Parker. I can't." Parker carefully slit the envelope open with the Swiss Army knife that he always carried with him around the farm.

A single sheet of bright yellow paper fluttered to the ground. Parker bent over and picked it up, unfolded the colourful paper. He read the message aloud. Lloyd's face turned white and waxy as Parker read the crudely printed note, some of the words misspelled:

WE HAVE MONAGRACE AND CHARLY. WHEN THE BAIL $$ IS RETURN THE WIMIN WILL RETURN. IF NOT, THEY WILL BE DED. YOU WATCH DOMINGO SO HE DON'T MAKE US LOOZ OUR $$ AND YOU DON'T LOOZ YOUR FRENDS!

No one moved. No one spoke. During the dreadful silence, not even a breeze whispered. Not a bird sang. Not even a mosquito buzzed. Nothing broke the stillness.

Finally, Lloyd broke the stunned silence, vocalised what everyone was thinking. "Dear Lord, what's happening? This is a nightmare. Who could have sent that pathetic note, and how in the name of everything that's Holy, did they know about the Mailbox? Or where to find the Mailbox?"

"I have to call Greg. We need to get back to the house. I left my cell phone in our vehicle. I need to call Gablehaus right away. The clock is ticking. I'll take the jump seats for the trip back. Go Parker! Step on it! GO! GO! GO!"

Parker started up the machine immediately and steered for home. He hollered at Lloyd, trying to make himself heard above the engine noise. "I'll drop all of you off at home, then I'll go in to the detachment and see if I can find something out, see what else, if anything, has happened."

They made it back to the farmhouse in record time. The two men scattered, leaving the women to assist Hilda and to unload the Rhino.

Parker ran, calling towards them as he raced past. "I'll be back asap, hopefully with news! I'll call as soon as I know anything more."

Lloyd was already on his phone, hitting the speed dial for Greg Gablehaus' cell number. Voice mail! Dammit, Lloyd thought as he left a message. He hung up and started to pace back and forth, back and forth across the living room. Susanna was just about to tell him to go outside and pace when his phone rang. He answered it on the first ring.

"Hey, Lloyd, this is Greg. Sorry I couldn't get to my cell before your message kicked in – I was otherwise engaged for the moment. I'm here now, though. Is there a problem?"

The sergeant listened carefully while Lloyd endeavoured to explain in short, disjointed bursts, what had transpired at the Mailbox.

Greg said, "Whoa, whoa, whoa, slow down, Lloyd! It'll just take longer to get moving if I can't understand what you're saying."

Lloyd tried to slow down. He started to repeat what he had just told the sergeant, but Greg Gablehaus stopped him. "Okay, I got you so far, Lloyd. Where are you now? Are you at home?"

Lloyd told him.

Greg asked, "Is that the farm close to where Domingo ran you off the road and then was apprehended a short while later?"

Lloyd said, "Yes."

"You've told me about your secret Mailbox before, Lloyd, from when you and Lacey were young, living in foster care. Does anyone else know about it?"

"As far as I'm aware, only Hilda, Parker, Susanna, myself, and Lacey know about it," Lloyd responded. "And you," he acknowledged.

"Stumpy knew, when he was still alive, but he wouldn't have breathed a word about it to anyone, ever!"

He looked at the women. "Have I missed anyone else that might know about the Mailbox?"

Greg spoke to Lloyd through the phone line. "Tell them to think hard. It's important."

Lloyd complied and then put his phone on speaker.

Lacey spoke up. "Hi, Sergeant Gablehaus, it's Lacey speaking. Charley knows, and I'm pretty sure Mona Grace knows, although they have never been to the actual location. I can't think of any other person who would know." She looked around the room. "Anyone else?" she asked worriedly. Although they all thought hard, no one could add to the list.

Greg asked to speak to Parker. When told that Parker had gone to the detachment to see if anything else had happened with regards to the Domingo fiasco, he said to forget it; he would check with the detachment himself.

Greg spoke through the phone to the group, although it almost sounded as if he was talking aloud to himself. "The first thing we need to do is to try and figure out who wrote that note and how it got into the secret Mailbox."

"And just how do we do that?" asked Susanna anxiously.

Sergeant Gablehaus answered her in a roundabout way, saying only, "I have a few ideas."

There was silence on the line for a short interval, then Greg said, "In the meantime, Lloyd, I'm wondering if you would come to East Van and help us out. I don't want to get into any details over the phone, but I know of a way for you to help, if you will?"

Lloyd looked over at Susanna, his eyebrows arched. She nodded affirmatively, mouthed that he should go.

"Sure, I can do that, Greg. I'll book a flight right away. Hopefully, I can be there tomorrow. I'll let you know once I've booked."

"I'll need a hotel room though. With Mona Grace miss – not at home, I will need a place to stay."

Greg said, "Don't worry about that, Lloyd. You can stay with my wife Bethany and me."

Lloyd asked, "Don't you think you should check with her first?"

Greg Gablehaus chuckled. "She's used to this. In fact, we have a spare room downstairs, reserved exactly for situations of this type. I will call her, though, just as soon as I'm off the phone here and give her a heads up."

"Call me back with your flight info, and I'll pick you up at the airport."

"Will do," Lloyd said. He hung up.

He called Parker's cell to find out where he should call to book his flight. He wasn't hopeful that he would get Parker on the phone, expected to have to leave a message; however, Parker answered the telephone himself. When Lloyd finished speaking, Parker told him not to worry, that he would have the detachment's front desk clerk book the flight. There would be a better chance of getting him on a plane much faster than if he tried to book it himself.

Parker said there was nothing the detachment could report other than what was already known. He said he was just leaving to come back home. He would ask that the flight details be relayed to the farm.

Within 15 minutes, someone from the detachment called with all the details of Lloyd's flight. He would be flying from Fort St John to Vancouver at eleven o'clock the next morning. Susanna agreed to drive him to Fort St John. Parker said it wouldn't be necessary, but if she wanted to drive him, Parker would be happy to go with them so Susanna wouldn't have to make the drive home alone. She happily accepted his offer. Immediately, Lloyd called Greg Gablehaus back. Greg said he would pick Lloyd up at the airport at noon.

"Well," Lloyd said, "I'm sorry, Sister, but we can't spend the night. I've got packing to do, and we will have to leave home very early in order to get to the airport and pick up my ticket and check in for that 11 am flight."

"Can't you at least stay for supper?" Lacey asked. Regretfully, Lloyd and Susanna said they must decline.

Domingo's trial was only a couple weeks away. It would have been nice, Lloyd thought to himself, if the timing had been closer to the trial date. It would have saved him a plane trip!

Lacey begged Hilda to stay overnight with her, so she would have company while Parker went with Susanna and Lloyd to the airport. Hilda was more than happy to stay.

When Lloyd and Susanna were ready to leave, Susanna went over to her sister-in-law and gave her a big hug, whispering in her ear as she did so, "It's just so exciting, being pregnant at the same time! We'll have so much fun with the little cousins as they are growing up! Once Mona Grace and Charley are safely found and Domingo is safely put away in prison, life will be wonderful, won't it?"

Lacey squeezed Susanna back and then went over to her brother and gave him a hug. "Be careful, Lloyd," she implored. "It's not safe on the streets of East Vancouver, especially with Domingo out on bail. Please, just be extra cautious!"

Lloyd hugged his sister tightly. "I will, Lacey, you know I will. Now, for Pete's sake, don't worry – you worry too much! It can't be good for the bump!" He gently patted her belly and then turned and walked out to the vehicle.

Both Susanna and Lloyd waved wildly as they backed out of the driveway and headed down the road towards home.

. . . .

Mona Grace opened her eyes. Her head throbbed. She reached up to the top of her head. Her hand came away, sticky with blood. Still not yet completely healed from her beating at the hands of Domingo, she hurt far more than she would have without that previous assault.

She lay quietly for a few minutes, trying to clear her head, get her bearings. When her vision had cleared somewhat, she glanced around. She was in a fairly small room. A single, small window was covered with a dark shade. It was impossible to tell if it was day or night.

Her head hurt! Her eyes watered as she desperately tried to remember what happened. Where was she? Why was she here?

Groaning softly, she tried to rise but was only able to half sit up. She leaned against the softness of a wall. What? The wall was soft?

Mona Grace was sitting on a single mattress on a hard, cold, grey-painted floor. A door to her left was open. A small bathroom – toilet, sink, and shower, nothing more. Not even a mirror above the sink.

To her right was another door with a small window very near the top. Bars, as well as a heavy mesh, covered that window. Mona Grace couldn't stand up yet, but she was pretty sure she wouldn't be able to look out through that high window – it was taller than she was. Briefly she wondered, what was the point in having a window that was too tall for anyone to look out of?

There was something else, but she couldn't clear the fog away enough to think what it was she was trying to remember. Finally, the pain exceeded her physical and mental capabilities. She slid down the soft wall, lay down on the mattress and passed out.

. . . .

Meanwhile, in another location, Charley woke up in a white metal, single bed, with safety bars attached on each side. She tried to reach her head to scratch a terrible itch but couldn't move her hands! Panicked, she realised her eyes were closed. Concentrating fiercely, she opened them slightly. Although the room was dim, she felt as if the sun was burning her retinas. Her eyes felt as if they were scorched. Salty tears burned as they washed down her cheeks, the liquid pooling under her chin. The itch continued without relief.

Tears continued to puddle under her chin until they overflowed and ran down her throat and neck. As her vision cleared, Charley dimly saw that she was restrained to the bed – each of her arms were secured to the side rails.

A door, she presumed, opened out into some sort of a hallway. That door suddenly opened inwardly. Someone wearing a gown and a mask approached the bed. It was impossible to tell if that someone was a male or a female.

Charley croaked, "Who are you and what the hell am I doing here?"

There was no answer from the apparition approaching the bed. Charley screamed loudly, shrilly. Her voice was husky and her throat hurt badly. It felt as if she had been screaming for days. She tried speaking to the apparition again, this time in a more conciliatory manner. "Please, tell me what's going on. Where am I? Why am I here? What happened to me?"

Too late, she realised that the person held a large syringe in a gloved hand. He or she grabbed Charley's arm. At the same time as the medication released from the syringe into her arm, Charley managed to lurch forward with all her might. She sunk her teeth deeply into the arm of the stranger. She tasted blood at the same time as a fist landed hard on her temple. Stars glittered and her ears rang. She sank into unconsciousness.

. . . .

99

True to his word, Greg Gablehaus was at the airport, waiting for Lloyd when he arrived. He shook Lloyd's hand and gripped his shoulder in a display of both welcome and affection.

"Thanks for coming, Lloyd. I can sure use your help."

They reached Greg's police vehicle, loaded Lloyd's luggage into the back, and then headed away from the Richmond Airport, towards the detachment in East Vancouver.

Traffic, as always, was heavy. Concentrating on his driving, Greg and Lloyd didn't have a chance for much conversation. Lloyd wasn't bothered by that fact. He simply leaned back in his seat and rested his eyes. Up very early to catch the plane, he welcomed the silence. His resting eyes soon became sleeping eyes. Greg glanced over once at his passenger, smiled grimly, then continued driving in silence.

The next thing Lloyd knew, they were at the detachment. Once Greg was parked in his private parking spot, he touched Lloyd gently on the shoulder. "We're here," he said softly.

Startled into wakefulness, Lloyd sat up so quickly that he hit his head on the roof. "What? Where am I?" he mumbled. Glancing over at Greg, he woke up completely. "We're here already?" he asked. "I must have fallen asleep; I'm sorry I was lousy company."

"Don't worry about it," Greg said. "Just be happy you had a chance to sleep. I'm afraid we are in for long days and maybe long nights trying to find the women. It's good you had your 40 winks."

Lloyd held his breath. "No word, then? You're saying you have no idea where Mona Grace and Charley might be."

Greg looked at Lloyd sympathetically. "Not yet, Lloyd, but we had a brainstorming session last evening and have come up with some ideas. Let's go into my office, and I'll fill you in."

Stepping out of the police car, he opened the back door and reached in. Standing up, he triumphantly hoisted a paper bag and a tray of coffee towards Lloyd. "You can leave your things in the cruiser for the time being," he said. "I thought we might need a bit of sustenance, so I stopped at Tim Horton's at the airport while I waited for you. I hold coffee and muffins in these workworn hands of mine. We'll need some energy while we plan our strategy."

Lloyd opened his mouth to utter a wisecrack about cops and Tim Horton's. He changed his mind when he realised that the delicious coffee aroma wafting enticingly towards him was just what he needed. He was not going to look a gift horse in the mouth by making fun of the location of the gift horse's stable!

Greg's office had been a beehive of activity since the last time Lloyd was there. Three felt boards were assembled and stood against the far wall, to the right of the door to the office.

The first board held a map of Vancouver. There were two specific areas highlighted. Lloyd recognised the first one. It was the location of the East Van Devils' clubhouse.

He pointed to the second highlighted location, looked at Greg, eyebrows raised. "The WARLORDS' den," Greg said. "As you can see, it is in a very prestigious residential area in West Vancouver, a much more prestigious location than that of the Devils'. We don't know how they manage it. Not one single person living in that ritzy West Van neighbourhood has complained about Vancouver's major crime gang living in their area. That gang is smooth, no doubt about it. It may be that they don't run any of their illegal activities out of their den. Maybe their neighbours don't care, or they are just too intimidated to do anything about the comings and goings, and large, loud parties. The West Vancouver Police have been trying for years to bust up that gang, but they are just too clever by half. It almost makes you wonder if they have an informant on the inside, you know, a dirty cop. God, I hope not!"

"We've tried time and time again to obtain search warrants to get a look inside the den, but so far, no judges have granted any. It's certainly not for lack of trying on the police department's part. The judges, to a man or to a woman, (to be non-biased, politically correct) have all said that there is not enough evidence to issue the warrant. We even dispatched a cruiser there. The officers rang the doorbell."

"The door was answered by a real-life butler! He was perfect for the job – tall, skinny, snooty, and very protective. He could stare down his nose and compete with the best of any movie actor butler. He was even wearing a hoity-toity butler's uniform, tuxedo tails and all! Impressed the hell out of those young rookies who had been sent to the door!"

"When told that they were investigating a telephone complaint, the caller claiming that there was an altercation going on at this address, 'Jeeves' responded that everything was fine, the television had just been turned up too loud and the fight was part of a television show. Everything appeared calm and orderly. Of course, the officers then had no choice but to leave the residence, without even having been invited into the main foyer. 'Jeeves' earned his salary that particular day."

Out of simple curiosity, and not for any useful reason, Lloyd asked Greg, "Was 'Jeeves' the butler's real name?"

Sergeant Gablehaus grinned before commenting, "Who knows! I'm pretty sure if it was, my rookies would have noted it for the file. From the description of the officers, 'Jeeves' just seemed to fit."

Greg continued, "Now the Devils, on the other hand, aren't so lucky. The judges in East Van hand out search warrants for their clubhouse like handing out candy to kids at Halloween. Not many weeks of the year where there isn't at least one Devils member in court for something or other. They are held so tightly under the WARLORDS' thumb it is painful to observe. Everything gets blamed on the East Van Devils. Perhaps it is to cover up the main gang's activities, but no matter how they work it, it is always a Devils member and not a WARLORD who takes the heat."

"There isn't a policeman on the force that wouldn't give up an early retirement just to see the WARLORDS brought down. Nobody even knows for sure who their leader is. Nearly everyone in the detachment has a different guess, but like I said, nobody knows for sure. It's the darndest, weirdest thing. It's almost creepy when it comes right down to it."

The second board had a blueprint pinned to it. Lloyd didn't need to ask what it was. It was clearly labelled, 'East Van Devils' Clubhouse, Main Level', followed by an address. Lloyd shuddered as memories of his escape from that building resurfaced. He recognised every room on the blueprint.

Underneath the first page, a second page was labelled, 'East Van Devils' Clubhouse, Upper Level'. The third and final page was labelled, 'East Van Devils' Clubhouse, Basement Level'. Clearly highlighted on each page of the blueprints, in a separate colour, was the dumbwaiter through which Lloyd had escaped.

Because of numerous, almost regular, search warrants, the sergeant had only one grey area pertaining to these blueprints. Flipping again to the third page, he turned and looked at Lloyd.

"I know recalling all this is difficult, Lloyd, but I need to ask. Please look at this last page entitled 'East Van Devils' Clubhouse, Basement Level'. Do you recognise the layout?"

"Yes, of course," said Lloyd. "Why do you ask?"

Greg asked, "Remember where the old mattresses were leaning against the wall?"

"Sure. They were right here." Lloyd placed his pointer finger on the correct wall.

Greg grinned grimly. "Look just to the left of that area, Lloyd. Between the coal furnace and where the mattresses were." He waited while Lloyd examined the page more closely.

"Good grief!" he exclaimed a minute later. "It's very indistinct, but it appears that there is a door behind the coal furnace! I missed that altogether!"

"What are you thinking, Greg? Do you think the women are being held behind that door?"

"It's only a theory, Lloyd." Greg shrugged his shoulders in neither a positive fashion nor a negative one. It was just a puzzled kind of shrug.

"We're trying to get a search warrant issued so we can see what's behind there. We should have it in our hands within the hour, that is if the judge grants it. At this point, I have no reason to think any differently."

"Now, Lloyd, listen. Don't beat yourself up about missing that door. I would bet dollars to doughnuts that it's camouflaged so cleverly that it will be almost impossible to see that it's there. Unless, of course, someone actually knows it's there and knows where to look to find the spot where it opens."

The third board also contained a set of blueprints but only two pages. One was labelled, 'THE WARLORDS' DEN, Main Level'.

The second page was labelled, 'THE WARLORDS' DEN, Upper Level'. A quick look at the plans for that level seemed to show only bedrooms and bathrooms, with a large deck facing the back yard, off the largest bedroom.

There was no basement level page, but the main level page showed a set of stairs leading from the main level back door and down a steep slope, towards the back of a very large yard. The stairs were obscured from view at the back of the yard because of giant Arbutus trees and heavy shrubbery, but they showed up again past the 'back yard forest', going down the side of the mountain, towards the ocean. The blueprint did not show anything past the property line, so it appeared on the blueprint as if the stairs ended in mid-air.

The sergeant let Lloyd study the map and the blueprints carefully. He leaned back in his chair and watched his young friend examine everything. Realising that this might take a while, Greg picked up a file from the stack of files piled high on the right side of his desk. Opening it, he began to read and make notes while he waited for Lloyd to finish his scrutiny.

He had pressed the 'DND' button on his desk phone so they wouldn't be disturbed. He had also placed a DO NOT DISTURB sign on the door to his office. Despite that, there was a knock on his door. With a frustrated sigh, he got up from his desk and approached the door, opened it harshly and bellowed, 'WHAT?' before the door was even completely opened.

A very young constable stood at the door, a brown envelope in his hands. He looked extremely intimidated. He stuttered when he spoke. "S-s-s-sorry, s-s-s-sir," the young man stammered, "b-b-b-but you wanted the s-s-s-search w-w-w-warrant im-im-im – right away if we g-g-g-got it." He was literally shaking in his boots as he handed Sergeant Gablehaus the brown envelope. "H-h-h-here it is, s-s-s-sir."

Greg felt sorry for the young guy. He suspected the more experienced constable who had accompanied him to the courthouse to obtain the warrant was rather cruel when he sent his junior partner alone up to see Greg.

"It's okay, son," Greg said to the constable in a much more moderate tone. "Thank you for being so prompt in delivering this to me."

The young fellow appeared only slightly more at ease. He saluted his superior officer, turned on his heel and marched down the hallway towards the stairs.

When Greg Gablehaus returned to his desk and opened up the warrant, he saw that Lloyd had finished his scrutiny and was standing in front of Greg's desk.

"Have a seat, Lloyd. You don't need to wait for an invitation. We're all equals in this investigation. If you think of something, speak up. If you have any ideas, speak up. The more brainstorming gets done, the quicker we will find Mona Grace and Charley."

"Well, we have our search warrant to search the basement of the East Van Devils' clubhouse."

He looked over his desk at Lloyd, his eyes unable to douse a twinkle that hovered in front of his pupils.

"Something tells me that you would like to accompany the other members of the team and me while we execute this search. Am I right?"

Overcome and humbled, Lloyd couldn't reply. He just nodded his head dumbly, like a young teenager on his first date, facing both the girl's formidable parents at the door. As often as Lloyd had nightmares since escaping from the clubhouse, he couldn't wait to accompany the police and observe the search.

While he waited for Greg to get off the telephone, Lloyd practised deep breathing to quell his jangled nerves. He also whispered a hushed prayer. *Please, God, look after Mona Grace and Charley until we can find and rescue them. Please keep them safe.*

Within 15 minutes, the full team was assembled. Sergeant Gablehaus and four other uniformed officers completed the official team. Lloyd felt honoured to be included in this group of highly trained policemen.

Sergeant Gablehaus directed the four officers to head to the Devils' clubhouse in an unmarked police car but not to exit their vehicle without a direct order from himself. "I'll be right behind you. Let's go find out what's behind the green door!"

Lloyd queried, "Green door, sir? I don't remember there being a green door anywhere in that basement."

"No, Lloyd, there's no such thing in that clubhouse as an actual 'green door'. You are too young to remember or even know, but there used to be a pop song about a green door. One of the lines said something like, 'Green door, what's that secret you're keeping?' I don't remember the rest. It's a really old song."

"I forget how young you really are. For that matter" – and here he looked at the rest of his team – "for that matter, I forget how young my team is!"

"Enough chatter, let's roll!"

In less than 10 minutes, all officers, plus Greg, plus Lloyd, were standing outside the clubhouse door. Sergeant Gablehaus rang the doorbell, taking care to stand to the side of the peephole.

The Devils' regular doorman, Bernard ('Brutus') Belcourt, known to all as 'the Tattoo Man', was, of course, in prison so there was no chance of him answering the door. Nevertheless, Greg did not want to take a chance that the replacement doorman would sound the alarm if he saw policemen standing on the doorstep. Hence, he stood to the side, at the same time signalling everyone else to stay out of the view of the peephole as well.

When a voice from the other side of the exterior door asked who was at the door and who he or she wanted to see, Greg stuck his shield in front of the peephole. "Police! We have a search warrant; open up! And don't even consider not opening the door. We will break it down if you don't open this door in the next 10 seconds!" He began counting, loudly and enthusiastically –

"1! – 2! – 3! –"

"Okay, okay, hold your horses," the doorman said, still from behind the closed door. "I'll open the door, but first, stick your warrant up your a-whoops! I mean, stick your warrant in front of the peephole so I can see it, please, sir." A flippant snicker made its way through the closed door.

Smart ass, Greg thought. He held the warrant up as requested and then resumed counting even more enthusiastically –

"4! – 5! – 6! –"

When he reached the count of eight, the door swung open.

A large, heavily muscled man, who could have been a brother to Brutus, stood in the doorway. Although heavily tattooed, Brutus had this biker beat by a mile. He wore a black leather jacket bearing the WARLORDS' colours.

Sergeant Gablehaus snapped at him in his most authoritative voice, "You're wearing the WARLORDS' colours. What's your name and why are you working at the East Van Devils' clubhouse?"

"Why?" said the smart ass. "Why do you need my name?" He spread his feet further apart, crossed his arms and glared balefully at Sergeant Gablehaus.

"Because I said so!" menaced Greg. "Now, either tell me your name and why you are working for the Devils when you are clearly a WARLORDS' gang member, or I will arrest you for impeding a police officer in the implementation of his duties."

The doorman muttered, barely but distinctly audible, "Imperialistic son of a bitch." Throwing a hostile look in Greg's direction, he said, "My name is Jose Sanchez, and I am working at the Devils' Clubhouse because their current doorman is – indisposed, shall we say."

Greg returned the glare. "Sanchez, are you related to Domingo Sanchez?"

"Why?" The smart ass smirked.

"Because I'm asking!" Clearly at the end of his patience, Greg called the smart ass's bluff. "Enough sarcasm! If you're not going to answer my polite questions, one of these fine officers will escort you back to the detachment, where you will remain until you do answer all the questions. And, sir, I can tell you that there will be a lot more questions if you don't answer mine here."

That caused a noticeable change in attitude. The smart ass, now known as Jose Sanchez, said in a civil, but barely civil, voice, "Domingo is my father's brother's son. I guess that makes him my father's nephew and makes him my first cousin."

Broadening his, until now slight Spanish accent, Jose Sanchez continued, "I am working at this clubhouse because Domingo he ask me, as a favour to him, to fill in for the Tattoo Man, at least until he can find a suitable replacement. I don't know how long that is going to take, but I am here until I am told otherwise."

Greg took a very deep breath and threw himself out on a limb. Not expecting an answer, he asked anyway, "Jose Sanchez, what is the name of your leader?"

Jose immediately said, without batting an eye, "My leader's name is Domingo Sanchez so long as I am working at the Devils' clubhouse."

Sergeant Gablehaus couldn't help himself. With a wry smile, he said, "Good answer, Jose, good answer. Now, though, tell me what 'you' know about what 'I' want to know. That is, who is your leader when you are working for the WARLORDS?"

Jose Sanchez made a zipper noise as he ran his fingers across his mouth, then said, "Hey, senor, you know I no can tell you. You want to get me killed or something? You can rape me, or beat me, or cut off my ear, but you know I no can tell you what you want to know, even though you torture me."

He changed the subject, "Now, let me examine your search warrant a little more closely and then I will tell you where you are allowed to be."

Oh well, nothing ventured, nothing gained, the sergeant thought to himself. *I didn't really think I'd get an answer, but it was definitely worth the try. Mr Jose Sanchez is definitely a fast thinker; he can think on his feet. Not likely to trip him up.*

The entire police team, including Lloyd, entered the clubhouse and headed down the stairs to find the invisible door.

Please, God, Lloyd thought to himself, *please let Mona Grace and Charley be in there, safe and sound.*

At the foot of the stairs, Greg Gablehaus turned to Lloyd. "Okay, Lloyd, since you are very familiar with this basement level of the Devils' clubhouse, why don't you do the honours here. Find the door and figure out how to open it. If, or rather when, you get it open, step aside and let the armed officers proceed from there. Got it?"

"Yes, sir!" Lloyd said respectfully. Greg handed Lloyd a powerful flashlight. Lloyd immediately headed over to the area behind the furnace and to the left of where the mattresses were still leaning against the wall. The space between the wall and the old coal furnace was small, but there was room for a good-sized man to squeeze into the space. Lloyd had a fair bit of room.

A visual check of the wall revealed nothing despite the fact that Lloyd shone the strong light over the entire space. Holding the flashlight in his left hand, he then began feeling the entire wall from right to left, top to bottom. On his third swipe, he felt an indentation in the middle of the wall, just deep enough for Lloyd to notice it and to repeat his last move. When he felt the indent once again, he pressed on it with his index finger, gently at first and then harder. Nothing. On a hunch, he measured the spot by placing his thumb into the dip. It was a much better fit than his index finger was. He then pressed the spot with his thumb one time. Nothing. Suspecting a code, he pressed two times. Again nothing. Suddenly remembering how he had knocked on the clubhouse door in a coded format to get the Tattoo Man to answer it, he pressed 'Shave and a haircut (pause), six bits' and voila! Open Sesame! The door swung inward, revealing a set of stairs descending downwards into nothingness.

As Greg had ordered, Lloyd immediately stepped out of the way to allow the members of the team to explore further. He gave them all time to reach the bottom of the stairs, watching to see which direction they would go next. They turned right. As soon as they were out of sight, Lloyd followed, holding on to the flashlight that he had not yet returned to Greg. The steps were old, crumbly, and very narrow. The last thing he needed would be to fall and break an ankle or something. He climbed down slowly and carefully.

At the bottom, Lloyd turned to his right, the same direction that the team had gone. Although he stood stock still and listened, he heard nothing. Lloyd was amazed at how five large men, dressed in full combat gear, wearing heavy boots and carrying weapons could proceed in such total and complete silence.

Deep in thought as he walked, Lloyd very nearly bumped into one of the officers. Startled, the policeman snarled in a vicious whisper, "Watch where you're going, man! You could get shot scaring a guy like that!"

"Sorry, officer," Lloyd whispered back. "I'll be more watchful."

A few steps ahead and then the team turned left, silently walking down even more steps. At the bottom was a large, very heavy wooden door, with a brass knocker attached above the latch.

Greg looked back, saw Lloyd, and whispered to him, "Do you think these guys are dumb enough to use the same password knock for every door in the clubhouse?"

"Sure do, Greg," Lloyd whispered back.

Greg stepped out of the way. With a sweeping bow, he instructed his young friend to 'be my guest'.

Taking a deep breath and holding it, Lloyd tapped out the 'Shave and a haircut…' code. He waited a minute, then rapped louder. Once more, and when there was still no answer, he stepped out of the way, allowing a member of the team to try to open the door. It wasn't locked! Opening it carefully, wincing at the loud, deep, creaking sound, the officers entered the room, sweeping their weapons first to the left and then to the right as they advanced further into the space. The last officer in closed the door behind him. He felt the wall to his left and to his right. On his right side, he felt a series of light switches. "Keep your eyes closed for a second, men," he said, "I've found the light switches, but I don't know how bright it will be when I hit 'em." His fingers on the switch closest to him, the officer stood still, calmly waiting for a sign from his sergeant.

"Now!" Sergeant Gablehaus ordered.

The officer flipped the first switch and a dim light turned on directly above the door, leaving the area suffused in a shadowy, almost as dark as before state. There were three more switches and when he flipped them, the area was as fully illuminated as if it was midday and the sun was shining full force.

Glancing quickly around, Greg whistled. "What the f – ?" Catching himself before the expletive could escape any further from out of his mouth, he said, "Hey, fellas, take a look!"

They stood in a large, square room that appeared to be approximately six metres long, six metres wide and six metres high. Against the wall to the left, deep wooden shelves spanned the length of the room. The same arrangement was mirrored on the wall to the right.

"Holy heck!" whispered one of the team. "Will you look at that!" Each of the wooden shelves held an arsenal of weaponry. Automatics, semi-automatics, sniper rifles, shotguns, handguns, even pellet guns were all laid out neatly, labelled with a complete description of each weapon. You name any type of firearm and it was there.

The shelves on the opposite side of the room contained an identical arsenal of weapons. All of the shelves, on both sides of the room, were completely filled.

The East Van Devils were apparently prepared for anything that might come their way.

The wall facing the officers on the far end of the room contained shelves also, but on each of the shelves, large wooden crates with pull-out drawers rested. On the outside of the drawer to each wooden crate was a label describing the contents in each drawer. These included various types and styles of knives, baseball bats, spiked clubs, brass knuckles, even a drawer full of Ninja nunchaku. Any weapon that might be remotely useful in hand-to-hand combat was stored and itemised.

Momentarily distracted from their main purpose, which was, of course, to find Mona Grace and Charley, the team picked up their dropped jaws and began a methodical search, hoping to determine a hidden room and praying that Mona Grace and Charley were in there. Although they searched for an hour, no sign of anything other than the single large room was discovered.

Disappointed at not finding the women but elated at finding the colossal cache of weapons, everyone exited the room and climbed the stairs out of the cavern into the basement once again.

There was no sign of the doorman. He had escorted them to the basement and then disappeared, conspicuous in his absence.

Knowing that Lloyd was familiar with every bit of the basement level, now that the secret door had been discovered, the officers made only a brief, cursory search.

Greg ordered, "Somebody please put police tape and a seal on that door."

"You" – and here he pointed to another officer – "call the detachment and have them send some forensic guys immediately to deal with all of the weapons. Tell them once they have itemised everything, to seize the entire lot and get them locked up in the exhibit locker at the detachment as quickly as possible. Tell them to make sure they are thorough."

Greg took a huge breath and then let it out slowly before he addressed his team. "Good work today, men. That is a huge discovery that can be credited not only to all of you but to our young accomplice here, Mr Lloyd Jordan. Thanks, Lloyd. I'm only sorry that Mona Grace and Charley were not here; however, we are not giving up. We will just go on to Plan 'B'. I'll discuss it with you, Lloyd, when we are back in my office."

A few minutes later, the hidden door dealt with, Greg instructed two of his officers to remain and guard the door while waiting for forensics to arrive.

"Once the forensic team arrives and you have shown them where the stash is, you can go home for the night."

Having instructed the two young officers, Greg then addressed the entire team.

"Thanks again, officers. You've had a very productive assignment. Take the rest of the day off."

Everyone chuckled because a quick look at their time pieces revealed it was already nearly 8 pm.

As Greg and Lloyd approached the detachment, they waved at the forensics guys, who were enroute to the clubhouse.

Stepping out of the cruiser, Greg's cell phone rang. He answered it, murmured a quiet response and then hung up. "That, my dear Lloyd, was Bethany. She has our supper nearly ready. What do you say we call it a night? It's been a long and eventful day. Tomorrow, bright and early, we'll get on with Plan 'B'."

Lloyd said, "Sounds good to me, sergeant. I'm bushed. Besides, I need to give Susanna a call after supper, make sure she is doing all right, you know?"

Greg smiled. "Sure do, Lloyd, I sure do. And don't worry! We're going to find Mona Grace and Charley, and they'll be fine. I feel it in my gut."

. . . .

Mona Grace lay on the floor, moaning softly. She had a splitting headache. She thought to herself, *I'll just rest here for a few minutes and then I'll attempt to stand up.*

A heat register was built in to the wall just above the rubber baseboard, beside her left ear. As she opened her eyes, she thought she heard something! She glanced towards the outside door to the space she occupied, but no one was there. Feeling extremely dizzy, she forced herself to lay still. She listened some more. It sounded like somebody was crying on the other side of the wall. After listening again, she called out tentatively, "Hello? Is anybody there? Can you hear me, whoever you are? I'm Mona Grace Ford. Please, if you can hear me, call out!"

There was total silence. Whatever or whomever Mona Grace had heard, she didn't hear anything now. Desperately, she leaned her ear against the register. The only sound she heard was a severe ringing in her ears. She tried to sit up so she could pound on the wall, but her vertigo progressed to the point that she fell back down to the mattress on the floor. She passed out.

. . . .

Charley opened her eyes, expecting to see the apparition with the syringe standing over her. There was no one there. Fighting to stay awake, she was suddenly overcome with a feeling of hopelessness, of helplessness. She hadn't felt this forlorn since she was held in the dilapidated old trailer in Hope. She had vowed never to let herself feel that helpless again, but it seemed that fate had other things in store for Miss Charlotte Ford!

She started to cry. No matter how hard she tried to stem her tears and wails, she just cried harder, louder.

Wait! She heard something! It sounded like someone was calling out to her. Charley tried to call back. No sound came out of her throat. She kept trying, but she had lost her voice. All too soon, the voice she was hearing stopped. Charley cried even harder.

She thought, *I have to get myself together if I'm ever going to get out of here, if I'm ever going to find Mona Grace* – she corrected herself, *if I'm ever going to find my mother.*

She heard someone at the door! Breathing deeply, she lay still and forced her eyelids to close. She feigned deep sleep.

. . . .

Greg and Lloyd arrived at the Greg and Bethany Gablehaus home. A quick glance around revealed a neat, well-landscaped two-storey home with an attached garage. Although the yard wasn't large, it was well designed and well-tended.

Greg took Lloyd's jacket and helped him bring his luggage in from the garage.

"Where are you, honey?" he called.

A pleasant female voice was heard from the direction of the back of the home. "In the kitchen! Bring Lloyd back here. I can't leave the gravy."

112

Mouth-watering aromas from the kitchen reminded the men that it had been a very long time since Tim Horton's muffins and coffee. They wasted no time heading to the kitchen.

Despite her prematurely silver hair, Bethany Gablehaus could have been in her mid-30s. She looked that young and stylish. In actual fact, she was older than her husband. She was closer to 50. Greg was only in his early- to mid-40s. She turned the burner down to low and turned her back to the stove.

"Well, well, you must be Lloyd! I've heard so much about you and your sister Lacey that I feel I've known you forever! Welcome to our home, Lloyd. I'm so happy to meet you at last." With that said, she walked up to Lloyd, gave him a firm hug and a friendly kiss on the cheek. Greg stood back and beamed. Once Bethany was done with Lloyd, she walked over and hugged her husband. After giving Greg a huge, noisy smooch, she turned back to Lloyd.

"Long day, wasn't it? You fellows must be really hungry, as well as exhausted. Have a seat at the table there. I've poured some wine. Lloyd, I hope you like red?"

Before Lloyd could answer, Greg told Bethany that Lloyd didn't drink.

"Oh, well then, how about a glass of water, juice or cola, Lloyd? We have a fair selection."

Lloyd said, "Thanks, Bethany! A Coke would be great, if you have it."

By the time the fantastic meal of salad, roast beef, mashed potatoes and gravy, asparagus, and home-baked buns was over, both Greg and Lloyd leaned back in their chairs, totally stuffed. When Bethany asked who wanted dessert, both men raised their hands in supplication, politely declining. There was definitely no room for any homemade apple pie for dessert.

Declining the men's offer to clean up the kitchen, Bethany waved them back down onto their chairs, stating in no uncertain terms that they had a hard day; they didn't need to do a single thing except sit at the table, drink either coffee or tea and visit. Bethany made short work of her kitchen mess.

Lloyd saw no signs of a mess anywhere. He figured Bethany must be another of those superb, organised women like Susanna – clean as you go was Susanna's strict motto. He had to admit, when he remembered to follow that motto, it really was much less work, especially in his carpentry shop!

Lloyd felt as if he had known Bethany Gablehaus forever. She was so easy to listen to. You didn't have to say much, just nod and smile. She did most of the talking. She didn't hog the conversation; she just had a lot to talk about. If she got too carried away and Greg wanted to say something, he grinned and playfully held up his hand like a student in a classroom. He then patiently waited for her to run out of breath.

Despite the disappointment at not locating the missing women, Lloyd relaxed in the remarkably stress-free atmosphere. The easy, loving banter going back and forth made him miss his wife more than ever. After a bit, he excused himself from the table, saying he needed to call Susanna. He explained to Bethany that his wife was pregnant and needed her rest, so he wanted to call her before it got any later. She totally agreed that was what he should do. She asked Greg to show Lloyd where his room was.

His room was spacious and comfortable. Down in the cool basement, it was nice and dark, and he knew he would have no trouble sleeping here, whether it was during the day or the night.

He called Susanna and talked her ear off, expressing his profound disappointment that they hadn't located the women. He had been so sure they would be found somewhere in the Devils' clubhouse. Skilfully changing the subject, Susanna filled him in on the everyday happenings at home. She told him not to worry about her; she was doing just great, thank you very much. She added, "Besides, Dad and Cora will be home soon. I won't be alone."

Once their telephone call had ended, Lloyd quickly washed, brushed his teeth and hit the hay. He was asleep practically before his head hit the soft and fluffy pillow.

Sometime during the night, he awoke with a strangled cry. Looking wildly around in the dark, he could see nothing. He couldn't remember where he was. He sat up and carefully felt beside his bed. On a night table stood a small reading lamp. He switched it on, blinking at the sudden brightness. Glancing at his watch, he saw that it was only 1:30 am. He walked across the hall to the bathroom, splashed water on his face and stared at himself in the mirror.

The face that stared back at him looked beyond exhausted. The only colour in the ghostlike, drawn features were heavy black circles surrounding the eyes. White-faced and messy haired, Lloyd shook his head. The remnants of his nightmare had slowly faded. He turned out the bathroom light, crossed the hall and crawled back into bed, leaving the lamp on. When he was sure the bad dream had ended, he turned off the lamp, prayed they would find the ladies before anything terrible could happen to them and went back to sleep.

The enticing smell of bacon floated down the stairs towards Lloyd's room. Yawning and stretching, he crawled out of bed. Once he had made his bed, he quickly showered and got ready to face the day. Just as he finished getting dressed, Bethany called from the top of the stairs, "Lloyd! Time to get up – breakfast's nearly ready!"

"On my way up, Bethany, thanks!"

"Wow," Lloyd said, "a person could get awfully fat eating at this house! You two obviously don't eat like this all the time or you would be bigger than your house!"

Bethany just smiled her sweet, complacent smile, got up out of her chair and poured Greg and Lloyd some more coffee in 2-Go thermos bottles.

"What!" Lloyd exclaimed playfully. "You're not going to let the police sergeant stop at Timmy's?"

She just grinned. "My coffee's better than Tim's, as you have probably already discovered. And my muffins are much better! I've packed you each a lunch." She looked over at her husband, shaking her pointer finger mischievously at him. "This man," she declared, "always forgets to eat unless I send some food with him." She turned to Lloyd. "Both of you make sure you eat! If you're going to be late, don't worry about supper. I've made up two TV dinners from last night's leftovers and you can just nuke 'em whenever you get home. I have a choir practice at the church and then some of us are going out for supper when we're done."

Greg and Lloyd both got up. "Let's make a mile, Lloyd," Greg said. "We need to put Plan B into action. Once we get to my office," he added. "I need some peace and quiet as we drive in order to get my thoughts together again."

"WHAT!" Bethany shrieked with amusement. "You can't get any peace and quiet at home? Really! I'm just as quiet as a mouse." With a giggle, she kissed her husband goodbye, whispered audibly, "Keep safe. Love you." She slapped his bottom (which made Lloyd blush) before Greg ruffled her hair and headed towards the garage.

Mindful of Greg's words about peace and quiet, Lloyd said not another word until they reached the detachment and were safely ensconced in Greg's office.

Greg quickly checked his messages, decided they could wait. He leaned back in his chair, thought for a minute, then spoke to Lloyd.

"I'll fill you in on what has happened so far. We attended at the clerk's office and obtained a certified copy of the receipt for the $500,000.00 bail money paid on behalf of Domingo Sanchez. The receipt showed that the money was received in the form of a bank draft. A bail assignment was signed by Paulo Santonio, accountant, agent on behalf of 02211947 Holdings Limited."

An extremely puzzled looking Lloyd interrupted, "Paulo Santonio! I thought he was counsel for Brutus?"

Greg grimaced. "He is. Mr Santonio is not only counsel for Brutus; he is counsel for any WARLORDS or Devils member who finds himself in need of a lawyer. He is also the accountant for the WARLORDS. The man may dress like a refugee from a dumpster, but he is pretty smart. He has a law degree. He is also a chartered accountant."

Lloyd commented, "If I was a gang member in the WARLORDS, I'm not sure I would want Paulo as my lawyer. To each his own, I guess."

"Be that as it may," Greg said, "he gets a lot of his scummy clients off."

"Now, continuing. With the certified copy of the receipt for the bail money, we were able to obtain a search warrant for the bank. The bank records show that the bank draft was purchased by Paulo Santonio."

"So, now, Lloyd, before we move on to Plan B, do you happen to have the anonymous note you told me about on the phone, the anonymous note you found in the Mailbox?"

"Yes, I have it with me in my backpack. Do you want to see it?"

"Please," Greg said. He waited quietly while Lloyd retrieved the note.

"Here you are," Lloyd said.

Greg shook his head sadly as he read the note aloud:

WE HAVE MONAGRACE AND CHARLY. WHEN THE BAIL $$ IS RETURN THE WIMIN WILL RETURN. IF NOT THEY WILL BE DED. YOU WATCH DOMINGO SO HE DON'T MAKE US LOOZ OUR $$ AND YOU DON'T LOOZ YOUR FRENDS!

"I'm shaking my head, Lloyd, because the note amazes me. The spelling is terrible, yet the printing is excellent, almost a work of art. Whoever sent this note wasn't very smart about it. I suspect that a member of either the Devils or the WARLORDS paid one of your homeless friends to print out the note. This person then recopied it, incorporating the same misspelled words as in the original note."

"What this second person did not do, was to camouflage the perfect printing. It shouldn't be too difficult to track the author of the note down, particularly if we can get a search warrant for the WARLORDS' den. It strikes me as the type of thing a gang leader might do; that is, to sit safely and anonymously at his desk in his fancy-schmancy office, copy the atrocious note, and then hand it over to a flunky to deliver it to the Mailbox. No way is he going to get caught. In that unlikely event, he would simply blame your Oppenheimer Park friend or whomever he paid to write the original note. The original note, that is, the one scribbled out with all the spelling errors, will be long destroyed."

Lloyd commented, "That brings up another interesting question, Greg, and that is, who knew where to deliver that note – who knew about the secret Mailbox?"

Greg simply shrugged his shoulders in a 'who knows?' gesture. "I'm sure that will come to light once we find Mona Grace and Charley. All in good time."

"May I have this?" Greg waved the original note in the air. "I'll make a photocopy of it for the file and an extra copy for you if you want it. I plan on using this original note as part of my application to the judge for a search warrant. With this note, together with disclosing to the judge the large arsenal of weapons found in the Devils' clubhouse, I am going to ask for two things. Firstly, a warrant to search the WARLORDS' den in order to determine if Mona Grace and Charley are being held either inside the house or elsewhere on the property."

"Secondly, I am going to ask for a warrant to have the bank disclose the bank account records for Paulo Santonio."

Greg leaned back in his chair, arms behind his head. "And that's where we are in this investigation."

"Following the money trail was the easy part. Now we are delving into the life and times of Mr Paulo Santonio. I figure his client must be the leader of the WARLORDS. If there is anything shady or unstable about him, be assured that his sin will find him out."

"I talked with BeeBee at length regarding the proposed Plan B. She wanted desperately to execute this plan herself, and I would have loved to let her. Unfortunately, as she will be appearing as a witness in Domingo's upcoming trial, there would be a definite conflict with her participation. There is also a pretty good possibility that her cover was blown during the execution of matters at the Devils' clubhouse, the details of which you are more than aware, having been part of the operation. She is too good an officer for me to risk her any further."

Lloyd was disappointed but completely understood. "What is the plan?" Lloyd asked.

"I'd like you to go back to Oppenheimer Park and speak with the residents there. You got to know some of them, if only slightly. I can't help but think that one or more of those people saw something on the day that Mona Grace and Charley disappeared. They won't speak to just anybody. Heck, sometimes they won't speak at all, but I think you developed a good rapport with enough of them that at least a few might speak with you."

"This could take more than a day or two. Depending on the mood, they will either speak to you now, later, or never. It's worth a crack, though. Are you willing to give it a try?"

"Of course. When do I start?"

Greg smiled with obvious relief. "As soon as we talk about how best to approach the subject with the residents of the park."

"And what is the next plan, Plan C, if this doesn't work?" Lloyd asked anxiously.

"One thing at a time, my friend. We'll jump into that fire if and when the need arises, don't you think?" the sergeant said noncommittally. "I think at the moment, we need to proceed full speed ahead in our search for the missing women."

For the next several minutes, Lloyd listened as Greg outlined the various questions Lloyd should ask, outlined the importance of making notes in a complete and timely fashion of any conversation he was able to elicit.

"I think one of your questions to your friends should be, 'Did anyone approach you in the last month or so and offer you money to write a note for him?'"

"Remember, don't push," Greg said. "The last thing you want to do is to scare them off. Word will spread quicker than mouse turds in an old barn if even a single, solitary resident of the park suspects something that might involve them."

Greg checked his watch. "How about we meet back here in my office about two o'clock? That's if you are able to, of course. You might well be in the middle of a productive conversation with one of your prospective witnesses. In that case, I'll just wait in my office until you get back here."

"Will do," said Lloyd.

Greg stood up, handed Lloyd a notebook and a pen. He said, "Good luck, Lloyd."

"Same to you, Greg," Lloyd responded. "See you at two, unless I luck out and am interviewing a potential lead."

The very first thing Lloyd did when he got to Oppenheimer Park was to perch himself on a bench, open his notebook and start a list of anyone he thought might possibly speak with him. He wrote down, 'the Whistling Man'. He then sat completely still, his idle hand poised above the notebook page. He suddenly realised that, although he recognised several characters from the area, he didn't know the given names of even one single person. It made him profoundly embarrassed to discover that he hadn't even considered introducing himself by name and then asking the names of the homeless people and calling them by their names! Just because they were homeless, alcoholics, drug addicts, unemployed, or had mental health issues, it didn't mean that they weren't real people with real feelings and a need to be recognised. Overcome with emotion, Lloyd bent his head down and covered his eyes with his hands while he tried to get himself back in control. He was totally disgusted with himself.

While he was sitting thus, he realised someone was standing right beside him, clearing his throat. A peek through his lowered eyelids revealed that this person was shuffling his torn sneakers-covered feet from left to right. The throat-clearing noises continued.

Lloyd lifted his head and stared into the eyes of this person. It was 'the Whistling Man'!

The man continued his precise shuffling, always in the same direction, rather like a box step being practised in dance class. It almost looked like he was in danger of wearing the box pattern deep into the soil beside the bench.

"Hey!" the Whistler exclaimed. "I know you! I know you!"

Lloyd stood up shakily. "Yes, sir, you do," he said. "But we've never been formally introduced, have we, sir?" He held out his hand. "My name is Lloyd, Lloyd Jordan. What's your name?"

The shuffling continued as the man gazed at Lloyd, his expression one of confusion, puzzlement, and a flicker of amazement thrown in for good measure.

"You want to know my name, know my name?" he asked incredulously.

"Yes, please," Lloyd said simply. "I'm Lloyd, like I told you. And yes, I would love to know your name. We can be better friends if we know each other's names, don't you think?"

An unsteady smile slowly crossed the Whistling Man's face. "Yes, yes, that would be fine. That would be fine. My name is – (and here, the man appeared to think really hard), my name is Tony! My name is Tony Thomas Hill, Tony Thomas Hill."

Lloyd held out his hand. "Nice to meet you, Mr Hill."

Tony looked at Lloyd's outstretched hand but didn't shake it. "Hands not clean, man," he said to Lloyd, wiping his hands on the legs of his pants. "Sorry…Lloyd?" He tried using Lloyd's name for the first time. A wide smile creased his friendly, weathered face. "You're Lloyd, you're Lloyd. I'm Tony, Tony Thomas Hill. I'm Tony Thomas Hill. Nice to meet you, Lloyd, nice to meet you!"

Lloyd's smile matched that of Tony's. "Nice to meet you too, Mr Hill."

Tony Thomas Hill's smile faded. "I'm just Tony, just Tony."

"Okay, Tony, just Tony, it is very nice to meet you!"

The sunny smile returned to Tony's face.

"Lloyd," he asked hesitantly, "whatcha doin' here?"

Lloyd asked, "You mean other than visiting with my new friend Tony?"

Tony nodded shyly, clearly happy with being called by his proper name.

"Well," Lloyd said, "I'm doing some work." He patted the park bench, asked Tony if he would like to sit while Lloyd explained what he was working on. Seeing Tony's hesitation, he said, "It's okay, man…I mean Tony. You don't have to sit close to me. It's just that telling you about my work might take a few minutes, and you'll get tired just standing there." Once again, Lloyd patted the bench, this time further away.

After lengthy consideration, Tony perched precariously on the very edge of the bench, as far away as possible from where Lloyd was sitting. He partially turned towards Lloyd and waited for him to speak.

"I have a very good friend. You might even know her. Her name is Mona Grace Ford. Her office is in the homeless shelter just over there." (Lloyd waved his hand in the general direction of the shelter).

"I also have a foster-care sister. Her name is really Charlotte, but everyone calls her Charley." Lloyd purposely didn't give Charley's last name. He didn't feel like going into a long explanation about the relationship between Mona Grace Ford and Charley Ford.

"Mona Grace and Charley are missing. I am searching desperately to find them before the bad people that took them can hurt them. Tony, I miss them so much and I am so worried about them."

Tony spoke to Lloyd in a hoarse whisper, "Who took them? Those women, who took them?"

Lloyd looked at the ground as he spoke. He had noticed that Tony seemed more comfortable if you didn't look directly at him. "I'm not positive, Tony, but I think it was either the East Van Devils or the WARLORDS gang that took them. It's complicated, but here's what happened."

Lloyd explained simply about the bail money and the WARLORDS' worry that Domingo would breach his bail and the WARLORDS wouldn't get their money back if that happened. He told Tony that the theory was that the WARLORDS were holding Mona Grace and Charley hostage until Domingo's trial was all done. When they got their bail money back, they would return Mona Grace and Charley, unharmed.

"Those are bad men, bad men, Lloyd," Tony whispered. He was clearly terrified by Lloyd's story.

Lloyd nodded in agreement, then took his copy of the note out of his backpack and showed it to Tony.

Tony held the note and painfully read the note aloud, with Lloyd's assistance. He then handed it back to Lloyd. Tony appeared shocked. "Who wrote that note, that note?" He stuttered slightly as he asked.

Lloyd told him that he didn't know for sure, but…here he told Tony the theory about a stranger approaching someone in the park, having that someone print out the note.

Tony said he was sure that nobody he knew could print so nice. Lloyd explained the rest of the theory, although he wasn't altogether convinced that Tony got it.

"Do you know anything about this, Tony? Did someone ask you to print a note?"

"NO!" Clearly agitated, Tony stood up and began his shuffling sequence once again. "I don't know, Lloyd, I don't know, Lloyd, nothing about the note, the note. I don't know nothing about this. It's bad, it's bad. Awful, awful."

Lloyd reached over to pat Tony's hand but stopped himself when Tony shied away. "Don't worry, Tony, I believe you. I just thought, you know, that seeing as you know all the people who use the park and the streets near here, you might have heard something. That's all. I didn't think you wrote the note."

"Although to be completely honest, I really wish you had. If I can find out who wrote that note, I could talk to them. If that happened, I could figure out who took Mona Grace and Charley and where they took them to. I could bring them back home. Understand?"

Although Tony still appeared somewhat upset and rattled, he had at least stopped his shuffling.

"I don't know Lloyd, don't know. But I can listen, I can listen. If I hear something I can tell you, tell you, right? I can tell you, right?"

"You sure can, Tony, my friend. I think I know a couple more guys I can speak with too. If they don't know anything either, then I might ask you if you have any idea about who I should talk to. Is that all right with you, Tony?" Lloyd waited with bated breath for Tony's answer.

"I guess so, guess so, Lloyd," Tony finally said. "I can listen and think. I'll listen and think."

As Tony turned to walk away, Lloyd stood up. "Thanks, Tony. I appreciate your help. I want to find those women soon."

"I know Mona Grace, Mona Grace. I really like her, like her. She is nice to me, nice to me. I don't know Charley though. I don't know Charley though."

Lloyd looked speculatively at his friend. "You'd like Charley, Tony. She's a great girl. Goes to the University of British Columbia. She's smart and nice. You would like her a lot, Tony. You'd like her a lot!"

"Okay, okay, Lloyd, I'll like her, Charley, I'll like Charley. Bye, Lloyd, Lloyd," said Tony. He began to whistle as he walked away. Lloyd could still hear him when he reached the other side of the park.

Lloyd picked up his notebook and checked his watch, then began to make notes about his first interview. When he completed his notes, he sat and thought for a minute. No one seemed to be hanging around in the park at the moment. He thought he might run into someone he recognised if he walked over to the shelter. He had two or three people in mind. If they were still hanging around the area, he should be able to spot them outside of the shelter.

The first person Lloyd noticed was a man whom he had seen on the day Lloyd had arrived in East Vancouver. The man still appeared to look the same as he had looked that first time. He was short and stocky, probably in his mid to late 50s. He had the purple, heavily veined, and bulbous nose of a copious drinker. If anything, and if possible, his nose was even more discoloured and swollen now than when Lloyd had initially seen him. This was the man who had spoken with Lloyd after seeing him break the ice with BeeBee. The Drinker (as Lloyd shamefacedly recalled thinking of him) had offered Lloyd a drink from an open liquor bottle he was waving around.

Lloyd approached the man. "Hello, sir, I don't know if you remember me? You came and spoke to me the first day I arrived in East Van. I had talked with a street woman named BeeBee. After I had talked with BeeBee, you came over and talked to me about her. Do you remember me?"

Lloyd paused, then exclaimed, "Oh, excuse me, sir, I'm asking you all these questions at machinegun speed and I didn't even give you my name! I'm Lloyd, Lloyd Jordan. What's your name, sir?"

Lloyd held his hand out to the fellow, who first wiped his grimy hand on the side of his pant leg before shaking Lloyd's. "Name's Mickey, Mickey McGuire. Want a drink?" He waved his almost-full vodka bottle precariously in the air.

Lloyd thought to himself that it must have been providential that he had come over here before the drinking man had drunk any more from that bottle, likely becoming incoherent. Remembering how pompous he had felt the last time he had refused a drink from this man, he simply answered, "Not just now, Mr McGuire. I'm working at the moment."

"Ah, well then, mustn't disturb a man fortunate to be working, should we?" He turned to walk away.

"Mr McGuire! Excuse me, please, but I really need to speak with you for a few minutes, if you can spare me the time. Can we adjourn to a quieter, less occupied spot? Oppenheimer Park, perhaps?"

Mickey McGuire squinted at Lloyd suspiciously. "Hey, man, you a cop? Whoops, sorry, you a cop, 'Lloyd'?" When Lloyd said that he was definitely not a policeman, Mickey raised his vodka bottle high in the air and whooped, "Hallelujah! Time for a drink!"

Lloyd caught the liquor bottle just as it slipped out of Mickey's trembling fingers. "Whew! Mickey, that was a close one! Would you mind if we go over to the park and talk for a minute or two before you have any more to drink? It's awfully important, awfully urgent."

Mickey glared balefully at Lloyd, then sighed and said, "Well, Lloyd, since you say you aren't a cop, then I suppose so, but let's get on with it. A guy gets pretty thirsty by coffee time."

"Would you like a coffee, Mickey?" Lloyd asked. "I can run into the cafeteria at the shelter and buy you a coffee."

"Nah!" Mickey scoffed. Remembering his manners, he said, "Thanks anyhow, but I've got my libations right here." The bottle once again rolled precariously, and Lloyd tensed, prepared to grab it. Mickey, however, settled down and headed off towards the park at such a fast clip that Lloyd had to jog to keep up.

Both men sat down on the park bench closest to the drop-off where Lloyd had seen the pumpkin truck more than once. Before he could start reminiscing though, he shook his head and devoted his full attention to Mr Mickey McGuire. Unlike Tony, who avoided eye contact at all costs, Mickey's eyes never left Lloyd's. He listened so intently that Lloyd was beginning to think that he had the complete attention of a man who certainly knew something.

Once he had disclosed all the happenings that he could regarding Mona Grace and Charlie's disappearance, Lloyd stopped talking and just stared at Mickey imploringly. Lloyd finally broke the silence. "Mickey, is there anything you can tell me? Did you perhaps see something one night while you were bedded down here in the park? Did anyone approach you and ask you to print out the note I told you about? Offer to pay you for your service? Or if you weren't approached, did you see someone else?"

Mickey answered Lloyd emphatically, "NO, NO, NO, and NO! Ain't nobody come up to me and asked me to write them no note."

Lloyd nodded his head slowly. "Okay, Mickey, I believe you. Would you do me a favour? Just keep an eye and an ear out for anything at all that you might see or hear, that might have anything to do with either Mona Grace or Charley's disappearance? Unless someone can help me out here, I'm terrified that something terrible will happen to them. Mickey, you know these gangs. They aren't above killing those women. We can't let that happen!"

"You know how dangerous the WARLORDS are, I'm sure, Mr McGuire. And I'm even more certain that you know that gang members don't necessarily follow the laws and rules of law-abiding citizens, so I'm positive you understand the depth and reasons for my concerns here, don't you?"

"I'll be back here tomorrow again, so maybe you can sleep on it and remember something or someone that might help. Okay?"

Mickey McGuire sat for another minute, staring into space, his brow furrowed in deep concentration. Finally, he stood up and said, "I'll sleep on it, Lloyd. If I come up with anything or anyone that can help you, you'll hear about it tomorrow. Now, sure you don't want a drink?"

Not waiting for an answer, Mickey turned on his heel and headed back towards the street where Lloyd had approached him, the bottle snug against his lips. Head tipped far back, somehow he managed a very large swig without walking into anything.

Lloyd sighed, tempted to give up, at least for today. The persistent nagger that lived in his brain booted him in the ass. Lloyd was ashamed. *Don't be ridiculous*, he chided himself. *Do you think Mona Grace and Charley have given up? If they have, then it's even more vital that you keep looking.* Disheartened but undaunted, Lloyd pulled back his slumping shoulders and prepared to find another interviewee.

Lady Luck was with him. He had approached the shelter and sat down on the bottom step, prepared to wait until he spotted someone he recognised. As it turned out, someone recognised Lloyd instead.

"Well, hello!" A surprised voice behind him made Lloyd turn around, in search of the source of the voice. He looked vaguely familiar, but – Lloyd must have looked puzzled enough that the man behind him came and sat down on the step, beside Lloyd. The man stuck out his hand and said, "Bed #9! I was in the shower line-up behind you the morning after our good friend (said very sarcastically) the Groper paid you a middle of the night visit. Remember me?"

"By the way," Bed #9 continued, "my name is Warren, Warren Widdifield."

"Lloyd Jordan," Lloyd offered, shaking the man's hand. "Pleasure to meet up with you again."

"So, what'cha doing around here again, Mr Jordan? The rumour mill had it that you moved to somewhere in Alberta. You back for good this time?"

Lloyd smiled enigmatically, neither confirming nor denying the rumour mill. "Just couldn't stay away, I guess," was all he said.

Warren Widdifield gazed thoughtfully at Lloyd. "Why are you really here, Lloyd Jordan? Must be some reason other than the charming company of the residents of East Vancouver."

Based strictly on a strong hunch, Lloyd was pretty sure that Mr Warren Widdifield knew something that would help out. He began once again to tell his story and ask for assistance. Warren listened, completely absorbed, until Lloyd was finished before he spoke.

"Whew! Quite the predicament you find yourself in, huh?"

"Well," Warren went on, "there are two things I can tell you. Firstly, I did not copy the note for anyone, but I'm pretty sure I know who did. Secondly, I saw something that I know will be of interest to you, if you want to hear about it."

Lloyd held his breath, hoping to tamp down his growing excitement until he heard everything Mr Warren Widdifield had to offer.

"Before I tell you, though," Warren said, "do you mind if we go over to Oppenheimer Park? It will be easier to explain things if we are at 'the scene of the crime' as it were."

Lloyd scrambled to his feet. He said only, "Lead the way."

A few minutes later, Lloyd found himself sitting on the same bench that he and Mickey had occupied a short time ago. He forced himself to remain quiet and not to appear excited, just in case this Warren fellow was making stuff up.

"First of all," Warren said, "about the note. Our friend, the Groper, is your man. I was walking through the park a week or so ago, looking for a place to drop my sleeping bag. I was scoping out a flat spot behind that huge arbutus tree over there." He pointed to the large tree with which Lloyd was very familiar. "I was pretty much hidden by both the tree and the near darkness when I heard the Groper's simpering voice. He was speaking to the driver of that pumpkin-orange-coloured delivery truck that comes around regularly. It says 'ZO'S HAULING' on the doors. Know which truck I mean?"

Lloyd nodded in the affirmative, although he said nothing.

"It caught my attention because that truck is usually here in the daylight, not in the late evening."

"Anyhow, the Groper guy said to the driver, 'Yeah? What's in it for me?' Then the driver said, 'I'll give you $100 if you print what I tell you on this piece of paper. That's all you have to do.' Then the Groper said, 'Show me the money.' The driver must have showed it to him cause the Grope said, 'Okay, man, I'll do it, but I have to sit down.' Then both of those guys came and sat down on this very bench. The driver told him what to write, something about someone having two people; I don't remember the names. Something about bail money and something about being dead."

"It took the Groper guy quite a while to print out the note. I don't think he has much education, and so, I doubt if he can spell very well. It was quite a while. I should know, because I was hiding while all this was happening."

"When the Grope was done (a lot of us guys call him the Grope; others call him the Groper), the driver gave him the money and asked him what his name was. The Grope said in his affected, giggly, soprano, falsetto, 'If you tell me yours, then I'll tell you mine!' The driver sounded disgusted, but he said, 'I'm Adam Draper. Who are you?' Then the Grope says, 'I'm Earl Turner, but you can call me Sugar. Everyone does.' The driver, Adam, made kind of a gagging sound and told the Groper guy to get lost and forget he ever did this little chore. He pretty much threatened the Grope that if he talked, he would regret it. The Grope walked away then. He didn't look back. And by the way, I have never heard anyone call him 'Sugar'. I don't know what that was all about."

"Oh, yeah! One other thing. The driver, Adam, called someone on his cell. I heard him say that he had the note and he would bring it over right away. He listened for a minute and then I heard him say that some dude named Lester knew where the mailbox was and he, Adam, would arrange for this Lester character to deliver the note to the mailbox when it was ready. He listened again and then said that he knew where the den was. He didn't need directions. He said he would be right over. Then I heard the truck start up and leave."

"That's all I heard, Lloyd. I hope it helps you in your search for those missing women. Everyone in this area knows and likes Mona Grace. If any of them know anything more, I'll send them over to the park to find you."

Warren Widdifield stood up and stretched. "And that, my fine friend, is all I can tell you."

Lloyd answered, "Well, I'd say that's quite a bit. Thanks, man – Warren – I appreciate your assistance."

He stood up and held out his hand. When he shook Warren's hand, a $50 bill magically transferred from Lloyd's hand to the informer's. Warren peeked into his hand, grinned broadly with delight and said, "Thanks! Like I told you, if I hear anything more, I'll be sure to let you know." He then walked back in the direction of the shelter.

Lloyd remained seated on the park bench, his head spinning. He picked up his pen and began making careful notes. He didn't want to forget anything that Warren Widdifield had just told him.

When he had completed his notes, he carefully read them over, looking for any errors or omissions. Finally satisfied that they were as complete and accurate as Lloyd could make them, he closed his notebook and sat, deep in thought. Although he had enough information to piece together some of the puzzle, he still desperately needed to find out who had picked up Mona Grace and Charley and where had they been taken.

He looked at his watch – FOUR O'CLOCK! Greg would be getting pretty antsy. Lloyd had missed their two o'clock rendezvous by two hours. He quickly tightened his backpack and headed for the detachment. At least, he thought, he wasn't going back without any information.

Finally, back in Greg's office, Lloyd handed over his notebook, waited while Greg read his notes. When he was finished, he whistled softly. "I'm impressed! You didn't waste any time, did you? I'm assuming that Adam is Adam Draper? He appears to be at least a part of this scheme. Are you surprised, Lloyd?"

Lloyd shrugged his shoulders noncommittally. "Disappointed, I think but not too surprised," he said resignedly.

Greg looked at Lloyd and asked, "What about this Lester fellow? Do you have any idea who that might be?"

"I've been thinking hard about that ever since Warren mentioned him," Lloyd mused. "The only Lester that I ever knew was a foster kid, Lester Laboucan. He was a foster teenager in the Petrie house, when Lacey and I were there. Lester was 15, I think; Lacey was 13; I was 17."

"Do you think Lacey might have told this Lester where the secret Mailbox was?"

"Knowing Lacey, I can say definitively that there is absolutely no way that she would have," Lloyd asserted. "I know that Lester was a really good kid, kind and helpful. He had been in foster care since he was a toddler. I figure since he never ran away and helped out where he could, he was an okay guy. Although he was extremely quiet and shy, I felt confident that he would keep an eye on Lacey when I left the Petrie's place.

"Lester might have followed Lacey when she went on one of her many trips to the Mailbox to check to see if there was anything in our secret hiding place.

He might follow her, either to protect her if need be, or just to satisfy his curiosity about where she went. He wouldn't squeal on her, that's for sure."

"Would Lacey perhaps know what happened to Lester?" Greg asked.

"I don't know," Lloyd said morosely. "I can give her a call and see. She did tell me that when Mrs Petrie was put in the criminal loony bin, that Lester and a set of young twins were moved to a different foster home than Lacey. She was pretty upset to be split away from Lester and the twins. She told me that when we were finally reunited. If I remember correctly, Lester had to change schools, so unless he played basketball or football or something where all the rural schools competed, I'm not sure how she would have been in contact. I do seem to remember that Lester played basketball. Don't quote me on that, but I seem to remember that he played, and he was a pretty good player."

"I'll call Lacey right after supper and check with her. There is a small chance that she'll know where Lester might be and what he ended up doing. I guess we'll never know for sure unless I ask, right?"

Greg stood up. "Speaking of supper, we should call it a day. You accomplished a significant amount today, Lloyd. I want to thank you for your assistance. So, are you done with your interviews now?"

Lloyd said, "Not quite. There is one more person I want to speak with. I'll go back to the shelter early tomorrow morning, before they boot everyone out for the day and try and have a talk with the fellow. Can I please have my notebook back in case I think of anything I missed, and so I can record what happens tomorrow?"

Greg handed him his notebook, cautioning him to keep it with him at all times. If he lost it, there would be no record of his interviews. Lloyd agreed and tucked it safely into his ever-present backpack.

Bethany wasn't back yet. Greg went directly to the fridge and removed two large TV dinners. He stuck them in the oven to heat, saying that he preferred heating the beef up that way rather than in the microwave; the meal didn't dry out as much.

He told Lloyd to make himself at home. He said he would be out in a few minutes, that he was just going to change out of his uniform.

"There's Coke in the fridge, Lloyd, help yourself. Turn on the television news channel, if you want, or whatever else you might want to watch."

Lloyd intended to 'eat and run' to his room and call both Susanna and Lacey, so he chose to throw on a pair of pyjama bottoms and a T-shirt before he watched

129

any television. He grabbed a can of Coke out of the fridge, then sat down, remote in his hand.

A picture of Mona Grace and Charley appeared on the television screen! It made Lloyd bolt straight up! He increased the volume. There was a short blurb about the missing women. The announcer asked the public to keep an eye out for Mona Grace Ford and Charlotte (known as Charley). Should they see or hear anything, the news broadcaster asked them to contact Sergeant Greg Gablehaus at the East Vancouver Police detachment.

When Greg came back to the living room, the first thing he noticed was how rigid and pale Lloyd appeared, sitting ramrod straight on the edge of the sofa. He was breathing rapidly and his eyes looked suspiciously moist.

"Are you okay, Lloyd?" Greg asked with concern. "You don't look well."

Lloyd replied, "I just saw a picture of Mona Grace and Charley on the news channel. Did you know it was going to be broadcast tonight?"

Greg looked sheepish. "I'm sorry, Lloyd. I got so engrossed with your interview results that I completely forgot that their pictures were going to be aired this evening. Just so you know, they are going to air the pictures and update the search progress daily for the next while."

Lloyd asked, "Is that a good idea? Maybe it will spook the abductor or abductors into moving the women, from wherever they are holding them now, to a new place."

"I don't think so, Lloyd. Remember, they aren't holding Mona Grace and Charley for a cash ransom. Well, at least not in the usual manner that ransom is dealt with. This ransom is a half million bucks, but all that has to happen is Domingo behave himself until his trial, not breach any of the terms of his bail, and then the women will be released. Simple, right?"

Lloyd stared at Greg dubiously. "Do you honestly think that will happen, Greg?"

"Which do you mean, Lloyd – that Domingo won't breach any of his bail conditions, or that whoever is holding them won't release them when the time comes?"

Lloyd stared steadily at Greg. "Lordy, Greg, I don't know what I mean. I know I'm praying that everything works out and soon!"

"I know what you mean, kid. Come into the kitchen and eat. Everything looks more positive on a full stomach."

After supper, Lloyd tidied up the kitchen with Greg. He then excused himself so he could phone Susanna and Lacey. He said if Greg was still up when Lloyd was finished with his phone calls, he would report to Greg as soon as he was finished. If not, he said he would tell him what Lacey had to say at breakfast.

He stacked up the numerous pillows that were scattered decoratively across the top of his bed. He then rested against the mound which Lloyd had managed to make very 'un-decorative'. In fact, it looked more like a mountain of mess.

Although he had intended to call Susanna first, he changed his mind. He dialled Lacey's phone number, his fingers tapping impatiently on one of the pillows as he waited for her to answer. Her voicemail clicked on. Lloyd figured she was probably outside feeding chickens or rabbits, or whatever you did in the way of evening chores when you had your own little hobby farm in the country. Certainly not like when they were at Bart and Gladys Bourke's farm, where Lloyd had to get up at something like four o'clock in the morning to feed the pigs and cattle and then do other, innumerable chores before he left for school.

"Hey, Lace, it's Lloyd. Can you please call me back on my cell when you get done doing your 'Old McDonald's Farm' stuff? I'm hoping you can help me. It's pertaining to Mona Grace and Charley. Call me back, no matter how late. Thanks!"

Susanna answered on the first ring. "Hey, luv! I've been waiting for your call."

Lloyd gave her a rapid-fire version of the day's events. He then told her that he was waiting for Lacey to call him so he needed to get off the phone. He told her that after Lacey called, he would call Susanna back.

Susanna let out a loud guffaw.

"What?" Lloyd asked.

Susanna said, "Lacey's here, Lloyd. Parker had to go to Regina for a couple of days. He's teaching some kind of a class to the recruits. Lacey came for a late supper. She did her farm chores early. I've convinced her to stay with me overnight and then, tomorrow, I'll go back with her and help her do whatever has to be done."

Lloyd said, "Don't overdo it, either of you! Don't forget, between the two of you, there are four of you!"

Susanna giggled. As usual, her giggle was so infectious, so carefree, that Lloyd could feel his mood levitating all the way up to the ceiling. "Get me my sister on the phone, woman!" he growled in a completely non-threatening manner, laughing before he even finished his sentence.

"Aye, aye, sir!" She then hollered so loudly that Lloyd's ears rang. "Lacey, the telephone's for you! You can pick up the phone on the hall table, just outside of the bathroom door." As soon as Lacey picked up, Susanna hurriedly said, "Talk to you later, Lloyd. Call me back when you're done talking with Lacey, okay?"

"Count on it," he said.

She hung up. She then returned to the kitchen and continued with preparing supper for Lacey and herself.

. . . .

Charley couldn't tell if her eyes were open or closed. The last shot administered by 'It', as she had begun to think of the apparition, had knocked her out more completely than any of the other shots.

The room was now in total darkness. Not a trace of light flickered anywhere, not even from under the hallway door across from the foot of her bed.

An uncontrollable itch caused her left eyelid to twitch. It was futile to try to scratch it, she knew, because her arms were secured to the bedrails.

She lay in the darkness, listening for a noise, any type of noise. Even the scratching of a mouse's tiny, filthy, creepy feet scampering across the floor would be more welcome than this total silence, this total darkness. Charley hated mice more than anything. They petrified her. *Dear God,* she prayed silently, *even the noise of a mouse would be welcome, I think, but maybe you shouldn't send one as a test of my faith!* Despite her desperation, she felt a wry smile flicker, briefly wrinkling her cheeks.

Her itch grew steadily worse. She gritted her teeth, trying to think about anything but the need to scratch. She was sure she would go crazy. Suddenly, without conscious thought, Charley lifted her left arm towards her head. Her arm moved upward; her hand reached her forehead! With a soft whimper, she sat up. When she tried to move her right arm, she had limited movement. That arm was still secured. Holding her breath, she tried again to move her left arm. The restraint was still wrapped around her arm, but it was not attached to the bedrail. The apparition must have been in a great hurry to leave. Charley was quite sure that 'It' must have been called away, had to run somewhere, and in the midst of the distraction, he neglected to restrain her left arm.

Completely forgetting about the itch, Charley concentrated fully on her unleashed left arm. She took great care to rearrange the restraint so that it would appear to be in its proper position the next time 'It' came into the room. This was very difficult to do, one-armed. It took a lot of twisting and jiggling before she finally was satisfied that her left arm looked as restrained as her right arm. She could only hope!

She lay still, puffing from the exertion, trying to slow down her breathing, to stifle any gasping noises. Stiff and still in the darkness, Charley made a huge decision. Clearing her rusty throat, she called out into the darkness. "Hello, is anybody there? If you can hear me, can you tap on your wall? Tap once for no; tap twice for yes."

She continued, "Who are you? – Oops, sorry, silly me! I guess tapping won't tell me who you are!"

Having corrected herself, Charley called out, a bit louder this time. "Do you know where we are?" She listened for several minutes, hearing nothing. Suddenly, she heard one tap. No, the person on the other side of the wall didn't know where they were.

This time, she called even louder, "Are you in a bed?" One tap. No, not in a bed.

"Are you tied in a chair?" Again, only one tap.

"Are you tied up on the floor?" One tap.

"Are you tied up at all?" One tap! Not tied up!

"Are you on the floor?" At last! Two taps.

"Can you lay down by the heat register so I can hear you better?" Charley heard a shuffling sound and then a timorous voice spoke, barely audible in its softness. "I'm Mona Grace Ford. Who are you?"

Charley could barely contain herself. She yelled, much too loudly, "It's Charley, Mama. It's Charley!"

Although she repeated herself, calling, "Mama? Mona Grace? Talk to me," there was no further sound coming from the other side of the wall.

Charley lay completely still, physically and emotionally drained. She prayed that Mona Grace's sudden lack of any response didn't mean that something bad had happened to her mother.

It would be a long wait until morning.

. . . .

At the same time as Charley lay exhausted and despondent in her bed, Mona Grace had heard someone approaching her room. She quickly dropped down on to her mattress on the floor, pretending to sleep. When the door from the hallway opened and a very large flashlight spread a stream of brilliant light that illuminated every nook and cranny of the room, she moaned and rolled over to face the wall, to try and hide her eyes from the glare.

A swift kick to her ribs brought her upright.

The person who stood at the side of her mattress was fully disguised from head to toe. An operating room cap covered every hair on his or her head; a face mask obscured every feature except for the eyes, which were hidden behind very dark sunglasses. Scrubs, a lab coat, gloves, and a pair of standard green booties worn over footwear made any chance of determining at least the gender of this person impossible.

"Who were you talking to?" Even the voice was disguised, emanating from deep down in the throat, emerging as a forced, squeaky falsetto.

Mona Grace struggled to rise, pretending she was awakened from a deep sleep.

"I don't know what you're talking about," she said, rubbing her eyes. "I was asleep until you turned on the flashlight."

"The patient from all the way across the hall and two doors down heard you." A momentary slip in the squeaky falsetto had Mona Grace believing that the person was a man.

"Oh!" Mona Grace said. "I was having a terrible dream. Maybe I screamed out in my sleep. I have been having some pretty wicked nightmares lately, as you can well imagine, what with being locked up in an unknown location and all."

She was leaning against the wall, hands on her stomach, wrists to elbows straight out from her sides, trying to make the vent in the wall less visible. She and Charley would be in some serious doo-doo if this fellow suddenly developed a brain and figured out that it was possible to hear another person through the ducts. *First time in my life, I've ever been happy to have a big butt,* she thought to herself.

"I'm really sorry if I disturbed the patient from all the way across the hall and two doors down. Please, pass on my apologies and tell that patient that I will try not to have any more bad dreams."

As she looked at the person (who, by now, Mona Grace was pretty sure was a man) standing above her, she wasn't sure if she imagined it or not, but she figured that there was some serious eye rolling going on behind those dark glasses!

Not even trying to disguise his voice, the man said, "Go back to sleep and shut up, for Christ's sake, before you wake up the others in this whole ward."

He slammed the door on his way out. Shaking, he leaned against the wall in the hallway, trembling so turbulently that his legs threatened to give out on him. He tried to convince himself that the woman in the room behind him was too strung out to have noticed that he had failed to disguise his voice. He took a few deep breaths to steady his nerves, then headed down the hall to report that everything was okay; that it had only been a nightmare, causing the woman to scream out, yell, and talk in her sleep.

Mona Grace lay quietly on her thin mattress on the very hard floor. Her mind rolled backwards, trying to recall every suspicious thing she had discerned while the man was in the room and speaking to her.

A few very important things stood out. Firstly, the 'person' was a man! He had made a huge error when he slipped and dropped the squeaky falsetto! His normal speaking voice was deep. No mistaking that voice for a female.

Secondly, and most importantly, she and Charley were in some sort of medical facility! She had definitely heard the man refer to a 'ward' as well as refer to the 'patient' from all the way down the hall.

When Mona Grace apologised for disturbing the 'patient' from all the way across the hall and two doors down, the man-in-disguise didn't correct her.

She suddenly thought of a third thing. Except for his expensive, prescription Serengeti Merano sunglasses, the man's disguise consisted entirely of medical apparel. Although not strictly a definite clue, Mona Grace thought it was a pretty good guess that the disguise was obtained from somewhere in this very building.

Without being able to see her watch face in the dark, it was impossible for her to estimate how long she lay on the floor, waiting. After what seemed like a complete lifetime, she placed her mouth to the register on the wall and spoke as quietly as she could, trying to enunciate clearly to compensate for her hushed voice.

"Charley? Honey, are you there?" Rats, she thought, it's not safe to yell or even speak loud enough for her to hear me. Before she could try speaking again, she heard two soft taps coming from the other side of the wall. Yes! Charley was there.

"Can you hear me? I don't dare speak too loudly because the man might come back. Two taps, Charley. Lord be praised! Now, listen carefully; I don't dare speak for too long. The person who came into my room was disguised, but he slipped up. He forgot to disguise his voice as he was leaving the room. Until then I didn't know if the person was male or female. He's definitely male."

"Also, we're in some sort of medical facility. He referred to 'the patient' and to 'waking up the whole ward'. Did you hear everything I just said, Charley?" (Here, Charley reached her left arm towards the wall, thinking, as she did so, *to heck with adjusting the undone restraint. It's more important to communicate with my mother*.) Two taps.

Before Mona Grace could say anything more, she heard the sound of a door opening, and Charley speaking very loudly, ostensibly so that Mona Grace would hear her.

"What are you doing here? It's the middle of the night. I'm very tired already. I don't need another shot. Please, just let me sleep. I can't go anywhere. I'm tied up to the bedrails, so how can I go anywhere?"

Mona Grace heard her daughter, loud and clear.

'It' stood at the foot of the bed, not saying anything but not doing anything either. Finally, in a squeaky falsetto, 'It' said, "Fine, no needle, just don't make me regret this. If you try anything, or make a fuss, you'll get a shot that will knock you out for days! Got it?"

For the second time, the man dropped his accent, saying, in a normal, deep male voice, as he backed out the door, "Remember, no funny stuff!"

"Thank you!" Charley said loudly.

And thank you, God, she prayed silently, *for not allowing that man see that my left restraint was messed up!*

Suddenly, the long dark night didn't seem quite so bad.

Afraid that the man might just park himself outside her door for the rest of the night, Charley took no chances. She made no further attempt to contact Mona Grace.

. . . .

As he waited for Lacey to pick up the phone, he fervently wished that he was there in person instead of trying to sort things out by telephone.

"Hey, Lloyd! Nice to hear from you."

"Hey, Lace!" Lloyd said. "How's it going?"

"F-i-i-ne?" his sister drawled out cautiously. "How's it going with you?"

Lloyd ran his hand through his hair, sighing audibly. "Kind of taking two steps forward and one step back, you know? I just come up with something that looks promising and then nothing comes of it. It seems like I've been back in East Vancouver for a month, but it's only been a couple of days. I miss home, that's for sure!"

Lacey chuckled. "So, Brother, rather than argue with me, you've decided that maybe I might be useful, is that it? I know you are calling me for a bigger reason than just to ask me how I am doing."

Lloyd snorted. "Something like that, I guess. You know me very well, Baby Sister." He paused for a few second, gathering his thoughts.

"Actually, Lacey, I really am calling for a specific reason. I've been speaking with some of the street people that hang out in East Van. I've been trying to track down the source of the threatening note that you and Susanna found in the Mailbox, the day we all went on that picnic."

Lacey asked, "Wow! How can you even begin to figure out where to start?"

Lloyd told her about Greg's theory that the poorly written note, containing numerous atrociously spelled words was printed by one of the homeless, after being paid well to do so. He expounded on Greg's theory that the scribbled note had been recopied by someone with exquisite handwriting – a big mistake on the part of whoever had rewritten it. The beautiful penmanship would stick out like a sore thumb, should anyone ever see it!

He told Lacey about the people he had spoken with. He told her how badly he felt that he hadn't bothered to find out the names of the homeless people when he was living among them, but now, he at least knew the names of some of them.

Using his notes as a guide, he told Lacey about interviewing the Whistler (whom he now knew as Tony Thomas Hill). He explained to Lacey that Tony couldn't help Lloyd. Nonetheless, Tony had promised to keep his eyes and ears open.

Lloyd told Lacey about the Drinker (now, thankfully, known as Mickey McGuire), how he also knew nothing but would use his eyes and his ears in case he heard anything that might be helpful.

Next, he talked to Lacey about Mr Bed #9 (Warren Widdifield). "Mr Widdifield was the most helpful interviewee," Lloyd told her. "He didn't write the note, but he knew who did write it. He said he saw the Groper waiting in the park, and then he saw the pumpkin-coloured 'ZO'S HAULING' truck drive up. Warren noticed the truck for not one, not two but for three reasons. Firstly, because of the brilliant orange colour, secondly, because it arrived at an unusual time, and thirdly, because Warren saw the Groper walk over to where the truck was parked. He heard the Groper speak with the driver. The Groper (whose real name is Earl Turner, but he said everyone calls him 'Sugar') was paid $100 cash to write out a note that the driver would dictate."

Lloyd paused for breath. For once, Lacey didn't interrupt his train of thought. He spoke again. "'Sugar' wouldn't write the note until he had the cash in hand. Once 'Sugar' completed the note (which took him a long time to write, according to Warren), he handed it back to the driver. He then immediately walked away from Oppenheimer Park."

"Now, Warren was hiding in the deep shadows of some large trees and thick shrubs while all of this was going on. I've hidden there myself. It's a perfect spot to see and hear everything that is going on at that end of the park."

"Not wanting to be seen, Warren continued to stay where he was. He said he heard the driver call someone on his cell. When that someone answered on the other end, Warren Widdifield clearly heard the driver say that it was Adam calling. Adam called the guy on the other end Lester, and he repeated out loud some of the things Lester was saying. He heard the driver, Adam, ask, 'Lester, do you know where that mailbox is, and can you deliver the note there when it's ready?' The dude, Lester, must have said yes because then the driver, Adam, said he would be in touch whenever the note was ready and he would give Lester a ride back to Alberta so Lester could put the note in the mailbox."

"I have to tell you, Lacey, I was so grateful to Warren for all the information he had so carefully and completely told me about, that I put a $50 bill in his palm when I shook his hand."

"At this point in my story, I need your help."

"I don't know about you, but I'm thinking that 'Lester' is Lester Laboucan. Do you remember him, Lacey? He was in the Petrie foster home with us. You were 13, Lester was 15, and I was 17. He's the only 'Lester' I know that might be aware of our secret Mailbox. In fact, he's the only 'Lester' I have ever known. I liked him. He was always quiet and polite, never got in trouble, not even with

Mrs Petrie! I think I might have even asked him to watch out for you when I was gone." Lloyd stopped talking, waiting to hear what Lacey might have to say.

It didn't take her long. "Of course, I remember Lester Laboucan, Lloyd. He saved my sanity after you took off and left me in that evil foster home, run by a crazy foster mother. He did watch out for me, and he watched out for the twins also. But Lloyd, believe me when I tell you, that, as much as I really liked him and trusted him, I NEVER told Lester where the Mailbox is. I wouldn't, and I didn't!"

Before Lloyd could reassure her that he believed her, Lacey started to cry. "It's okay, sis, I believe you," Lloyd soothed. "But let me ask you this: is there any chance that Lester might have followed you sometime when you went to the Mailbox to check for a note? Maybe he stayed just far enough back that you wouldn't have seen him?"

Lacey sniffed and thought hard. "Maybe," she said. "I kind of recall one particular day. I was just leaving to go check the Mailbox, when Lester asked me where I was going. I told him nowhere in particular, I just needed to get out of the house for a while. Mrs Petrie was being meaner than usual, and I needed to get away. Lester asked me if I wanted company, and I told him thanks for the offer, but I just wanted to be alone." She stopped, aghast. "Oh! Lordy, do you think he might have followed me that day? I know he was worried about me, because he had heard Mrs Petrie threaten to punish me for something earlier. Oh, Lloyd, I feel sick!"

"All the time I was walking to the Mailbox, I remember I felt kind of creepy, like someone was watching me, so I kept looking around. The hair on the back of my neck felt really weird. You know how people say when something creepy is happening, that the hair on the back of their neck stands up? So, I was feeling creeped out, but I never saw anyone, even though I kept looking. I remember feeling grateful that Lester would worry about me, even though I never thought he would stalk me!"

Lloyd said, rather distractedly, "Hmm, I don't think he had any intention of harming you, Lacey. You're right; he was probably just keeping an eye out so you would be safe."

"Tell me, Lace, did you ever see Lester after the Petrie place was shut down? I know you weren't in the same school after that."

"Let me think," Lacey pondered. "I did see him from time to time. He played basketball, I remember. Sometimes during school hours, buses would bring teams to our gymnasium to play against our local team. I saw him a few times but never had much conversation with him beyond a 'Hi, how are you doing?' or 'How are the twins doing?'. There were a few weekends where a bunch of teams would come and compete. I didn't go to those tournaments because I didn't feel comfortable imposing on my new foster parents. Thinking back, I'm sure they wouldn't have minded driving me."

"Funny, isn't it, Lloyd? Lester was so nice to me when all that crap was going on in the Petrie place that when we got split up, I really, really missed him. But I haven't even thought about him for the longest time! That makes me feel selfish."

"Did you ever hear what happened to him when he finished school? Where he went? What he did for a living?"

"You know, Lloyd, come to think of it, I did hear something. I can't remember who told me. It might have been my bus driver, but I don't know that for sure. Anyhow, whoever it was, said that Lester quit school after Grade X and moved to Vancouver! He apparently got a job at some insane asylum or somewhere like that. He'd be very good, I think. He was such a caring, gentle guy. I really missed him when he and the twins had to go to a different foster home than I did."

For the first time, Lloyd felt something other than apprehension. "Thanks, Lacey!" he said. "I'll keep in touch, but right now, I need to talk to Greg. Please tell Suz that I'll call her back after I speak with Greg, if it's not too late, otherwise I'll talk to her again tomorrow."

Chapter 6
Lester and Emily Laboucan

After speaking with Lacey about Lester Laboucan, Lloyd quickly called Greg Gablehaus' cell number. After ringing several times, the voicemail message kicked in. Swallowing his disappointment, Lloyd left a call back number, hung up, and waited for Greg to call him back.

At midnight, Lloyd knew that he wouldn't receive a call back before the next morning, at the earliest. He got ready for bed, crawled in, and spent a restless night dreaming of all the terrible things that could be happening to Mona Grace and Charley while everyone else was safe at home in their nice warm beds.

Lloyd woke up early. He tried to be quiet as he got ready to leave; however, Bethany was already up. He asked her if Greg was home. She replied that he was working nights and usually didn't get home until mid-morning sometime. "Ah," Lloyd said. "That explains why he didn't return my call last night. He was probably too busy at the detachment."

"What would you like for breakfast, Lloyd?" Bethany asked him. Lloyd apologised and told her that he would love to stop for breakfast, but he had to be somewhere and didn't have time to stop and eat. Bethany made him promise that he would grab a bite of something as soon as he was able. Lloyd promised her that he would.

With a quick wave, Lloyd left the house. He still needed to speak with Earl Turner (also known as 'The Groper'; also known as 'The Grope' and also known – to himself at least – as 'Sugar'). Lloyd wanted to arrive at the shelter before the residents and the street people scattered for the day. By 6:30, he was sitting on the steps of the shelter, trying not to appear as if he was snooping. Still, his gaze was obvious as his eyes darted furtively around the street, searching for Earl Turner.

It was not an interview that Lloyd was looking forward to. He still had bad dreams in which 'The Groper' was touching Lloyd's shoulder in the middle of the night, asking him if he wanted company to keep him warm! *Well, at least I made my refusal abundantly clear*, Lloyd thought. *He shouldn't proposition me in broad daylight, I sincerely hope*! Lloyd prided himself in believing that he was not prejudiced in any shape or form, whether it be race, colour, creed, or lifestyle. No matter how painful it was for him to admit it, even to himself, he had discovered that he was definitely prejudiced when it came to being propositioned by another person of his same sex!

Deep in those thoughts, Lloyd jumped a foot when a sugary, simpering voice, aimed directly at Lloyd's right ear assaulted and interrupted his reverie. "Well, if it isn't the sweetie from his first night at the shelter! Nice to see you again, sweet stuff. What are you doing back in East Van? Rumour has it that you moved to Alberta."

Swallowing nervously, Lloyd held out his hand. "Hello, again, Mr Turner. I'm just back in East Van for a week or so. Listen, I owe you an apology. I never introduced myself before. I'm Lloyd, Lloyd Jordan. It's nice to officially meet you."

Earl Turner shook Lloyd's hand heartily and said, "Lovely to meet you also, Mr Lloyd Jordan." He then sat quietly, his eyes never leaving Lloyd's face as he waited for him to speak.

Clearing his throat, Lloyd said, "I'm hoping, Mr Turner, that you can help me. It's concerning two women who are missing, and there are a lot of people who are looking for them. You know Mona Grace Ford? She is one of the counsellors at the shelter. Well, she is one of the missing. The other woman's name is Charlotte, but she goes by 'Charley'."

Earl looked puzzled. In a normal, ordinary, deep voice, he asked Lloyd, "What's that got to do with me, if I may ask? I certainly know nothing about this."

"Well, you may not remember anything, Mr Turner, but I think I might be able to jog your memory a little. Would you answer some questions for me, please?"

"I'll try, Lloyd. I like Mona Grace Ford, and I would hate to have anything happen to her. Ask me anything. If I can, I will answer you."

Lloyd asked Earl if he had eaten breakfast yet. He had. The early morning air was chilly and so, when Lloyd offered to buy him a coffee, Earl accepted gratefully. Lloyd asked him if he wanted to drink it inside the shelter cafeteria. Earl preferred to be outside. Asking Earl to please wait, Lloyd ran into the cafeteria. A few minutes later, he emerged carrying a cardboard cupholder. Two large coffees and two giant cinnamon buns filled the tray.

"Let's go over to the park and have a more comfortable seat, okay, Earl?" Lloyd asked.

Earl simply nodded and began walking the short distance to Oppenheimer Park. Side by side, the men did not speak until they reached the park and sat down on the bench closest to where the pumpkin truck and Adam Draper had been.

The sight of the pull-out where Adam had parked evoked a startled, uncomfortable sound that escaped from between Earl Turner's lips. "I can't help you, man," he said to Lloyd. "I don't know what it is you want, but I can't help you." As he tried to rise up from the bench, Lloyd gently grabbed his sleeve and pulled him back down.

"Yes, I think you can help me," Lloyd said calmly, quietly. "I know you talked with the driver of the pumpkin orange delivery truck that has the name 'ZO'S HAULING' on the side of it, the day before yesterday. I also know that, in exchange for you writing a note, you were paid in cash. A $100 bill, I believe." Noting Earl's white face, Lloyd softly inquired, "Memory coming back a little, Earl?"

Earl nodded mutely. A second later, he asked, "Lloyd, you seem to know everything that happened. What more can I possibly add?" He adjusted the frayed collar on his shirt nervously. It appeared to be choking him. "Besides," he added, "I was told not to say nothing to nobody. The guy sounded as if he meant business, that Adam guy – the driver of the delivery truck, that is."

"Just tell me what the note said that you wrote out for Adam. I know you might not remember it word-for-word, but it's very important. Don't worry; Adam will never find out that you talked with me. You just keep out of sight for a couple of days and all this should be over. Please, Earl, can you remember what the note said?"

Earl whimpered. He looked around the area very carefully. He even walked over to the giant old arbutus tree and checked around there. Satisfied that there was nobody else around, he came back to the bench and sat down. He looked Lloyd directly in the eyes and held his gaze. "Lloyd," Earl said, "I remember every word of that note. Once I wrote it for that guy, I knew it was wrong. I knew there was something terrible going on, but it was too late. I had already written the note and got paid for it." Earl looked as if he was going to burble forever, and he was growing more wired by the second. "Earl, look at me," Lloyd said, firmly drawing the nerve-ridden man back on topic. "What did that note say?"

With a shuddering breath, Earl droned:

'WE HAVE MONAGRACE AND CHARLY. WHEN THE BAIL $$ IS RETURNED THE WOMEN WILL RETURN. IF NOT THEY WILL BE DEAD. YOU WATCH DOMINGO SO HE DON'T MAKE US LOSE OUR $$ AND YOU DON'T LOSE YOUR FRIENDS!'

Earl put his head in his hands and sobbed pitifully. "Lloyd, I can't read or spell too good, but my memory is excellent. That note has to do with Mona Grace and that Charlotte woman, doesn't it – I knew the second I finished writing it, that it had to do with something real, real bad. Every time I close my eyes, I can see the note and the words of it run around my brain. I know who Domingo is. He's the leader of the East Van Devils. They are bad men. If they find out I talked with you, I'm done for." Earl raised his head from his hands. He shuddered vehemently, begging Lloyd to not ask him any more questions, to just leave him alone. He then got up from the bench and, still sobbing, walked away from Lloyd and out of the park.

Before Lloyd could process Earl's information, his cell rang. Answering it, the caller identified herself as calling on behalf of Sergeant Greg Gablehaus. She said, "My sergeant asked me to call you and request that you come to the detachment and meet with him at ten o'clock this morning. Can you make it?" Lloyd checked the time on his phone. It was only 8:45. Assuring the woman that he could certainly make it, he hung up the phone. Neither of the cinnamon buns he had purchased earlier had been eaten. Lloyd bought himself another coffee and returned to Oppenheimer Park to eat the buns and drink the coffee while he waited for the clock to crawl forward towards ten o'clock and his meeting with Greg.

At 9:30, Lloyd was unable to wait a moment longer. Just as he arrived at the detachment, he spotted Greg getting out of his vehicle, trying to balance a tray full of coffee, a paper bag, and two Tim Horton's boxes full of a combination of muffins and doughnuts. Lloyd thought, *Tim Horton's must really love the Vancouver City Police*! He stopped and waited for his friend. "Hey, Lloyd!"

Greg greeted him enthusiastically while handing him the paper bag and both boxes of doughnuts and muffins to carry. "Sorry about not getting back to you earlier. Not only was I on night shift but it was a full moon and all the crazies came out to howl! What a night!" He looked and sounded exhausted.

They entered the detachment. Stopping at the front desk to pick up his phone messages and mail, Greg handed all the coffees, except for two, and both boxes of goodies, to the woman at the desk. Her previously unsmiling face burst into a large grin as she accepted the offerings from her sergeant.

They then proceeded to Greg's office without a word passing between them.

Once in his office, he pressed the DND button on his phone so they could converse uninterrupted. With a deep sigh, Greg rubbed the base of his neck as he leaned back in his chair.

"So, my young friend, tell me about your call to Lacey and then your interview at the park this morning." Lloyd looked at the sergeant, his eyebrows raised. Greg grinned wickedly. "One of my team spotted you sitting on a park bench with a fellow from the shelter. Can't keep anything a secret in East Van. There are eyes and ears everywhere!"

"I'm beginning to believe you, Greg," Lloyd said wryly. He reached inside the paper bag and chose a carrot muffin. Picking up his coffee, Lloyd reversed Greg's suggested order. He began with 'The Groper'. He told Sergeant Gablehaus everything. He ended with a terse comment. "It's strange, don't you think, that Earl Turner could recite the contents of that note word-for-word, but he couldn't spell or read worth a darn."

Greg shrugged. "I guess if you don't do any writing, it must be difficult to be a neat printer as well as a good speller."

Lloyd then told Greg about his conversation with Lacey. When he was done, he leaned back in his chair, his eyes never leaving Greg's tired face. The only movement from the sergeant was the tapping of his fingers on the arm of his chair. Finally, he reached for the phone and spoke briefly to the person on the other end. "I need someone to do an immediate search of a LESTER LABOUCAN. He's probably in his mid- to late-20s, and he apparently worked, or still does, for a psychiatric facility for criminals somewhere in the Vancouver area. I need the results as soon as you have them, and I need them to be complete. Phones numbers, addresses, present and previous employment, including reasons for leaving. Thanks. My DND button is activated, so please run your results up to my office." After disconnecting, he said only, "Now we wait. As usual, Lloyd, you've outdone yourself. You have a real knack for extracting information from people. It is a very useful trait to have. Are you sure you don't want to be a cop?"

Lloyd grinned. He was already digging in his backpack as he spoke. "I'm sure of that, Greg! I'll leave that stuff up to you. Why don't you close your eyes for a bit? You look wiped. While you snooze, I'll make my notes of this morning's visit with Earl Turner. Maybe by the time I'm finished, the report on Lester will be here."

When there was no response from Greg, Lloyd looked up and smiled. The sergeant was already sawing logs, so sound asleep that his mouth hung open and noisy snores echoed around the office.

Very fastidious, it took Lloyd quite some time to complete his notes. When the knock came, Greg didn't stir. Lloyd opened the door. The same woman who was at the reception desk earlier stood there, an envelope in her hand. Lloyd put his finger to his lips in a shushing motion, as he nodded towards where Greg was still sleeping. The woman nodded and wordlessly handed the envelope to Lloyd before leaving.

Lloyd sat back down; the envelope still held in his hand. Although he was itching to read the contents, he nevertheless waited for another half hour for Greg to wake up.

Stretching mightily, Greg yawned. "What time is it?" Lloyd told him it was 1:15.

"What! I slept for two hours? No wonder I feel better! Now, that report on Lester Laboucan should be ready." He reached for the phone. Lloyd interrupted him, handing him the envelope.

"It's unopened. I must tell you, though, Greg, that it was very difficult not to have a peek before you woke up."

It was not only difficult, it was maddening. Greg just smiled and then got up and went to the bathroom, leaving Lloyd to gnash his teeth as he sat and waited helplessly for the sergeant to return to his desk.

After an excruciating 15 minutes, Greg finally came back. He picked up the envelope and removed a single sheet of paper. Lloyd held his breath until, just as he was sure he would pass out from lack of oxygen, Greg handed the report over for Lloyd to read.

Lloyd skimmed the single page report, then he read it more carefully. His hands were shaking as he gave the report back to the sergeant.

"I don't get it, Greg," Lloyd said quietly. "This report says that Lester Laboucan is a member of the WARLORDS. I simply don't get it. The Lester Laboucan Lacey and I lived with was about as far from a gangster as you could imagine. He was so soft and gentle. He wouldn't harm a flea. What the heck happened to him?" For several minutes, Lloyd simply stared out of the window.

Greg finally demanded Lloyd's attention. "Look, Lloyd, whatever happened to Lester, the fact of the matter is that he 'is' a member of the most notorious, evil gang on the B.C. coast. It also says that he is employed at the Forensic Psychiatric Hospital in Chilliwack, and previously, he worked at Riverview Hospital. I don't know much about the existing Forensic Psych., but I do know that Riverview closed down in 2012. The B.C. government announced plans last year to reopen the Riverview psychiatric hospital in Coquitlam as a 105-bed, mental-health and addiction-wellness centre, but it's anyone's guess as to if and when that will actually happen." He quickly checked the report once again. "Yeah," he murmured, almost to himself. "He went to the Forensic Psych. just before Riverview closed."

Lloyd interjected, "I wonder why it closed. Do you know what Riverview is used for now?"

Greg answered Lloyd, "It closed because of funding problems. The Riverview premises are extremely old. Some of the beautiful old buildings were crumbling badly. The wiring was ancient, as was the heating equipment. There was no money for repairs. It had become a danger to anyone who had to live or work there. After numerous and various attempts to secure funding, the facility closed. Now, it is a tourist attraction. Tour buses loaded with vacationers come to photograph the beautiful buildings. The architecture of the old buildings is something else. No one is allowed inside any of the buildings, but visitors are free to wander around the grounds and take photos."

"Vancouver has become well known as a great location for making movies, documentaries, and a number of television series. Riverview has become a film makers' dream as far as a filming site goes. At any time, day or night, you could come across a production being filmed among the hauntingly beautiful old structures. It has been said that spirits of the most violent prisoners haunt the halls in each building in Riverview. There are those who swear that they have seen them. I don't know about ghosts, but you should really take a look at Riverview, Lloyd. It's well worth taking a tour."

"Now, we can go a couple of different ways regarding an idea that is brewing in my brain. There is a home address here for Lester and as well, there is his current place of employment. I'm thinking of paying Mr Laboucan a friendly visit. My first thought was to go by myself. I'm thinking if he does know anything about the missing women, he might be more inclined to speak with you, particularly since you haven't seen each other for a long time. Maybe you can get him to open up about his affiliation with the gang. He probably, no, definitely, won't name the gang, but it wouldn't hurt to ask him about it. Maybe he'll slip up and mention the name of the leader. I know, I know, it's a longshot. But my fine young friend, a longshot is all we've got at the moment."

Greg leaned back in his chair, tapping the arm with his pen. "So, do you want to come with me?"

Lloyd said enthusiastically, "Can a fish swim?"

Looking at the clock, Greg said, "It's already two o'clock. We should probably grab a bite at some fast-food place on our way. That way, we won't have to fib to Bethany." He grinned broadly. "Where would you like to eat, Lloyd?"

Lloyd smirked. "I'm not too fussy. A burger sounds good right about now." He smirked even more as he added, "But you better pick, because I know they don't serve burgers at Timmy's!"

"Very funny," Greg said as he turned the cruiser into a McDonald's drive-thru.

After their lunch, they drove towards the Forensic Psychiatric Hospital in Coquitlam. From information he had read on the Internet, Lloyd knew that this facility housed approximately 190 patients. Pulling some notes he had made from out of his trusty backpack, he read them aloud to Greg.

"The goal of the programs offered by this facility is to restore fitness to attend court proceedings and/or reintegrate patients gradually and safely into the community. The hospital also serves individuals who have been transferred temporarily from correctional facilities to be assessed or receive treatment for a mental illness under the 'Mental Health Act'. The facility consists of 9 clinical units (5 secure, 3 closed and 1 open unit)."

"The Forensic Psychiatric Hospital provides specialised assessment, treatment and case management services:

$\rightarrow$ at the 'Forensic Psychiatric Hospital', a secure inpatient facility located in Coquitlam, BC (a suburb of Vancouver)

$\rightarrow$ at six 'Forensic Regional Clinics' located in Vancouver, Victoria, Surrey, Nanaimo, Kamloops and Prince George.

These services include:

$\rightarrow$ Court-ordered assessments

$\rightarrow$ Inpatient and community-based services to persons found Not Criminally Responsible on Account of Mental Disorder (NCRMD) or Unfit to Stand Trial

$\rightarrow$ Psychiatric/Psychological Pre-sentence Assessment Reports

$\rightarrow$ Hospital treatment of adults with mental health disorders who are in conflict with the law and in provincial correctional centres, admitted on temporary absence to the Forensic Psychiatric Hospital

$\rightarrow$ Court-ordered assessment and treatment of individuals on bail, probation and conditional sentences."

As they approached the facility, Lloyd stared out the window. Located in a peaceful, park-like setting, a stately old building came into view. His stomach trying to tie shoelaces with his intestines, he breathed in deeply while counting to three; then he exhaled slowly while counting to eight. Surprisingly, it worked. By the time Greg parked the cruiser and they were walking up to the main doors, Lloyd felt calm and composed. *What was there to stew about, anyhow*, he thought. *Either Lester knows something, or he doesn't.*

Greg was not in uniform so, as they approached the main reception desk, he took his badge out and handed it to the woman at the desk. "Sergeant Greg Gablehaus. I'm here to see Lester Laboucan, please."

Checking her computer, the woman looked puzzled. "I don't see any Lester Laboucan listed as a patient here, sergeant. Are you certain he is in this facility? There are several other forensic regional clinics in B.C."

"Oh, no, I'm sorry, ma'am," Greg said. "Mr Laboucan is not a patient; he is employed here."

The woman smiled warmly for the first time. "Well, that certainly explains things, doesn't it?" A few keystrokes and a new list jumped on to her screen. "Ah, yes, here he is, Lester Laboucan. He is employed here, as an orderly." She pulled up a picture on the screen. "Ah, yes! I recognise him from his identification photo on his staff nametag; I'm bad with names but good at recognising faces." Click, click, click. "Oh, dear! You've just missed him. Mr Laboucan was here this morning, but he suddenly felt ill and had to go home. May I tell him about your visit, when he returns to work?"

"No, thanks, ma'am, we'll try to catch him at his residence. Thanks for your help though, Mrs" – Greg squinted at her nametag – "Mrs Reid; you've been very helpful."

Motioning for Lloyd to follow, Greg exited the building. Until they were safely seated in the cruiser, he said nothing. Then, "If I had a search warrant, I would look at Lester's employment records."

Lloyd asked, "What for?"

"Just a hunch is all. I suspect that Lester misses a fair bit of work. When the gang has something for him to do, everything else, including paid employment, would have to wait."

Lloyd mused, "If that's the case, I don't see how Lester can hold his job. He's been here since 2012, and I don't know how long he was working at Riverview before that place closed, but I'm pretty sure it was for a fair amount of time."

Greg responded, "Well, just another thing to ask him when we find him. Let's head for his residence now. Who knows? He might even be there."

Lester lived in a very nice 11-storey apartment building. Lloyd figured it was probably no more than two or three years old. He was briefly confused when Greg drove right past the building and parked a long block away, completely out of sight of the building, muttering as he parked, "Damn! I should have brought an unmarked car! Just being extra cautious, Lloyd; humour me, please." He added, "Oh, and no matter what, follow my lead."

Lloyd said, "Okay, whatever you say, Greg. I'll back you up."

When the men finally reached the main door, it was opened by a rather rough-looking doorman, complete with a uniform of sorts. He wore black dress pants, a short-sleeved dress shirt, a tie, and a swanky pair of grey snakeskin cowboy boots. Both of his arms were completely covered with sleeves of intricate tattoos. He also had gaol house tatts on all of his fingers. Although red flags went off in every direction as Greg spoke with the man; the doorman was very polite, almost professional. "Do you have an appointment with Mr Laboucan?" the fellow asked in a slightly stuffy voice.

Before Greg could say anything, Lloyd piped up, "I'm his foster brother, and I'm here to surprise him. Would you please tell him that Lloyd Jordan is here?"

Lloyd peered at the doorman's nametag. "Thank you, Carlos," Lloyd said, in an equally stuffy voice. *Two can play at that game*, he thought.

"Certainly, Mr Jordan; I'll buzz his suite." Although Carlos tried to hide which suite number he punched, Lloyd caught it – Suite JR-9. He filed that number away in his memory until he could write it down in his notes.

A quiet, gentle voice spoke through the lobby speaker. "Yes, Carlos, what is it?"

Carlos announced Lloyd's arrival. There was silence for a full minute before Lester ordered Carlos to let him in and key the elevator to stop at the ninth floor. "Yes, sir," said the doorman, "he does have another gentleman with him."

"No problem. If he's with Lloyd, he's welcome here also. Let them up, please, Carlos."

As the elevator began its ascent, Lloyd opened his mouth to speak. Greg made a shushing motion and pointed to a dark corner of the elevator. Lloyd didn't see anything, but he kept silent, shut his mouth. He'd ask Greg later what that was all about.

The elevator opened directly into the vestibule of Lester's full-floor suite. Lavishly furnished, there were several large vases filled with fresh flowers scattered about. A voice from the back called out, "Turn to your left and have a seat in the living room, Lloyd. I'll be right out!"

Lloyd and Greg walked into the living room and gaped, open-mouthed; one entire wall was floor to ceiling windows. The view was spectacular; you could see for miles. Despite the lavish furnishings, the men took a seat, prepared to perch precariously on the edge of the sofa cushions. Surprisingly comfortable, they settled back. 'Wow!' Lloyd mouthed silently to Greg.

They only had to wait for maybe five minutes before Lester entered the living room. Lloyd stood up as his foster brother rushed towards him. "Oh, man! Lloyd? Is it really you? I thought you were dead, man. It's been so long! It's amazing to see you, sitting here in my apartment in the flesh." He turned and looked at Greg. "Hello? Who might you be?" he inquired.

Lloyd blushed deeply. "Sorry, Lester, I got so excited at seeing you that I forgot to introduce you to my..." Before his searching for a word became obvious, Greg smoothly continued on Lloyd's behalf.

"Hi, Lester; I'm Lloyd's carpentry apprentice. My name is Greg. It's great to meet you!" He reached out his hand and the two men shook hands. Noticing that Lester appeared somewhat dubious, Greg calmly clarified. "Something I always wanted to learn. I was working last Christmas as a salesman for an auto dealership in southern Alberta, but I hated it! It might be that I'm suffering from mid-life crisis, having just turned 40, but I truly hated my job! Then I saw an ad in the newspaper for a carpenter's apprentice. I called for an interview and voila! You are looking at a first-year apprentice! And boy, is Lloyd ever a great teacher. Anytime you want to learn a new trade, he's your man." Lloyd was thinking, *What the heck? Who is this masked man*? He'd never heard Greg babble before, but he was definitely doing so now! Lloyd did remember that Greg had said to follow his lead, so he just listened to him babble until Greg ran out of breath.

Lester asked, "Can I get you guys anything? A coffee, a Coke, or something stronger?"

Greg asked for a coffee, black and unsweetened. Lloyd asked for a Coke. Lester pressed an intercom button; the drinks were delivered in no time by a beautiful young woman. Lester smiled lovingly at her before introducing her to the men. "This is my wife, Emily. Emmy, Lloyd is one of my foster brothers from when we were in the same foster home in Alberta. It was a long time ago. I thought he was dead."

Emily smiled sweetly at Lloyd and said, "Oh, Lloyd, how nice to meet you! Lester talks about you and your sister, Lacey, a lot! Is your sister here with you?"

Lloyd told her that he was sorry to say she was not. They exchanged pleasantries for a few minutes and then Emily walked over to her husband, gave him a warm kiss and a quick hug and announced she was going shopping. "Bring your sister with you next time, Lloyd. It was lovely to meet you!" With an airy wave, she left.

After a few more minutes of idle chit-chat, it became very clear to Greg that nothing of interest was going to be happening as long as Greg was there. Looking over at Lloyd, he said, "Well, my young carpentry boss, would you mind if I leave you both to catch up while I go for a run? I didn't get it in this morning and I'm feeling a little sluggish. Just call me when you're ready to leave and I'll pick you up."

Lester suggested that Greg come back in an hour. He immediately walked over to the elevator, opened the doors and held them until Greg got in. Lester then went to the floor-to-ceiling windows that were located all along the front side of the building. He watched until he saw Greg exit the building, do some stretches, and begin to jog away from the apartment. When he was certain that Greg was actually gone, his shoulders visibly relaxed. He turned away from the windows, took a seat facing his friend, and said, "Well, Lloyd, we have a lot of catching up to do. Start at the beginning – from when you ran away in order to search for our missing foster siblings. From television and the newspaper reports, I know they were eventually found, but I know nothing after that."

An obscure premonition niggled like a worm on a hook in Lloyd's head. Not entirely sure why he didn't trust Lester, he erred on the side of caution. He gave Lester a brief summary of his life after he left foster care, but he cautiously and specifically left out any reference to either the East Van Devils or the WARLORDS. He did, however, tell him about Lacey's heroics in rescuing their missing foster sisters. He also told him that Lacey was now married and expecting a baby. He told him about marrying Susanna and that they were also expecting their first child, just a month before Lacey and Parker. He talked about his carpentry business and how much he loved both the business and the awesome log home that had been built by his father-in-law. He leaned back in the comfortable sofa and stretched. "Lester, life is good." He looked around the room. "Well, my life is good, although it isn't as good as your life, by the look of things."

Finally, he told Lester about Mona Grace and Charley being missing. "I don't know what could have happened to them, Lester," Lloyd said gloomily. "I'm at a complete loss. Although Charley took off from foster care before I really got to know her all that well, I still consider her to be one of my foster siblings. Mona Grace was my landlady when I first came to Vancouver. I owe her a ton, Lester, and I'm just sick with thoughts of how those two women might be suffering!"

Lester asked him how Mona Grace and Charley were connected. Lloyd told him that Mona Grace was Charley's mother, that they had found each other after many years and were just trying to catch up on all the missing years. He then put his head between his hands. Although it embarrassed him, several heavy teardrops leaked out from between his fingers.

Lester uncomfortably cleared his throat, bringing Lloyd upright, mortified to show such a lack of self-control. "Sorry, Lester; I'm okay. Tell me about you. What's been going on with you since I saw you last?" While he waited for Lester to speak Lloyd thought, *Nothing legal, I'm pretty sure. With the limited education Lester has, he couldn't begin to rent a place as fancy as this, let alone own it.*

Lester said, "Not much to tell, Lloyd. I've been really lucky, though. The last foster parents I had, after Lacey and I got sent to different homes, were like a lot of foster parents. They were all about fostering just for the money, money, money. There was no nurturing going on. The only good thing that happened at that place was that the twins were adopted by a wonderful family and so they were two of the few who experienced a happy ending away from the whole foster home crap. Finally, after I finished the 10th grade, I ran away. I ended up in East Van, living on the streets, resorting to begging or dumpster diving in order to survive. One day, a big, black, fancy BMW drove through the neighbourhood. It stopped beside me. The windows were tinted so I couldn't see inside. I started to walk away. The back door opened and a very distinguished-looking man stepped out. 'Wait, please,' he said to me. 'I want to talk with you.'"

"Curiosity got the better of me. I waited. He asked me questions. What was I doing? Where was I living? How was I managing to feed and clothe myself? How far had I gone in school? Stuff like that. I asked him his name, but he changed the subject. He asked me if I would be interested in working for him. He said he owned several places in and around the City of Vancouver. If I was interested in finishing my Grade XIII, he would find me a job and a place to live. The only criteria at the time was that I work hard and finish my high school education. I could do that by correspondence if I wanted. He could get me a job as an orderly at a forensic psychiatric hospital. Normally you need, at the very least, your high school diploma in order to become an orderly, but the guy said he could get around that. The job would be for minimum wage until I finished my courses, but then I could be trained for a higher-paying job. Now, I must tell you, the streets of East Vancouver are not a pleasant place to live. This fellow in the fancy black car sounded mighty convincing. He told me that until I finished my correspondence classes, I could live in a residence he owned. Its purpose was to house homeless kids like me until they could get on their feet and afford to move. Once I graduated, he would put me up in my own apartment. Although the guy seemed like he was on the up and up, I asked him to give me the address of the homeless kids' place so I could check it out. He said his driver could take me there, but I said no, said I didn't quite trust either him or his driver yet. I said I would find the place myself. I thought that would be the end of it, that I had probably pissed the guy off enough that he would disappear. He just put his head back and laughed. He told me that he admired a kid with guts, a kid who would exercise a high degree of caution, yet still not be afraid to say what he's thinking. He handed me a card. It had an address on it. He said it wasn't far from where we were, so he would meet me there in an hour. I went to that temporary housing place, had a look around, talked to a few of the kids that were bunking there. The three or four kids I talked to seemed to think the place was okay. They said a teacher came every day to help anyone who was having trouble with their correspondence lessons. They told me I could take as many classes as I could manage; so, if I worked hard at it, I could graduate before the standard length of time it took to complete three years of high school. It is the only time since I've lived in B.C. that I regretted not living in Alberta, where you only have to go to Grade XII. Anyhow, I worked my tail off and graduated in just over 18 months. While I studied, I also worked at Riverview as a junior orderly. Are you familiar with Riverview?"

Lloyd swallowed, decided it would not advance Lester's trust in him to be caught in a big lie, so, fingers crossed behind his back, he said simply, "I am. I took a bus tour of the place. The architecture is stunning. The place closed in 2012, I believe." He thought, *that's only a partial lie. I fully intend to take a bus tour of Riverview and soon! But please! Don't ask me anything more about it!*

"That's right, Lloyd. Anyway, I worked at Riverview from the day after the boss stopped me on the street in his big, black car until the day it closed. The next day, I started at the Forensic Psychiatric Hospital, and I'm still there."

Lloyd asked, "How long have you and Emily been married? She seems very nice."

Lester grinned shyly. "Isn't she something? We've been married just over a year. I was introduced to her by the boss and lucky me! There was an instant spark between us. We got married six months after our first date. She works for the same company that I do, but we work in different areas."

Lloyd caught the slip. Lester had nearly said 'gang' instead of 'company'. Lloyd gently steered him back with another question. "So, you finished your high school; you're working in a forensic psych facility, and you are living in a veritable mansion on the ninth floor of a palace. You must be rolling in the dough, if you don't mind me saying so! How do you manage it, Lester? I'd like your secret formula!"

Lester grinned widely, but he never turned his eyes away from Lloyd. He was trying to determine if Lloyd believed him when he said, "Turns out I married a woman with relatives in the right places. She comes from money; we both make good money, and we both work for a very generous boss. Also, we both love nice things, especially me, who came from nothing. We are both of the same

155

mind, which is, that you can't take it with you, so you might as well live life while you can."

Right then, Lloyd decided it was time to sink or swim. "Lester," he said, "don't take me for a fool. Nobody can work as an orderly and live where you do. Come on, man, level with me. How many jobs are you working to afford this place?" He chuckled, hoping to convince Lester that he was on his side, that he considered him lucky. He did not want Lester to suspect that he had an ulterior motive for his visit, so he added, "Might as well make hay while the sun shines, huh? In other words, before the babies start arriving, better work as hard and as long as possible so you'll still be comfortable with only one income. Get what I mean?"

Lester smiled briefly. "Spoken like a true, first-time father-to-be. Oh, just so you know, we won't be having any babies of our own. When Emily heard how I was raised in foster care, she agreed with me that, instead of bringing more babies into this world, we will foster as many kids as we can. And you can bet your boots, Lloyd, it won't be a home like any that you and I experienced. The foster kids that we take in will know what real love and attention are like."

Lloyd was moved to tears. After a minute, he said quietly, "That's wonderful, Lester. I wish you and Emily all the best. I know you'll be great foster parents."

Glancing at his watch, he stood up. "Well, Lester, this was great, seeing you again. Hopefully, we can get together again soon, and you'll have a chance to meet Susanna and see my sister again."

Lester said simply, "I'll make it happen." He walked over and patted Lloyd on the back. "Can't wait to do this again, man. Thanks for stopping by." Looking at his own watch, he yelped, "Yikes! I better get going – job #3. It's a new job so I don't want to be late." He walked Lloyd to the elevator, keyed in the main floor for him and then stepped out.

"You're not coming?" Lloyd asked.

"Nah, I'm on a fitness kick. I always take the stairs. Besides, they come out right beside where my car is parked. See ya!" He turned and jogged down the hall to a door that had an EXIT sign above it.

Lloyd waited at the front of the building until he was sure that Lester was gone. He then called Greg and told him he was ready to go. Greg told him he was already sitting in the car, parked in the same place as they had earlier. As Lloyd hurried up the block, he didn't notice that Carlos had come out of the building and stood watching Lloyd until he could no longer see him. Satisfied that Lloyd was leaving, retracing his steps from when he had arrived earlier, the doorman went back inside and promptly forgot about Lloyd and Greg.

Approaching the spot where Greg had parked earlier, Lloyd noticed that he was now parked right across the street from where he had been, and he was facing in the opposite direction, ready to leave on an instant's notice.

Lloyd got in. He asked Greg (with a slight smirk) how his 'run' was. Greg smirked right back. "I'll have you know I try to run at least five kilometres a day, Mr Smarty, and today I ran a full seven!"

"Oh!" Lloyd responded with a note of surprise in his voice. "I didn't know that about you. Good for you. I should be so diligent."

"I have to," Greg said simply. "East Van requires a lot of running. I don't just have a desk job. We are often short-handed. Lots of times, I go out in response to trouble calls from our officers. If I didn't keep in shape, I couldn't function at my job."

They drove back to the detachment and switched out the patrol car for Greg's personal vehicle, an older 'Jeep green' Cherokee. Greg was prepared to head home. All of a sudden, Lloyd excitedly barked, "Follow that big black Navigator, but don't let him see you! Hurry, don't let him get away!"

Calmly and smoothly, Greg switched lanes. He held back while keeping the vehicle constantly in his sight. "Mind telling me what we're doing, Lloyd?" he asked, making a casual, right-hand turn, three vehicles behind the black SUV. Fortunately, traffic was heavy, making it easier to follow unnoticed but more difficult to follow without complete concentration. A couple of blocks further down, Greg managed a quick glance at his friend.

"Lloyd?" he queried.

Lloyd said, "That's Lester. He told me that after I left, he was going to a 'job #3'. He said it was a new job, and he didn't want to be late. I'm hoping we can tail him without being noticed, at least until we can figure out where he is heading."

"Gotcha," Greg said. The driver had sped up. Greg became silent, concentrating on following Lester without drawing attention to his green Jeep Cherokee. The Navigator was taking a very circuitous route, so, even if Greg and Lloyd had the tiniest, hazy inkling about where Lester was heading, it would be very difficult to know for sure that they were on the right path.

All of a sudden, Lloyd choked out, "I know where he's going!"

"Where?"

Lloyd said, "To Riverview. But what he's doing there? Well, we'll just have to figure that out. I have a strong hunch. With Riverview closed down, the buildings are all empty. Or, are they? See where I'm heading with this, Greg?" Lloyd looked at his friend anxiously.

Greg was grim, still following the Navigator but finding it more difficult to keep from being noticed.

"I do, Lloyd. Hey, look! There's a movie company shooting today! Talk about luck! As long as Lester doesn't recognise us, we can mingle with the crowds and follow him until we find out what he's up to!"

Very shortly, they reached the beautiful grounds and stately, if somewhat disreputable, old buildings scattered throughout. Several buildings stood between Greg's vehicle and Lester's. Lester turned towards the third building down and disappeared around the building. Greg quickly pulled into a lot marked 'Cast only', just past the building and parked. An attendant started to approach, speaking loudly, "Hey, man, you can't park here!" Greg flashed his badge and the parking attendant shrugged his shoulders, turned around, and walked away.

Leaping out of the jeep, Greg reached into the back seat and picked up two ball caps. Throwing one at Lloyd, he said, "Put this on backwards. If you look around, you'll notice the movie extras are all wearing caps, some backwards, some properly. Now, run to the corner of the building and take a peek around the corner. I'm right behind you. Just, for heaven's sake, don't let Lester spot you or it's game over for us."

Doing as he was told, Lloyd peeked around the corner. A row of thick, fairly tall lilac bushes grew alongside the building's outer wall. Although it appeared to Lloyd that there was no entry into the building from the end where Lester was standing, he was wrong. Lester was bent over, concentrating hard, running his hand along the wall about three metres from the ground, pushing his way sideways through the tangle of branches and leaves. He was searching for something. Suddenly, he pounded on a spot on the building wall that, from where Lloyd was observing, appeared slightly darker than the rest of the wall. Suddenly, a door swung open, and Lester disappeared. Lloyd raced towards the door, catching it just before it closed. Greg was right behind him and managed to squeeze through at the very last moment.

Squinting in the unexpected dim light, both men lost precious seconds before they could see well enough to proceed down a long hallway. Reaching two elevators, Greg looked up and watched as the elevator closest to him inched slowly upwards, finally coming to a stop at the fourth floor.

Greg turned to Lloyd and spoke in a hoarse whisper, "I think we need to leave now, Lloyd. We need to block that outer door we came through so that we can get back in. I have just the gadget back in my car. It's a rubber gizmo, shaped like a ball. When I put it just below the lower hinge, it flattens enough that it is not visible but doesn't allow the door to close completely. Fortunately, this old building is a mottled mixture of paint and peeling paint, so my gizmo will blend in perfectly."

"That's all well and good, Greg, but why don't we just go up to the fourth floor now and check things out?"

"Because we need backup," Greg said in his 'I'm the sergeant and this is the way it has to be' tone of voice. "It's not safe for just one of us to go up while the other waits here. Also, if we both go up, Lester could come back down in the second elevator and wait, ambushing us when we get back down."

Bitterly disappointed, Lloyd nonetheless agreed with Greg that it was probably the right way to proceed.

Sensing how despondent Lloyd was, Greg said, "Remember, Lloyd, Lester told you that this 'job #3' was a new job, that he didn't want to be late. That tells me that he'll be back to do whatever it is he has to do. I think we should wait until dark, return with some backup, and find out just what's going on at floor #4 – what do you think?"

Lloyd simply nodded, at a loss for words.

. . . .

Charley opened her eyes, startled to see her captor standing silently at the foot of her bed. She hadn't heard him come in. She stared at him, saying nothing.

"I had a visitor today, Charley. Someone I think you know. It's too bad, but I got the distinct feeling that I was being followed when I came here just now. I'm sorry, but I'm going to have to move you and your mother this evening, when it gets dark. Too bad, because this was a perfect spot. See you later." He set a paper bag on the bed beside her, saying, "I bet you're starving. Here's something to eat. I suggest you eat it all; I don't know when I can get you more food." He then reached over to free her from the restraints that held her prisoner to her bed. "Tsk, tsk," he clucked when he discovered that one arm was already freed.

"Aren't you the tricky one! You better not try anything or not only will I drug you until you overdose but I'll kill your mother." He turned and left Charley's room, heading next door to see Mona Grace.

. . . .

Mona Grace lay on the floor, staring at the door. She wasn't surprised to see her captor standing inside the doorway. She hadn't heard him open the door. She stared at him, saying only, "What do you want?"

"I had a visitor today, Mona Grace. Someone you know. I'm sure that I was followed when I came here just now. I'm sorry, but I'm going to have to move you and your daughter to a safer place this evening, after dark. Too bad, because this was a perfect spot. I'll be back when it's dark."

Mona Grace spoke up, "Who was it? Your visitor? Who was your visitor?"

He said, "It was Lloyd Jordan. It's too bad that he wasn't more discreet. He was one of my foster siblings, you know. I always considered him to be a brother, even though he disappeared before I got to know him very well. I liked him a lot. Too bad he has been snooping around in all the wrong places." Just as he had in Charley's room, he left a paper bag beside Mona Grace, urging her to eat while she could. Forgetting to turn out the overhead light, he left Mona Grace shivering with apprehension, the bright light hurting her eyes.

. . . .

Greg had called Bethany to tell her they were on their way, but that they had to leave again later in the evening. By the time Greg and Lloyd got home, his wife had supper prepared and waiting. She had been a cop's wife long enough to know that if and when Greg could tell her about his day, he would but in his own sweet time. He said nothing about the events of the day. Instead, they talked about Domingo's upcoming trial. Lloyd assured him that he was as prepared as he could possibly be to testify against Domingo Sanchez. What he did not say aloud was what he was thinking, and that was, *I hope they find the bastard guilty on all counts, put him in prison and throw away the key!*

As the twilight faded towards darkness, Greg was on the phone arranging for backup. He ended his call with: "I'll need six plain clothes backup officers, in two unmarked cars. I want all six officers wearing Kevlar, helmets, night goggles, and be fully armed. Bring a paddy wagon to bring up the rear. We will be following a suspect who will have two civilian captives with him, so all precautions must be taken to ensure the captives are unharmed."

"There is a movie crew shooting tonight so we will have lots of people milling about the area. On the plus side, it won't be a problem being inconspicuous with all the extras on site, particularly because they are filming very close to where we will begin to follow our suspect. On the minus side, even though he will have the two women with him, it won't be much of a problem for our suspect to evade us in the crowd." He ended the call by giving the address for Riverview and telling them to be at a specific location by no later than 20:15.

"Time to go, buddy," Greg said to Lloyd. "Put this on under your jacket." He tossed a Kevlar vest to Lloyd. He also handed him a helmet and said that before he could exit the jeep, for any reason, he would have to wear it. He was only to get out of the jeep if and when Greg ordered him to. Under absolutely no other circumstances was he to get out of the jeep. Lloyd's teeth chattered as he agreed to follow all of Greg's instructions.

They arrived at the 'Cast Only' parking lot, which was the rendezvous point. Greg stopped beside the parking attendant and flashed his badge. He told the young man that there were two unmarked police vehicles right behind him, and they needed to enter the lot, turn around at the end of it. All three cars would then park near the entrance, away from the other vehicles, ready to go at a moment's notice. Greg handed the young man a $20 bill and asked him to please not allow anyone to park in such a fashion that the cars would be blocked, preventing them from exiting. The attendant, whose name tag read 'Billy Gray', grinned happily, pocketed his $20 and assured Greg that he would do exactly as he had been asked. Once turned around and in position, Greg stepped out of his jeep and walked back to speak with the leader of the backup team. Once he had filled the officer in on the plans, he asked about the paddy wagon he had requested be available. The officer told him that it was ready for the action, that it was parked a couple of blocks away. The driver was in radio contact with the officer; the vehicle was running. "Good!" Greg commented.

Returning to the jeep, he told Lloyd that they had only about 20 minutes until sunset. In that short time, they were going to sweep the fourth floor for any sign of Mona Grace and Charley. If anyone approached them, they planned to pose as visitors. Lloyd said, "Great! With eight of us checking, we will have the floor covered in plenty of time."

"You're not coming," Greg said tersely. Before Lloyd could protest, Greg said, "We need you right here, man. In case Lester gets in ahead of us, brings the women out, and returns to his vehicle before we get to ours, you need to get a description of the car, the plate number, and tell me which direction he headed out. It's the only way we won't lose him. Understand?"

"Yes, sir, understood," grumbled Lloyd. "I do understand how important it is, Greg," he said in a much more reasonable tone of voice. "I also understand that I don't have the training to carry out this manoeuvre."

"Thanks for that, Lloyd," Greg said. "Don't worry, between all of us, you included, we're going to get Mona Grace and Charley back. The licence plate number is vital, so if you think you might forget it in the excitement of a chase, write it down." He left the jeep and took off running towards the lilac bushes, waving for the rest of them to follow him.

The gizmo that Greg had used on the door so that he could get in again worked like a charm. Within seconds, all seven policemen were inside the building and standing outside the elevator doors. Using hand signals, Greg directed three of the officers towards the elevator on the left; the remaining three would come with Greg in the elevator on the right. He was counting on both elevators being in use when Lester came for the women. Arriving at the fourth floor, they jammed the elevator doors open so they were held in place and could not descend back to the main level. Having already discussed the plan of action back at the parking lot, the officers split. Three of them ran to the far end of the floor. One officer stood guard at the end of the hallway; a second officer started looking into the rooms on one side; the other officer took the opposite side. Before they opened a door, they made a fast note of the name on the outside of the door.

Greg and the remaining officers, started at the opposite end. Praying that they would complete this mission before Lester arrived, they silently began to search every room.

It was a long hall. There were six rooms on each side, 12 rooms in all. Someone was asleep in every room. *Either asleep or drugged*, Greg thought to himself.

Greg and his group searched the side of the hallway with the even-numbered rooms. After dealing with door #2, Greg opened door #4. Bingo! Charley looked at Greg with terrified eyes. He made a shushing motion, and she recognised him as he approached her bed. She clapped her hands over her mouth and held them there. In a quiet, urgent voice, he explained what was about to happen.

"Do you know where your mother is, Charley?" Greg asked.

Charley nodded and pointed to her right. "Next door," she whispered. "Sergeant, are you sure this is going to work?"

"I am." Greg said. The unruffled tone of his voice calmed Charley. She listened carefully to his instructions and then, she repeated them back to him, at his request. In that instant, she just knew that she could and would follow his instructions, and they would see positive results.

Greg spoke faster. "Now, I've got to go see Mona Grace and then we need to get out of here before Lester comes for you. I'll see you later this evening. If you do exactly as I just told you, you'll be back in your own bed by tomorrow night." He patted Charley's shoulder and then stepped out of her room and hurriedly opened door #6.

"Greg!" Mona Grace spoke very loudly. Greg shushed her, finger to his lips. As he had with Charley, he hurriedly explained what would be happening tonight. "Charley is aware of the plan," he said. "I said this to her, and I'm saying it now to you – I'll see you later this evening. If you do just what I've told you, you'll be back in your own bed by tomorrow night. Now, I know you heard me, but I want you to repeat my instructions, just for my own peace of mind. Speak quickly but quietly. We are running out of time." Greg listened, nodded, then gave her shoulder a reassuring pat before he disappeared out of the door.

Back in the hallway, an officer whispered to him that the rest of the rooms had been checked and everyone was ready to go. "Did you make sure that the elevators were no longer disabled?" Greg whispered. When the officer replied in the affirmative, Greg gave a 'thumbs up' and then pointed towards the EXIT sign. *Take the stairs and be careful. Wait for me to check the main floor,* he mouthed inaudibly. The officers filed through the doorway and descended silently down the stairs towards the main floor.

Near the bottom of the stairway, the men stopped and leaned against the wall on one side to make room for their sergeant. They waited for Greg to check and ensure the coast was clear. Just as soon as he cracked open the door and looked towards the elevators, the entrance door opened! Not moving a muscle, Greg watched as Lester approached the elevators. Although he didn't appear to be carrying anything, his left hand kept patting his jacket pocket, as if to reassure himself that whatever he carried in that pocket was still there.

As soon as the elevator doors closed behind Lester, Greg motioned for the six officers to hurry and leave the building. The last one out, Greg took a last glance at the panel above the elevator, to reassure himself that Lester had made it to the fourth floor.

Once outside, he waved them towards their vehicles. As silent as shadows, the officers swiftly glided through grass that badly needed mowing, their footsteps muffled by the lawn as well as the voices that echoed from the movie shoot in progress, just next to the far side of the 'Cast Only' parking lot.

As they approached their vehicles, Greg recognised the shiny black Lincoln Navigator parked along the yellow curb in front of the building. *Well, he mustn't plan to be very long, parked in a no parking area like he did*, Greg thought. Smiling sardonically, he mused, *If I wasn't so anxious to find out where Lester was taking Mona Grace and Charley, I would ticket and tow the Navigator, just because I can.*

Double-checking the licence plate, he went back to his Jeep Cherokee. As Greg reached for the door handle, a hand tapped him firmly on the shoulder, causing him to jump. *Whoa! Slow down! I need to get myself under control*! he thought, before turning to his right. The officer in charge of the backup team handed Greg a handful of papers. A quick glance indicated the fourth-floor room numbers, and the names that had been posted on each door. "Thanks," he said to the officer. "Now, get ready to roll. Lester should be out with the women any minute now. By the way, that illegally parked black Navigator belongs to Lester Laboucan, our suspect. Whatever you do, don't lose him!" He quickly got in his jeep. Once seated, he handed Lloyd the papers.

"What's this?" Lloyd queried.

"Room numbers and names of the occupants of each room on the fourth floor," Greg said. "When this mission is over, I'll need to combine them into a single list and figure out who these people are and what they're doing in an abandoned centre."

Lloyd whispered frantically, "Here he comes! He has the two women with him." Looking sideways at the sergeant, he asked him, "With all the backup you have, why can't you just jump out and grab Lester, and have the other guys grab Mona Grace and Charley?"

"Because, Lloyd, that's not the plan. We'll discuss all this later, during a debriefing. In the meantime, remain totally motionless. Either duck down or do not move! When the three of them are in the Navigator and start to drive away, put your seatbelt on, zip your lip, and hang on tight!"

Both Greg and Lloyd turned to stone, remaining stationary as they watched Lester scan the area thoroughly before opening the rear door and motioning the women to get in. Charley seemed to say something, and Greg watched with bated breath as Lester simply patted his jacket pocket. Whatever he had in there, it shut her up. Charley quickly got into the shiny black beast, scooted over to make room for Mona Grace, and sat still. Mona Grace appeared to get in without any comment.

After another look around, Lester got in the driver's side, put the car in gear, and drove away.

"Do you think the women will try and jump out at a red light, make a run for it?" Lloyd asked Greg.

"Nope, they won't," Greg said. "For now, please don't talk to me. I need to fully concentrate on remaining unseen while still following Lester. You need to help by keeping your eyes peeled for anything unusual. There is nothing that makes me think that this will go off without a hitch. Your extra pair of eyes is both welcome and necessary."

After leaving the Riverview grounds, Lester sped up. Traffic was far from heavy and so it was difficult for Greg to follow closely enough not to lose him yet remain unobtrusive. Greg pulled over and allowed the first backup vehicle to take over the tracking. Several blocks further on, that vehicle pulled over, allowing the second backup vehicle to take over.

They proceeded uneventfully for a fair distance. Suddenly, Greg gasped. "Holy, holy, holy! We're heading to the WARLORDS' den! Talk about luck!"

He picked up his mic and spoke to the driver of the car behind him. "I know where he's going. Keep him in your sight and follow him. I'm going to take a shortcut. If, God forbid, you should lose him, here's the address in North Van. Let the second backup know what's going on." Having given the address for the den, Greg turned off the route Lester was taking. Once out of sight, he sped up and raced towards North Vancouver and the den of the WARLORDS.

Greg knew exactly where to go. He also happened to know that the property next door to the den was vacant, a FOR SALE sign prominently displayed on the front lawn. He also knew that the driveway on that property began at the street and followed along the side of the house furthest away from the den. A very large lot, all three vehicles would be able to park at the side of the house without being seen.

As soon as Greg reached the driveway entrance of the house next to the den, he parked and cut the motor. Reaching into the back seat, he retrieved a shrunken copy of the blueprints for the WARLORDS' house. Studying the main floor level, Greg muttered, "Damn! Just what I figured."

Lloyd stared at the sergeant. *Greg must be really upset about something*, he thought. *He rarely swears.* "Something wrong, Greg?" Lloyd questioned.

"I hope not," Greg answered. "But just as I remembered, the backyard plans only show as far as the property line, and nothing shows up in the small forest of trees at the back, southwestern side of the property. I'm thinking there's got to be a small cabin or some sort of enclosure there. I'm going to go see. Hopefully, I can check it out and then hide if anyone seems to be heading that way. You need to stay here and let the rest of the team know where I am." With that said, he took off, running quickly but quietly through the darkness.

Not until he was in the middle of the dense trees and underbrush that grew between the vacant house and the den, did he reach for his tiny but powerful flashlight. Before he could turn it on, he tripped over what he thought was a tree root. *Aaagh!* He groaned silently as his hip struck something hard. Gritting his teeth against the stabbing pain, he rose to his knees and turned on the light, holding it close to the ground and away from the house. He had crashed down on a metal handle attached to a round wooden cover. Before he could try to remove it, though, he heard something. He immediately extinguished his light and backed further into the trees. He sat down, completely hidden, hip pounding painfully, and waited to see what would happen next.

He didn't have long to wait. Within five minutes, he heard Lester's voice and saw the beam of a powerful flashlight approaching the entrance to the copse. Willing himself to ignore the pain, Greg waited. Soon he heard Lester say, "Okay, ladies. Stand still while I open this cover. Don't try anything funny or you'll regret it. Remember, I've a tranquiliser dart in my pocket and won't hesitate to use it if you try to escape. I'm an excellent darts player and as a result, I rarely miss when it comes to tranquiliser darts." Greg heard a pitiful moan, but the thick underbrush muffled the sound, and he couldn't tell who had moaned.

With a loud grunt and a crash backwards, Lester narrowly missed falling into Greg! If he hadn't been able to regain his footing, it would have been bad! Only by exercising super-human self-control was Greg able to remain silent, even though his heart rate had sped up so much that he was sure Lester could hear it pounding! Again, upright and steady, Lester reached into the side of the hole that the wooden cover had previously concealed. Feeling around in the darkness, he suddenly felt what he was searching for. A light switch. Flicking it on, he next flicked a switch beside the light switch. Mona Grace and Charley watched in horror as a ladder slowly unfolded, stopping securely on the floor at the bottom of the hole.

"Now, ladies, you're going down there." Lester pointed. Charley gasped loud enough to be heard as far away as where the cars were parked. "Be quiet," Lester hissed. "Don't make me drug you and throw you down the hole. At the bottom, there is a double bed, a small kitchen table, two chairs, and a small television set. There is a refrigerator stocked with food and drinks. There is even a small bathroom. Sorry, no shower, but there is a toilet and a sink, and cold running water. You will be living a mini-life of luxury. I will come back tomorrow and check on you. If you need anything or want something special, make a list and I'll take it with me. Now, please, ladies, down you go."

Charley looked at her mother. "I'll go first, Mum. That way, if you slip, I can catch you."

Mona Grace looked at her daughter and laughed, albeit a sickly sound. "Honey," she said to Charley, "if I was to fall on you, you'd be squished like a bug. Don't worry; I'm not going to fall. Let's check out this minus five-star accommodation, shall we?"

Charley nimbly climbed down the ladder. It was only about six metres to the floor of the hole, but it seemed much further to Mona Grace as she awkwardly inched her way down the ladder. No sooner had she reached the bottom and stepped off, than Lester flicked the second switch again and the ladder rose, folding itself up. Charley reached as high as she could, but the ladder was out of reach.

"Nighty-night!" said Lester just before he replaced the heavy cover.

Waiting until he was sure Lester wasn't coming back, Greg rose painfully to his feet and limped heavily back to his jeep before the backup team could come and look for him.

Greg relayed what had just transpired.

Lloyd asked, anxiously, "We're going to get them out now, right, Greg?"

"Not yet. Don't worry, the ladies are safe down there." He told Lloyd what Lester had said regarding the 'amenities' in the underground accommodation.

He continued, "They have food and drink. They also know what the plans are and so they will be patient while they have to stay imprisoned for a bit longer. They are aware that it is only until the search warrant is executed, and they will then be released."

Lloyd said, in a somewhat bitter, exasperated voice, "What the heck is the plan anyway? Everyone here, including the captives, knows the plan except for me! Please, sergeant, fill me in!"

Greg let out a gigantic sigh. "The plan is, Lloyd, that now we are applying for a search warrant to search the WARLORDS' den and the surrounding grounds. Our reason for the search warrant is that we have good and sufficient reason to believe that Mona Grace and Charley are now being held either in the den or somewhere on the property."

"But," Lloyd interrupted with a loud protest, "we already KNOW where they are. Why the search warrant when we could just march over there right now and release the women! I don't get it." Lloyd stopped, suddenly aware that he was whining like a five-year-old child whines for candy or a toy in a store.

Greg said, "Yes, we could do that, but then we wouldn't get a good look inside the den. We are looking for other things besides Mona Grace and Charley, Lloyd. We're also looking for accounting records, drugs, illegal firearms; basically, anything that will prove that a major gang operation is being run out of this residence." A signal on his phone indicated an incoming text. Greg noted that it was coming from his superior, Staff Sergeant Brown. As soon as he read the text, he spoke to the rest of them. "Okay, guys, here we go." Greg read the text aloud. "Search warrant granted. Justice made warrant as all-inclusive as possible."

"Listen up!" Greg ordered. "My officer is 10 minutes out. As soon as I have the warrant in hand, we will be knocking on the door!"

"Oh! Hang on. Another text from Staff Sergeant Brown!" He read this second message aloud:

"WARLORDS' leader had a heart attack early yesterday morning. Succumbed shortly after admission to St Paul's Hospital. New leader already chosen. He arrived at the WARLORDS' den last night. Good luck with search."

Anxious, but totally prepared for what lay ahead, Greg and his backup team waited calmly. Lloyd also sat tight but not so calmly. He fought with himself mentally in order to keep his composure.

"Lloyd! Do you still have your Kevlar on?" Greg asked. "I shouldn't be letting you in with us, so make damn sure that you do exactly as you're told by any one of these officers, or your ass will be booted out the door faster than you can imagine. Got it?"

"Yes, sir, I do."

The officer with the search warrant had arrived. Greg unceremoniously grabbed it, muttering a gruff 'thank you' as he read it through. Greg then spit out a terse command. "Everyone! Helmets on! Weapons in hand but do not draw, aim, or fire without a specific command from me. We will search the entire den first, then the yard, and finally, the underground prison, at which time we will rescue the women. Got it everyone?"

"Yes, sir!" came the response, loudly and in perfect unison.

Chapter 7
The Brothers Gablehaus

Approaching the impressive front doors, Greg rang the doorbell, stepped back and waited for what seemed much longer than necessary. *Although*, he thought to himself as he glanced around, *this darn place is as big as a hotel, so it would be a fair bit of a walk to reach the front door.* Just for good measure, and to, hopefully, annoy the doorman, he leaned on the bell.

The massive doors swung open and the snooty uniformed butler stood there, looking down his pompous, homely, pointed nose at Greg. "Yessss?" he drawled in his affected butler's voice. "What may I assist you with, sir?"

Greg shoved the copy of the warrant at the man, retaining the original document in his vest pocket. "Stand aside, sir," he said in a deadly calm voice. "We have this warrant to search the entire premises at this address, inside and out, including any other buildings located on the property." Noticing the butler reaching for something under a hall table, he snapped, "Don't even think about ringing that buzzer. In fact, you can come with us and answer any questions we might have."

"My first question is this: I hear your big boss had a heart attack yesterday morning and died. I also hear that his replacement is already here. The first place I want to look is in the room where your new big boss is." Greg made an attempt at a formal, if very awkward, bow, swept his arm in front of him and pseudo-politely said, "After you, kind sir!" He turned back to his men and said quickly, "As soon as you see which room 'Jeeves' here takes me to, search the rest of the premises. You're looking for anything gang related, from hookers to drugs or drug paraphernalia, to weapons. You know what to look for without me listing everything for you. Check everywhere; leave no stone unturned. This is the first warrant we have been able to obtain. We may never get another, so – search within the house until I'm ready to go outside with the rest of you."

Greg turned to Lloyd. "Stick with me, Lloyd. Just stand back and observe. I could easily need a witness. If I do, you're it!"

Greg and Lloyd followed the butler, leaving the six officers to begin their search. At the end of the hallway, an elegant sunroom gleamed in the rapidly fading light. When they reached the entrance to the sunroom, the butler turned right and led the men to the end of another very long hallway. The fancy double doors reminded Lloyd of the entrance to Domingo's living quarters in the East Van Devils' clubhouse, but this was so grandiose that it inspired awe, beginning at the far end of the long hall. Lloyd's jaw literally dropped. He was so overcome that he had to pinch his arm, hard! He reminded himself that all of this was obtained through the proceeds of crime.

'Jeeves' knocked on the door and waited until a voice from behind the doors hollered, "For heaven's sake, man, just knock and enter. I've only been here a few hours and I've spent half of my time waiting for you. Just knock and enter," he repeated wearily. "I've had a stressful day and don't need to stand on formality with you. Open the damn door and come in."

Three men were in the room. How something so ostentatious could yet display such elegance simply boggled the minds of both Greg and Lloyd. After a minute that seemed to stretch into several, they finally closed their dropped jaws and came back to earth. The first person they noticed after their jaw-dropping, blinding first impression of the office, was Lester. He was sitting in a leather chair in front of a massive cherrywood desk that was piled high with paperwork – mostly bank statements and ledgers, it appeared. It was obvious to both Greg and to Lloyd that they were interrupting a pretty important meeting. Lester paled when Greg and Lloyd entered the room. Panicked, he tried to rise but was firmly pushed back into his chair. "Watch Lester, Lloyd," Greg ordered.

Sitting beside Lester was the sleazy lawyer/accountant, Paulo Santonio. He too tried to rise. Greg slapped him on the shoulder. "Don't even think about it, man," he quipped, in a pseudo-congenial manner.

Finally, both Greg and Lloyd turned their complete focus towards the third man.

Lloyd felt his gorge rising as he recognised the man behind the imposing desk. He reached for Greg and supported him when Greg's legs threatened to, rather than simply tremble spastically, collapse completely. Greg and Lloyd both stared at the man across the desk.

"Fred?" Greg said, his voice feeble with shock. "What are you doing here?" Not waiting for an invitation, Greg collapsed onto a third leather chair, to the right of Paulo Santonio. He cleared his throat with great difficulty, his face wan and waxen.

Greg's brother briefly looked as shocked as Greg did. The knot in his tie threatened to choke him. Fred reached up to loosen it, his hands shaking a little.

Momentarily at a loss for words, Fred swallowed nervously before he tried to speak. After a few false starts and a span of deep breathing, a complete change came over him. Fred vanquished his nervousness, straightened into his normal ramrod-straight posture before he leaned back in his office chair. Suddenly, Fred Gablehaus appeared to be in total control, an imposing picture of what the big boss of one of the largest gangs in the country should be.

"I'm replacing the leader of the WARLORDS," he stated in a very imperialistic tone. "He, fortunately for me, died from a heart attack yesterday. I got the call immediately after his death and here I am!"

Momentarily ignoring his brother and Lloyd, Fred turned towards Lester and said, "Lester, I know you want to get home to Emily. Your father-in-law's death must have shaken you both. Go home. Be with your wife. We can sort out my expectations of you later."

Aha! Lloyd thought. *That explains Lester and Emily's extravagant lifestyle! Her father – the now deceased leader of the WARLORDS! How fortunate for a poor little foster kid; truly a 'from rags to riches' life story. He should write his memoir.*

'Poor' Lester looked like he wanted to jump out of the window if it would get him out of this situation more quickly. As he reached the doorway, Greg's voice stopped him. "Sit back down, Lester; I'll deal with you shortly, after I finish with your new big boss and his flunky counsel/accountant. Watch him, Lloyd."

Greg turned back to Fred and Paulo. "Just so you know, and don't get all huffy on me, I have a very carefully worded search warrant that enables me to search this entire house and the surrounding grounds and buildings. If we find what I expect we will, your newly acquired kingdom will collapse around you like a set of dominoes. You can claim the dubious record of holding the position as leader of the WARLORDS for the shortest length of time, namely 24 hours. In fact, that might make you the record-holder for the shortest period of time of ANY gang leader." He paused and then, in a controlled voice, he spoke again. "I suggest you pack up everything on your desk. The search warrant authorises me to seize anything that might be relevant to the investigation into the criminal activities of the WARLORDS."

"Now, I am going to continue with my search of your new digs, my ex-brother. Don't go anywhere. I will post an officer in this room with you to ensure that you do not destroy anything." As he turned to leave the room, he said, "Happy packing!"

For the next several hours, Greg moved about in a fog. So many unanswered questions, the biggest, how could he not have seen this coming? He thought that he and his brother were as close as two brothers could possibly be. Greg was starting to doubt his ability to be the excellent judge of character that he, and others, had always believed he was.

Chapter 8
The WARLORDS

Greg was so deep in thought that he walked right by one of his backup team. The officer had been standing just outside the doorway, waiting for Greg. Unaware of why his sergeant was so upset, he quickly hurried after him. "Excuse me, sir!" he called. When Greg didn't answer, the officer called again.

"Oh, sorry!" Greg said. "I didn't hear you. What do you need?"

"We've finished searching the house, sir," the officer said. "I just wanted to tell you that we are ready to search the grounds when you are."

Greg glanced at the officer's nametag. "Cst. Thomas," Greg said, "did you search the second floor?" The officer nodded.

"Every square metre, sir. Nothing up there but beds and bathrooms. Even the dresser drawers were empty."

Greg said, "Please pick one of your more senior team members to come here immediately." He waved towards the office, indicating where he wanted the member to go. "Have that officer, with Lloyd's assistance, ensure that the men inside that office are not trying to hide anything or shred anything, that they do not leave that room. The new head of the WARLORDS has been instructed to pack up everything on his desk. Your man needs to guard that room and the men in it until we are finished searching the grounds and outbuildings. That same officer will be in control of all the packed items. The items will become exhibits in the case against members of the gang. Any filing cabinets are to be seized, as well as anything else in that room that looks like it could be of assistance in proving criminal activities. Get the keys from the new big boss. Your officer will retain custody of the said documents and filing cabinets until he signs them over to the detachment exhibit clerk. I'll wait here for your officer. Got it?"

"Certainly, Sergeant; right away, sir," the constable said. Cst. Thomas took off running for the back door of the mansion, returning in record time with a middle-aged officer whose nametag read 'Cpl. Peters'. Once Cpl. Peters had been fully briefed regarding his responsibilities, Greg and Cst. Thomas assembled the rest of the team and headed outside.

The first place they searched was the detached triple-car garage, including a loft, which was accessible by a pull-down ladder. Nothing up there except for a couple of dusty canoes. The rest of the large space was clean. A thorough search of all three garage bays revealed nothing. They then searched the three vehicles that were parked outside the garage doors, from top to bottom, front to back. All three vehicles were a metallic black. Each car was a new BMW 750 IL. Nothing found that shouldn't be there.

Once those searches were completed, they advanced to a garden shed near the back of the property. The shed was the size of a double-car garage. *That's odd*, Greg thought to himself. *I'm pretty sure that the WARLORDS have a lawn care company to look after this large yard. Why would they need a garden shed at all, let alone one that large?* "Listen up, men!" he called to his backup. "I have a strong gut feeling that this building needs to be searched by the entire team. Search it board by board, tile by tile."

"Yes, sir!" the men responded in unison. A double garage door on each end of the garden shed opened with automatic openers. If it hadn't been getting darker outside by the minute, Greg could tell that in the daylight, with the doors open, there would have been lots of light to search by. As it was, they discovered a light switch that turned on several interior floodlights.

"Here's something interesting, Sergeant Gablehaus," observed Cst. Thomas. "This pegboard full of small tools has hinges on the left side. When I tried to open it, though, nothing happened. Could you take a closer look, please?"

Greg walked over to the area in question. Taking his small flashlight from off his belt, he shone it carefully along the right-hand side of the pegboard, beginning at the top and examining the crack between the board and the wall all of the way to the bottom. About 2/3 of the way down, a glimmer of something shiny caught his eye. "Hand me that flat screwdriver, somebody," he said. Cst. Thomas quickly obliged. Greg pushed the flat part in as far as it would go. He heard a 'click' and the floor of the garden shed began to slide sideways, causing the officers to quickly jump to a non-moving one-metre border around the movable area of the floor.

"What the...?" Greg said. Once the floor stopped moving, a ladder unfolded and stopped at the bottom of the space below the floor. Shining his flashlight down the hole he could see that the walls and the floor at the bottom were all cement. Pointing to an officer, Greg ordered him to stand guard on the main level of the garden shed and to alert him if he heard anyone approaching. He then climbed down approximately four metres, got off of the ladder and moved to the side, to make room for the rest of the team.

Once they were all down, Greg spotted a switch on the wall, just to his left, out of sight of the ladder. He flicked it on and the 'wall' directly across from the ladder slowly slid to the left. Once the 'wall' was open half-way, a bright light came on automatically. Aided by the light, a hallway was indistinctly illuminated. The team cautiously advanced, Sergeant Gablehaus in the lead. Once they reached the end of the hall, a door appeared on the right. There was a button to the left of the door. When Greg pushed it, the door slid open, and lights came on inside the door. Holding up his arm, he signalled for the men to wait in place while he went inside with Cst. Thomas.

It took only a brief look for Greg to whistle softly. "BINGO!" Turning to the constable, he said, "I hope you have a camera. Start taking pictures." He turned to the rest of the team and said, "Come on in and have a look. There's room in here for everyone to stand. We've hit the big time!" To himself, he added, *Shades of the East Van Devils' secret stash in their Clubhouse; only this is at least three times bigger! PLUS, all these drugs!*

One side and one end of the large room held shelves full of firearms of every sort, together with ammunition. Each weapon was safely secured in its own spot, matching ammunition nestled at the stock end of the firearm.

The other two sides of the room held glass-faced, refrigerated cabinets, full of illegal drugs, and drug paraphernalia of every description.

The last cabinet was not refrigerated, but it had a glass door. Inside the locked door, each of the five shelves contained stacks of bills of varying denominations. Held together by rubber bands, like denominations banded with like $1,000, $100, $20, $10 and $5 were visible, one denomination per shelf. Each shelf was full. It was impossible to even begin to try and figure out just how much cash that single cabinet held.

A single sheet of paper was taped on to the door of each of the cabinets, a record of some sort. Although the men searched the room thoroughly, they could not locate keys for the drug cabinets, nor for the money cabinet.

Greg ordered Cst. Thomas to make sure he took pictures of everything on the shelves and pictures of each of the cabinets. "When you're done, seal off this room with police tape. We're going to need these exhibits to be picked up as soon as possible. If keys to the cabinets are not located, the entire cabinets will have to be removed as exhibits. In fact, have the exhibit team remove the cabinets and drugs. Have one of your men stand guard until these items can be taken to the detachment's exhibit storage. Also, have your teammate continue to guard the main floor of this garden shed, to ensure nobody enters, and to ensure that the exhibit team doesn't fall down the hole. I want it left open so the exhibit guys can have instant access to the lower stash. They better bring a moving van; they've got their work cut out for them transferring not only paper but furniture, firearms, ammunition, and drugs."

Cst. Thomas motioned for one of his officers to remain. Greg and the others left the area and climbed back up into the garden shed. They left the floor open so that the members who came to remove the exhibits could proceed quickly. Cst. Thomas advised the guarding member that he was to continue to do so until the exhibit team arrived and loaded up all the exhibits from the lower level under the garden shed.

Outside once again, the only remaining building to be dealt with was the underground fortress where Mona Grace and Charley were being held. They searched the forested area, proceeding towards the underground chamber, until they reached the round wooden cover. "Don't trip!" Greg barked. "It hurts like heck if you crash into this heavy wooden cover – the metal handle is deadly." He signalled for some help. Between Greg and the remaining three members of his backup team, they quickly and efficiently removed the heavy cover. With a minimum of fumbling, Greg found the switches that turned on the lights and lowered the ladder. He quickly descended, anxious to see Mona Grace and Charley.

As he stepped off of the ladder, the two women nearly bowled him over; they were so relieved to see him.

"Are you both okay?" Greg asked. Charley said her mum seemed to have a few lingering effects from whatever drug Lester had injected into her while they were held captive in Riverview. Mona Grace insisted that she was just fine, that the drugs were most certainly out of her system by now. She said she just was feeling dizzy and weak from all the emotional upheaval of the past few days; after all, any person who was kidnapped could not avoid suffering some sort of physical and mental trauma. Once again, they assured Greg that they were both fine.

Greg pointed at the ladder. "Then, up you go, my friends. Let's get you some fresh air."

As weak as they were from being held captive, first at Riverview and then in this sophisticated 'hole', they nimbly scrambled up the ladder in racing speed time. It was only when they were safely out of their underground prison, standing on solid ground, that they began to tremble. One of the officers ran to his vehicle and returned with two blankets and two bottles of water.

Greg climbed out and off of the ladder. He directed one of the remaining officers to go below and photograph everything, including the switches at the top that turned on the lights and lowered the ladder. He also directed that once those pictures were taken, the cover be placed back over the hole. It was to be photographed also. "I'd hate to have to pay the power bills," Greg quipped, trying to diffuse the emotions that suddenly, embarrassingly, threatened to overwhelm him.

Mona Grace stared at the men surrounding her. "Thank you," she said simply, tears clouding her vision. "We thought we would have to wait until tomorrow, and we were not looking forward to the wait. We were afraid that Lester would come and move us again. Thank you for rescuing us today."

She turned, frantically looking for Charley. "I'm right here, Mum," Charley said softly. "We can relax; it's over."

Greg cleared his throat and the women turned to him. "Not quite, ladies, not quite yet. We'll have to go down to the detachment and have you fill out your statements. We're also going to have to discuss your safety between now and the time this mess is all sorted out and the trials are over. But for now, let's simply take one thing at a time, step by step."

He asked Cst. Thomas to escort Mona Grace and Charley to his jeep and remain with them for a few more minutes until Greg returned. He signalled for the two remaining backup officers to come with him.

Entering the opulent office, Greg strode over to Lester. "Lester Laboucan, stand up!" he snapped. "Lester Laboucan, you are under arrest for the following offences: for kidnapping and unlawful detention of Mona Grace Ford and Charlotte Ford; for administering an illegal substance to Mona Grace Ford; for illegal possession of drugs and drug paraphernalia; for illegal possession of weapons and ammunition and for benefitting from the proceeds of crime." Greg nodded at one of the two backup officers. The officer approached Lester and handcuffed him, reciting his rights as he did so.

Greg then turned to Paulo Santonio and spoke. "Paulo Santonio, stand up!" Tersely, he said, "Paulo Santonio, you are under arrest for the following offences: for the kidnapping and unlawful detention of Mona Grace Ford and Charlotte Ford; for illegal possession of drugs and drug paraphernalia; for illegal possession of weapons and ammunition and for benefitting from the proceeds of crime." Without waiting for instructions, the second backup team member stepped forward and cuffed Mr Santonio.

With the strangest, simultaneous feelings of both regret and relief, Greg turned his attention to his brother. "Fredrich Gablehaus, stand up!" His heart felt heavy in his chest as Greg began, "Fredrich Gablehaus, you are under arrest for kidnapping and unlawful confinement of Mona Grace Ford and Charlotte Ford; for illegal possession of drugs and drug paraphernalia; for illegal possession of weapons and ammunition and for profiting from the proceeds of crime." Steeling himself against the jumble of emotions that threatened to embarrass him further, Greg placed the handcuffs on his brother himself, intentionally tightening them until Fred winced.

Greg turned and spoke to Cpl. Peters. "Corporal, I would like you to wait for the exhibit team to get here. Once they have removed everything, you are free to return to the detachment. Get 'Jeeves' here to let you out. Once you have completed your necessary paperwork, go home and try and get some rest. Tomorrow promises to be a day full of headaches, albeit the events of today proved to be an outstanding feather in all of our caps. Thanks for your assistance today, Corporal." Greg held out his hand and shook the officer's hand warmly.

Nodding at 'Jeeves', Greg smiled grimly and said, "Don't leave town. We'll need to speak with you. It can be either as a witness or as a gangster – it will be your choice. But one way or the other, we'll be in touch. Leave your real name, a contact number, and an address where you can be reached."

For the first time today, a crack appeared in the butler's armour. The top half of his face appeared to fall down to his chin as he thought about the implications of his future actions. Greg said, "All I'm saying, is think about it! Have a good night." He turned, whistling merrily as he said one more thing, "I'll let myself out!"

Back at the police detachment, Greg assembled four police officers who would, in teams of two, provide 24-hour protection for the women.

Mona Grace looked gratefully at Greg but said quietly, "Domingo can have someone get to me even though he is in gaol."

"I know," Greg said grimly. "That is why I checked with my good wife, and that is why you and Charley will be hidden at our home." He added, "Lloyd, of course, is staying with us also, until he testifies." Mona Grace started to speak, but Greg, anticipating her protest, held up his hand to silence her. "There will be no argument. That's how it is going to be until we are sure you will be safe. It's either this, or we will hide you out in a hotel. Your choice!"

Mona Grace knew better than to argue. She sat back, looked at Charley, and then she went over to Greg and gave him a heartfelt hug. "I know it's not enough to say thank you, but it's all I've got. Thank you, everyone."

Sergeant Gablehaus handed each of the women a pad of paper, directing that they write out their statements, beginning with the abductions and ending with the events of today, as it pertained to them.

A couple of hours later, the ladies had completed their statements and handed them over to Greg. Standing up, he said, "I'll be right back. I just want to leave these on my typist's desk so she can type them out first thing in the morning. I'll bring them to you at my home to review and sign, rather than risking someone seeing you come into the detachment. The gangs have eyes and ears everywhere."

When he returned to his office, he yawned and stretched. Glancing at his watch, he said, "Well, everyone, it is already close to 4 am. Let's go home and try to get at least a few hours of shut eye before we continue, shall we?"

No one protested. It had been quite the day and night!

Chapter 9
Belligerent Bessie

Although he was bone weary, Sergeant Greg Gablehaus had been unable to catch more than an hour or two of sleep. Finally, he got up, dressed, and quietly left the house. By nine o'clock, he was sitting at his desk.

Deep in thought, he jumped when an officer standing in his doorway coughed as he tried to attract Greg's attention. "What?" Greg said, much more roughly than he intended. The young officer, visibly nervous, for a moment said nothing.

"I'm sorry, Constable," Greg apologised. "My team and I have had a long day and night. I shouldn't have been so gruff. What can I do for you?"

"It's me that should apologise, Sergeant. My team leader gave me these papers to bring to you. He said to tell you that they are the names and room numbers from Riverview. He said you would know what they are, Sergeant."

"Thank you." Greg motioned for the young officer to come forward and hand him the papers. Once he had turned the papers over to Greg, he simply stood there, waiting. After several minutes, he coughed, and Greg finally looked up. "You can go, Constable," Greg said, waving his hand in a shooing gesture, as if waving away a pesky fly. He then continued looking at the papers that had been handed to him.

There were 12 pieces of paper. On each piece, a backup officer had messily scribbled down a room number and a name from the fourth floor of the supposedly empty building at Riverview.

Before he could begin to try and decipher the mess, Greg's phone rang. While he was dealing with the call, a soft tap on his door had him look up and smile broadly. He pointed at the chair in front of his desk, wordlessly inviting his visitor to sit down.

It was several minutes before he finished the phone call. Hanging up, he stared over his desk and said warmly, "Good morning, BeeBee. What brings you in so bright and early?"

"Well, I am just hoping, Sergeant Gablehaus, that you will fill me in on the happenings yesterday. It's killing me not to be part of the team, even though I know it is a safety precaution."

Greg filled her in on the events of the long day and night. When he was finished, he suddenly struck the heel of his hand on his forehead. "Wow! I just had a brainwave! There is some investigation work that still needs to be done over at Riverview. With Lester cooling his heels in the clink, if you want, you can take over that part of the investigation, bearing in mind at all times, that the gang will probably have you under surveillance." Greg handed her the loose papers, explaining what they were. He explained that there was a total of 12 rooms on the fourth floor, odd numbers on the left, even on the right. "Might I suggest that the first thing you do is to put these in some semblance of order and then type up a chart so the names can be read easily. What we really need to do is try to figure out why the WARLORDS have all these people in a condemned building. Now, here you go. When you have the list organised and typed out, come on back to my office and you and I can brainstorm."

"Certainly, Sergeant!" Usually calm and unflappable, BeeBee spoke excitedly and left immediately, anxious to compile an easily digestible list.

Besides being beautiful and brainy, BeeBee was very efficient. In no time at all, she had the scraps of paper assembled into a pile. It took a bit longer to complete the chart, but when she was finished, it looked like this:

WARLORDS – RIVERVIEW BUILDING – FOURTH FLOOR – OCCUPANTS

ROOM # (ODD)	OCCUPANT	COMMENTS
1	TURNER, E.	Pervert; tie hands to head of bed, gag
3	McGUIRE, M.	Booze hound; keep him happy

5	JORDAN, P.M.	Chain to bed; gag
7	SANCHEZ, J.	Overdose – RAT
9	SANCHEZ, D.	Restrain, tape mouth, sedate, blindfold
11	BELCOURT, B.	Restrain, tape mouth, sedate

ROOM # (EVEN)	**OCCUPANT**	
2	VACANT	Leave vacant unless ordered to fill
4	FORD, Charlotte	Injected sedation required – x4
6	FORD, Mona Grace	Do not harm, no matter what!
8	VACANT	Leave vacant unless ordered to fill
10	GRAY, B.	Bribe – could prove useful
12	JORDAN, A.M.	Druggie – keep happy – DO NOT overdose!

After assembling the chart, BeeBee spent a fair bit of time trying to figure out the characters. She knew who Mona Grace and Charley were, of course, but aside from a strong feeling that she should recognise the others, try as she might, she couldn't place them. Finally, with a shake of her head, she made some extra copies of the chart and headed back to Sergeant Gablehaus' office.

Greg spoke first. "Well, the first thing we now know is that Lester Laboucan is the son-in-law of the leader of the WARLORDS. Rather, he 'was' the son-in-law of the leader of the gang until yesterday morning, when his father-in-law died."

"Thanks to Lloyd, who paid a visit to Lester, we also know that Lester was the person holding Mona Grace and Charley on the fourth floor of that vacant building in Riverview and Lester, personally, moved the two women to the underground area on the grounds of the WARLORDS' property in North Van."

Ignoring the chart for the moment, Greg spoke. "There's got to be a connection here. BeeBee, I think, between you and Lloyd, you should be able to figure out what that connection is pretty quickly. Do you mind if I call Lloyd and have him come down here and meet with us? I don't want to step on your toes, having just asked you to take control of this part of the investigation."

"No, Sergeant," BeeBee said. "No problem. In fact, I welcome being able to work with Lloyd again."

Greg picked up the phone and called home. Bethany told her husband that Lloyd was in the shower, but she would pass on his message. Lloyd should be at the detachment within the hour.

"Thanks, babe," Greg said. He listened for a minute, and then, blinded by tears, his voice harsh and pain-filled, he said, "Love you too. Talk to you later."

Embarrassed, BeeBee was looking everywhere but at her friend/co-worker.

With a heavy sigh, Greg leaned back in his chair and stared off into space before he spoke. "I left out one thing when I was telling you about the events of yesterday, BeeBee. The new leader of the WARLORDS is my brother, Fredrich Gablehaus."

An involuntary gasp sounded loudly across the desk. "Oh, Greg, I am so sorry!" BeeBee managed to sputter.

"Yeah, me too," Greg said sadly. "I did have the dubious pleasure of arresting him and cuffing him myself. I never in a million years would have guessed that he was affiliated with 'any' gang, let alone one as large and powerful as the WARLORDS. I haven't spoken with him yet, other than to read him his rights, but I fully intend to have a chat with him in cells sometime today and find out what the hell he thinks he is doing. He's a cop, for Pete's sake, and as far as I know, he was a damn good one. I'm just sick about the whole thing, not to mention embarrassed. The sad thing is, his counsel will have him out on bail before morning. Being the new gang leader will have its advantages, no matter how corrupt and rotten he may be."

BeeBee sat silent. After all, what could she say that would ease the suffering her friend was enduring? Suddenly, she stood up. "Be right back, Sarge." She left the room and headed for Tim Horton's. She returned, bearing coffee and goodies, at the same time as Lloyd arrived. After an exuberant greeting, they walked together towards Greg's office.

The three of them drank their coffee, speaking little and skirting around the fact that Fred Gablehaus was the new 'Big Chief' of the WARLORDS.

Finally, Lloyd asked, "What's up, Greg? Bethany said it sounded important, so I hurried as quickly as I could."

Greg pointed to a sheet of paper on the corner of his desk. Lloyd picked it up. It was a copy of the chart. He skimmed over it quickly. Both Greg and BeeBee, having read the contents earlier, studied their copies more slowly.

Suddenly, there was a loud outburst from Lloyd. Greg stared at him, frightened by the ghastly pallor of his skin. Ignoring Greg and BeeBee's concerned looks, Lloyd said, "Follow along on your copies. I can tell you who these people are, just by the comments written beside the names."

With hands that shook so hard that he could barely hang on to the chart, Lloyd started, "Room #1, E. TURNER. This guy is also known as 'The Groper' or 'The Grope'. Incongruous as it may seem, gang members don't like perverts; hence, in the comments column – Lloyd adlibbed – tie his hands to the head of the bed so he can't fondle himself or anyone else who comes into his room and gag him to quell the sound of his simpering voice."

Lloyd continued, "Next, we have Room #3. McGUIRE, M. Mickey McGuire, I found to be a very pleasant man to talk to; however, as it so rudely says under the comments column, Mr McGuire is, unfortunately, a raging alcoholic. From the comments here, I'm pretty sure he won't be sober when we get there."

Clenching his jaw so tightly he got an immediate headache, Lloyd said, "Room #5. May I introduce you to my biological sperm donor, Mr Paul Martin Jordan. If you refer to the 'Comments' column, it tells us that Mr Jordan will be chained to his bed, with a gag in his mouth."

Lloyd fought to control the feeling of nausea that threatened to overtake him despite his determination to keep in control.

He continued, "Room #7 is Jose Sanchez. Mr Sanchez is, or maybe was, the temporary doorman/enforcer for the East Van Devils' clubhouse while Brutus is otherwise occupied in prison. From the comments, the WARLORDS appear to consider Mr Sanchez a 'RAT'. Hopefully, the cavalry will arrive before an overdose happens."

"Room #9," Lloyd said, "I would be willing to bet that D. Sanchez is Domingo. It would seem that the boss of the East Van Devils is worth a great deal of bail money. It would be interesting to know what they intend to do with Senor Sanchez and when."

Lloyd looked at his co-workers. "Last room on this side of the hallway is #11. I think our friend Bernard 'Brutus' Belcourt has been creating quite a fuss in Riverview Building #4; hence, restraints, mouth taped shut, and 40 winks with the aid of sedatives."

He drained the rest of his coffee before moving down to the bottom half of his chart.

"Room #2 is empty. For some reason, the WARLORDS don't want to fill this bed at the moment, who knows why."

Lloyd spoke again, his voice strained, "Room #4 is where we located Charley. She was lying restrained to a hospital bed, frightened almost to death. She had been sedated; she thought, at least four times in order to keep her in the dark as to who her captor was. Although Charley had run away from foster care, it appears she remembered Lester's name but few, if any, other details about him. If he hadn't bothered to disguise himself, it likely wouldn't have made any difference in her ability to recognise him."

Lloyd continued on, referring to both rooms #6 and #8. "Mona Grace was in Room #6. There was a very thin mattress on the floor, no other furnishings in the room. She told me she could feel her hipbones grinding through the mattress and into the cement floor. Although she knew that Lester Laboucan was married to the daughter of the now-deceased WARLORDS' gang leader, she couldn't recall ever meeting Lester personally." Speaking briefly about Room #8, Lloyd simply said, "The room next to Mona Grace was vacant, as was Room #2 next to Charley. For some obscure reason, the WARLORDS isolated the two women as much as possible from the other inhabitants of Riverview Building #4."

"I'm pretty sure that Room #10 houses Bobby Gray. Young Mr Gray is the parking lot attendant for the 'Cast Only' parking lot outside of Building #4.

Considering he accepted a $20 tip already, the comment, 'Bribe – could prove useful' doesn't surprise me."

At this point, Lloyd got up out of his chair and started to pace. Several times he tried to speak; several times nothing came out of his mouth. His face was ashen, he was sweating profusely, and his breath erupted in short, panicky gasps.

BeeBee jumped out of her chair and walked over to where Lloyd was preparing to change direction and pace back to the other side of the room.

"Lloyd!" she said, but Lloyd didn't appear to hear her. Fearing a full-blown panic attack, she motioned to Greg to come and help her as she tried in vain to get Lloyd to settle down. Greg came around his desk and stood on one side of Lloyd, placed his arm around his shoulders. BeeBee did the same on Lloyd's other side. Surrounded by concern and the love of his friends, Lloyd finally stopped pacing.

Once again, he tried to speak. "R-r-r-room n-n-nu-um-b-b-ber #12…" Large, terrible tears spouted from his eyes and ran unheeded down his cheeks as he gasped for air.

BeeBee said softly, encouragingly, "Yes, Lloyd, what about Room #12?"

Lloyd stared at BeeBee. Turning to Greg, he finally articulated, "I think Jordan, A.M., is my mother, Anna Marie, but it doesn't make sense. My father told me she died from a drug overdose, but who else could it be? How can I be sure? Oh, I need to be sure. I have to go to Riverview and see for myself." Lloyd struggled to free himself from well-meaning hands and leave.

Greg tightened his grip, spoke harshly. "Lloyd, listen to me! We are going to go back there and check. First of all, of course, we need to arrange for backup to accompany us. Remember, we are dealing with the WARLORDS here, and they won't hesitate to shoot first and ask questions later. Now, sit down while I make the arrangements. Actually, do you want to phone Susanna and Lacey? If so, go ahead and use my phone."

Still in a state of shock, Lloyd didn't seem to comprehend Greg's suggestion. BeeBee reached over and took Lloyd by the hand. "Lloyd, look at me," she said. "Greg asked you if you wanted to use his phone and call Susanna and Lacey while he makes backup arrangements. Why don't you do that? We'll be on our way to Riverview very soon, but if you can't calm down, we won't be able to take you with us." That worked! Lloyd seemed to crumble into himself. Suddenly, he seemed much smaller.

"I don't think I should call them until I see for myself if my mother is truly the captive in Room #12."

BeeBee nodded. "Now you're thinking!" BeeBee exclaimed. "That makes perfect sense, Lloyd. While we're waiting for Greg, why don't you go into that bathroom and wash your face. By the time you're finished, we should be ready to go."

Lloyd did manage to get up out of the chair, unaided. He slowly walked towards the bathroom, looking for all the world like a 90-year-old man. Part of the way there, he stopped, turned, and stared helplessly at BeeBee and Greg. BeeBee nodded, encouraging him without words. Finally, he reached the bathroom, went inside and closed the door.

Chapter 10
Brutus Belcourt the 'Tattoo Man'

"Okay, backup in place," Greg announced when Lloyd came out of the bathroom. "Kevlar vests everyone. Let's roll!"

This time, Greg didn't take an unmarked vehicle. He climbed into a cruiser. BeeBee jumped into the front passenger seat and Lloyd sat in the back, behind the screen. He felt somewhat like a criminal being escorted to a gaol cell might feel, but he didn't mention it. He said nothing the whole way. He was taking no chance that talking might distract Greg's attention from a speedy arrival at Riverview. He wasn't going to give the sergeant an opportunity to ban him from this operation as a result of anything he might say or any argument about how Greg was handling things; therefore, he sat, mute, praying silently. He even crossed his fingers, for luck.

Lights and sirens not activated, Greg nonetheless sped towards Riverview, praying the entire way that the inhabitants of those 10 rooms were still there, unharmed.

They arrived in record time. Greg drove into the unattended 'Cast Only' parking lot, followed closely by an unmarked van containing six backup officers. Walking briskly over to the van, Greg ordered the officers, "Wait here and keep a careful eye out. If anyone approaches that hidden door into the building, stop them before they can gain entry. Detain them for trespassing. They will either be members of the WARLORDS or people hired by that gang. No matter which, they will definitely be armed and up to no good. No matter what, do NOT let anyone else into that building without further orders from me. Get it?"

In perfect unison, the officers replied, "Yes, Sergeant Gablehaus, got it!"

Waving at BeeBee and Lloyd to come with him, they quickly approached the hidden door. Silently, Greg opened the door and the three of them entered the building. Both elevators rested on the main floor. They got in and Lloyd pressed

'4'. Although the elevators were, in fact, fairly speedy, the elevator car that they were in appeared to inch its way towards the fourth floor. Lloyd's ragged breathing intensified as they approached their destination. Forcing himself to slow down, to take deep, slow breaths, he managed to appear calm as they stepped off the elevator and on to the fourth floor.

Greg motioned to both BeeBee and Lloyd. Huddled together, Greg's voice was barely above a whisper. "I know, Lloyd, that you want to barge in to your father's room and run straight to the room where you believe your mother is, but I want to go into Room #11 first. If it is indeed Brutus held captive in that room, he will know, first of all, 'who' put all these people in these rooms and, second of all, probably 'why'. Once we have spoken to him, depending on what he tells us, if anything, we will check out Rooms #5 and #12."

Lloyd opened his mouth to protest, wisely decided against it and clamped his jaws firmly shut.

"Here we go," Greg said, "let me do all the talking." A stern look aimed at Lloyd convinced Lloyd that Greg wasn't kidding around.

They stealthily approached Room #11. Opening the door without a sound, all three squeezed into the room, BeeBee and Lloyd standing well back from the bed.

In the semi-dark room, the person in the bed appeared to be either sleeping or drugged. Greg went over to the single window and pulled up the shade. Weak sunlight filtered through the very dirty window pane; the intensity broken by thick bars on the outside. Still unable to see clearly, Greg closed the shade to the outside world and flicked on the light switch. The room was now bathed in a bright white light. The unshaded bulb was mounted directly above the bed. Greg walked to the head of the bed, harshly ripped the tape from the mouth of the man in the bed.

Both eyelids flew open, and two dark, frightened eyes peered up at Greg. "What, what?" the man said. "Who are you?"

A fierce look plastered across his face, Greg said, "Well, well, well, if it isn't Mr Bernard Belcourt. How ya doing, Brutus?" Motioning BeeBee to stay back so as not to allow Brutus to have a good look at her, Greg motioned Lloyd to come and stand beside him.

"You!" Brutus snarled as he looked at Lloyd. "You're the little shit who ratted out your very own father! 'You' should be lying in this bed, you son-of-a-bitch!"

Greg quickly reached over and grabbed Brutus by the ear, twisting it sharply. "Never mind that, Brutus. You have more important things to tell us, starting with who put you in here and why?"

Brutus just stared at Greg, saying not a word.

Pretending not to notice his reticence, Greg asked, "I also want to know about the other captives on this floor. Were you all put in here at the same time? Why? Who put you in here? How long have you been here? Do you know what's going to happen to you? To the others?"

He continued, "Why are you in restraints? Why was your mouth taped shut?"

Not a word escaped the lips of Bernard Belcourt.

Lloyd opened his mouth to speak. Greg elbowed him sharply and Lloyd closed his mouth.

Glaring at Brutus, Greg said, "That's a ton of questions, Brutus, for you to ponder over. You might like to know, though, that I'm pretty sure that all hell is about to break loose. The new 'Main Man' has arrived at the WARLORDS' den and was busy planning what to do about all you fourth floor residents. That is" – Greg chuckled – "until he was arrested yesterday."

Brutus finally spoke, "Well, then, if the Big Boss is in custody, I guess I don't have to worry for a while, do I?"

"Oh, I wouldn't count on that, big guy. He had lots of time to issue orders before he was arrested. In fact, it wouldn't surprise me a bit if a posse of your gang members were on their way here, as we speak, to deal with all of you, one way or the other. In fact, if you don't want to talk to me, then we'll just leave right now and you can wait for doomsday." Greg turned, bent his head in the direction of the door, and started towards it.

"Wait! Wait, please," Brutus called out in a voice filled with terror. "Don't leave me here, trussed up like a pig ready for the dinner table! I'll tell you what you want to know. Just don't go!"

Greg pulled up two chairs, sat down, and motioned Lloyd to take the other. BeeBee stayed out of sight, sitting down on the dirty floor and leaning against the wall.

With an exaggerated sigh, Greg asked, "Who put you in here, and why?"

Brutus said, "Lester Laboucan, acting on the orders of his father-in-law."

Greg said, "When?"

"What day is it?"

Greg replied, "Friday."

"Well," Brutus said, "we've been here a week today."

"All of you?" Greg asked.

"All except for Mona Grace and her kid. They came, I think, later. Tuesday, maybe?"

Greg asked, "One guy, Lester, brought all of you, or did he have help?"

"He didn't need any help. The big boss spoke to us, said if we tried any funny stuff, Lester had orders to shoot to kill. We went along willingly after that."

"Just so you know, your 'big boss', as you call him, is dead. Heart attack."

Brutus stared at Greg, excitement brimming in his dark eyes.

"Don't get too excited, man." Greg chortled. "You have a new big boss, and he is meaner than a snake with a rat stuck in its throat. You'll be wishing you had the old boss back again if you cross the new guy."

Despite the restraints which had Brutus secured very tightly to the bed frame, he managed to shrug his shoulders. "Shit!" he said.

Greg, once again, questioned Brutus, "Why are you here?"

Brutus said simply, "The WARLORDS figure that everyone here has crossed the boundaries in the gang's rules and regulations, one way or another. They think that I shared some of their plans, the ones I knew about anyway, with the East Van Devils."

"And did you?" Greg queried.

"So, what if I did," was his answer. "The East Van Devils gang is a subsidiary of the WARLORDS. I still can't see what the problem is if I share with my own gang."

Jeez, this guy is missing more than a few brain cells, Greg thought to himself. He stood up. "Well, just lie tight for a bit, Brutus. We're going to check out the rest of the people on this floor. We'll be back."

"Wait!" Brutus wailed. "What if Lester comes back? You can't leave me here!"

"You've got a very loud voice," Greg said. "Just holler and I'll come running!" Greg grinned sarcastically and left the room with Lloyd and BeeBee, leaving Brutus wailing like a banshee.

"Lloyd," Greg asked, "do you want to check out Room #12 or do you want to speak with your father first?"

Lloyd answered, "Room #12, please. If it is my mother, then my father has some serious explaining to do."

He stared at the door to Room #12, only a half-dozen steps away, on the other side of the hall from Brutus. Holding his breath, Lloyd slowly turned the knob.

As were all the other rooms that they had checked, this room was also very dim. The shades were pulled and the light was off.

The person lying in the bed beside the window was so emaciated that she barely created an outline under the threadbare blanket that covered her up to her chin. Lloyd drew closer, peering through the dim light, trying to determine if this pathetic skeleton of a woman was, in fact, his mother.

Greg walked over to the window and pulled up the shade. Raising his eyes in Lloyd's direction, he mouthed, "Better?"

Speechless, unable even to nod in Greg's direction, Lloyd went to the very head of the bed. He reached for and held her hand, which trembled feebly. She peered up at her son; however, she did not appear to recognise him.

In a quaking voice, she asked, "Did you bring my medicine? I need it!" She withdrew her scrawny hand from Lloyd's. He noticed how prominent the thick blue veins appeared in her tiny appendage. The woman in the bed became more and more agitated. "You promised! You promised I would get my medicines if I came here. You said I wouldn't have to go looking for them anymore, that you would bring them!" Tears escaped unbidden from bloodshot, jaundiced eyes that blinked continuously. She tried to speak louder, but her voice enervated, dropped from heart rending, barely heard softness, to completely mute. Seemingly exhausted and without hope, the woman picked at her frayed blanket compulsively. Lloyd could see where she had managed to pick a hole all the way through. He thought to himself that she must have been picking at that poor blanket the entire time she has been here.

Lloyd pulled the covers back, then, discovering she was naked under the blanket, quickly covered her up again. That short glance, however, had determined that there were needle marks on both arms, and even in the veins of her feet. He turned towards BeeBee and asked her if she would be so kind as to examine the woman further for more signs of drug injection sites. While BeeBee complied with his request, he turned his back. Even a poor creature like the woman in the bed deserved a bit of privacy while her bare body was being scrutinised.

When she finished with her examination, BeeBee carefully covered the woman up once again. "Every place possible to inject has been used, even between her toes and in her groin." BeeBee stopped, cleared her throat, and said sympathetically, "I'm sorry, Lloyd."

Reluctant to ask but knowing it was necessary, Greg asked Lloyd, "Is it her, Lloyd? Is this woman your mother?"

Stricken, Lloyd said, "I don't know! Isn't that appalling; I can't even say for sure that this poor woman is my long-missing mother."

Before Greg could comment, the woman suddenly squirmed, trying without success to release her arms from the restraints. "Hey, guys, I used to have a son and a daughter." She seemed to be sobbing but in a very alarming way. Her features crumpled; her eyes bulged in their sockets. This woman gave every appearance of uncontrollable grief, but no tears escaped.

In a split second, Lloyd was back at the head of the bed. With herculean effort, he managed to ask her, in a deceptively calm tone, "What is your name?" She said nothing, just continued to pick at the blanket. Lloyd tried again. "You had a son AND a daughter? What were their names?"

The woman stared up at the ceiling for several minutes, silent as a proverbial tomb. Lloyd once again asked his question and once again, she would not, or could not, speak.

BeeBee stepped forward and tapped Lloyd on the shoulder. "Do you mind if I try, Lloyd? She seems to relate better to me. Probably because I am a female. Something seems to have happened that she shuts off any and all males." Waiting for Lloyd's assent, she finally pushed Lloyd gently over to where Greg was standing, just out of range of the sorry woman.

BeeBee reached carefully for the woman's hand. Once she was holding it between both of her own hands, she rubbed comfortingly and spoke in a very soothing tone. "So, ma'am, you have two children. You are very fortunate. I would like to have children someday, ma'am, but I think I'll wait until I find a husband first!" She laughed softly. The woman in the bed either did not, or could not, get BeeBee's attempt at levity. BeeBee simply continued to gently massage the unfortunate hand of the woman in the bed.

After a while, she tried once more. "Excuse me, ma'am, what is your name?"

The woman's head turned restlessly from side to side. "It's not ma'am, not ma'am. My name's —" Here she seemed to forget what she was saying. She settled down deeper into her threadbare pillow and started to hum a tune. At first, it sounded like nothing anyone had heard before. Suddenly, she stopped, looked at BeeBee and said, "Did you bring me my medicine?"

"I'm sorry, ma'am, I didn't. I wish I could have brought it to you, though, ma'am."

"Not ma'am," the woman said. "Not ma'am, it's Anna, Anna Marie." Before Lloyd could react, BeeBee shot him a warning glance and motioned for him to stay back. Greg put his arm around Lloyd and held him firmly in place.

BeeBee said, "What a pretty name. Anna Marie. Do your friends and family call you Annie?"

"No! No! No!" she said emphatically. "Not Annie, hate Annie, hate it! Anna Marie is my name! Not Annie!" Her agitation was reflected in the feverish tone of voice and her trying to throw herself from side to side. If not for the restraints, she would have thrown herself completely off the bed and down on to the floor.

"Anna Marie," BeeBee said, so quietly that Anna stopped her thrashing and strained to listen to the kind woman who stood by her bedside.

"Anna Marie, what are the names of your children?"

Anna squinted her eyes almost totally shut, thinking hard. "My children, my sweet children," she wailed. "I left them. I left them all alone. I had no choice." With a wretched, feeble yet horrifying scream, Anna cried unceasingly. She kept repeating, "I left them all alone, all alone."

BeeBee was not one to give up. Firmly, she grabbed Anna's hand and firmly she spoke once again. "Anna," she said in her stern, no-nonsense, police woman's voice, "what are your children's names?"

Deep sigh. Peevish tone of voice. "Lloyd and Lacey."

BeeBee asked, "Lloyd and Lacey? What is their last name?"

A continual peevish tone but Anna did answer. "Jordan."

Lloyd could be restrained no longer. Shaking off Greg's arm, he stepped up to the bed, standing next to BeeBee. He stared at Anna, lying weak and helpless in the bed, in the beginning throes of withdrawal.

"Do you know me, Anna Marie?" Lloyd asked. Weak eyes gazed at him, glazed over, uncomprehending.

Lloyd asked again, "Do you know me, Mum? I'm Lloyd. I've been looking for you for a very long time." Choking, Lloyd could say no more. He just stood close to the headboard and waited for some response, any response, from Anna Marie Jordan, who lay relatively still despite rapidly approaching delirium tremens that threatened to intensify. Anna Marie, through no fault of her own, would likely have to endure the oncoming DT's – tremors and terrifying delusions – cold turkey. They would become so severe that poor Anna Marie would be totally incapacitated unless and until she got some medical help.

"You're not 'my' Lloyd," she said finally. "'My' Lloyd was a little boy. He was 13 when I left him. You're not 'my' Lloyd." Sweat covered her entire body as she turned her head away from Lloyd, the once tiny droplets beginning to run together to form larger, wetter, bubbles of perspiration.

Greg was on his cell to the lead member of his backup team. "Get an ambulance here, STAT," Greg said. "Room #12, fourth floor. We have a severely addicted woman beginning withdrawal." Glancing at his watch, Greg said to both Lloyd and BeeBee, "Ambulance is on its way for Anna Marie."

"We are running out of time," Greg continued. "We need to check the rest of the captives, reassure them that help is coming, that we will get them out of here and take them to a safe place. BeeBee, you check the even-numbered rooms; Lloyd, you and I will do the odd-numbered rooms, but we'll start with Room #5. Can you control yourself in there? You have to promise me you can and you will, or you won't be allowed in your father's room."

Grimly, Lloyd clenched his teeth and muttered, "Understood, Greg. I understand. But, for God's sake, let's get going before the WARLORDS come to move them all."

Before leaving the room, Lloyd once again took his mother by the hand. "Don't worry, Mum. Help is on the way. You'll get your medicine very soon now." With tears in his eyes, he turned his back on his mother and walked out of the door.

Greg stood outside Anna Marie's room in order to give Lloyd some privacy. Just as Lloyd reached the door, they heard a tremendous roar from Brutus Belcourt's room. Before Greg could open the door, Brutus opened it. He roared again, catching both Lloyd and Greg completely unaware.

"Whoa, there, Brutus!" Greg said. "I suggest you take it easy. How the heck did you get loose anyway?"

The 'Tattoo Man' lowered his head and charged towards Greg's stomach. At the very last possible second, Greg stepped neatly out of the way. He stopped; Brutus did not. Completely out of control, he crashed head-first into Anna Marie's door, knocking himself completely off his feet. Before he could get up, Greg had roughly wrenched Brutus's arm behind his back. Yowling in pain, Brutus couldn't move. Greg quickly, efficiently, handcuffed Brutus's hands behind his back. Ordering him back to his bed, Greg once again restrained the big man, only this time he attached the restraints not only to his arms but also to his legs. Brutus would not be going anywhere anytime soon, unless he could figure out a way to drag the bed to the door and through it.

"Cool your jets, Brutus," Greg said. "And, by the way, thanks for all the information you provided today. You've been a big help, and we just might take that into consideration when your trial date arrives."

Brutus snarled, baring his teeth like a rabid dog. "You tricked me, you dirty bugger. Trust a cop to trick a guy! Only thing you can trust about a pig is that they'll trick you every chance they get!" He muttered something else, unintelligible except for the 'stupid fuckers' that he repeated again and again.

"Hmm." Greg murmured, "On the other hand, maybe not! I would suggest you settle down and pray that the Vancouver police rescue you before the WARLORDS do. I'm pretty sure you want to keep breathing, so, if I were you, I'd just shut up and pray!"

Greg turned his back to the out-of-control giant before smirking and rolling his eyes.

"Come on, Lloyd," Greg said. "Let's go down the hall to Room #5 and you can have a chat with – what is it you call your father again?"

"My biological sperm donor," Lloyd said acridly. "Yeah, let's see what he has to say for himself."

Both men started off down the hallway, Brutus's ferocious howls echoing behind them.

Chapter 11
Paul Martin Jordan

Standing outside the door to Room #5, Lloyd began to hyperventilate. He was so angry that he didn't know if he could control himself enough to keep calm while trying to question his father. He bent over, hands on his knees, his breathing rough and ragged. Greg stood quietly by, patting Lloyd's back, waiting for his friend to settle down. After several minutes, Greg, in his sergeant's voice, sternly ordered Lloyd to stand up straight and use his training to get the job successfully done! His teeth still chattering, Lloyd stood up straight, took several additional deep breaths, and finally said, "I'm okay, Greg, truly. Let's do this!"

Just before Lloyd opened the door, Greg told him that he would let Lloyd take the lead but only so long as he maintained control. The second it looked like Lloyd was about to lose it, Greg told him, he would be kicked out of the room. Once Greg was certain that Lloyd understood completely, he nodded tersely, indicated that Lloyd should open the door. Pulling his shoulders back, Lloyd turned the knob and entered the room.

As in the other rooms on this floor, the blinds were pulled down and it was very dim. Lloyd yanked the blind and it ripped free of his hand, hurtling its way to the top of the window, stopping with a loud crack. Lloyd then turned on the overhead light before turning to face the man in the bed.

Paul Jordan lay on his back. His mouth was taped shut so tightly that the skin around the tape was a stark white. Both arms and both legs were chained securely to the guardrails of the bed, allowing no room for movement whatsoever. An unpleasant ammonia odour wafted from the sheets, assaulting Lloyd's nose. Although there was a small bathroom just off the back of the room, Paul had no way to access it, trussed up as he was.

Lloyd stood at the side of the bed, saying nothing. He waited for Paul to open his eyes. When he did so, he stared blankly at his son. Muffled mutters could be heard from behind the tape, but whatever words he was trying to convey were incoherent. Lloyd let him lay there and rant; Paul grew more frustrated by the second. Finally, Lloyd reached over, grabbed a corner of the tape and ripped the tape off Paul's mouth – slowly, so that the pain would last. The tape was stuck hard! It gave Lloyd some degree of satisfaction to hear his father whimper and then yell once the tape was fully removed.

"What the hell are you doing here?" Paul growled at Lloyd. "Who the hell do you think you are, barging in here like you have?"

Lloyd grinned, an awful, bitter smile contorting his face, totally beyond his control to alter.

"I can leave, if you like. Leave you here to await whatever the WARLORDS have in store for you." Lloyd turned as if to leave, a feeling of satisfaction growing when he heard his father whine.

"No, no, no, son! Don't leave me here! For God's sake, if you have any compassion, don't leave me here!"

Greg was watching Lloyd carefully. When he saw that his legs were threatening to give out, he quickly shoved a chair under Lloyd so he wouldn't fall. Greg then pulled up a second chair and sat, waiting patiently for Lloyd to continue.

"So, Paul," Lloyd began, deliberately not referring to him as a relative of any kind, "why are you here, trussed up and tied up like a whole pig ready for the roasting pit?"

Paul Jordan snapped his mouth shut, resolutely refusing to answer his son.

"Fine, then," Lloyd said. "We'll tell you what we told Brutus. It wouldn't surprise us one bit if a posse of your gang members were on their way here to deal with all of you, one way or the other. In fact, if you don't want to talk to us, then we'll just leave right now and you can wait for whatever fate has in store."

Turning to Greg, Lloyd simply said, "Let's go. We're not going to get anything out of him."

Both Lloyd and Greg turned towards the door but before they could take a step, Paul's plaintive voice reached out. "Okay, okay, don't leave me here! I'll tell you whatever I can." The man looked positively apoplectic. His eyes bulged out, red-rimmed and watering; his complexion was pasty. "Please," he whimpered again. "Ask me anything. I'll answer you if I can."

"Now we're getting someplace," Greg said. "Go ahead Lloyd."

"Who put you in here, and why?"

Paul said, "Lester Laboucan, acting on the orders of his father-in-law."

Lloyd asked, "When?"

"Is this Friday?" Paul inquired.

"Yes," Lloyd agreed.

"Then we've been here a week today."

Lloyd asked, "Why are you in here?"

"Because," Paul said, "the leader of the WARLORDS asked me, no, ORDERED me, to come and work for them as their accountant."

Lloyd queried, "What did you tell him?"

"I told him no."

Lloyd asked, "Is that the only reason you are here?"

Almost as if the responses had been memorised, they were so close to Brutus's, Paul said, "The WARLORDS figure that everyone here has crossed the boundaries in the gang's rules and regulations, one way or another. Because I'm the accountant for the Devils, they think that I was able to access the WARLORDS' plans, and to get information out of some of the WARLORDS' men and to pass on the information on to Domingo, I'm pretty sure that's why they ordered me to come and work for them – so they could keep a close eye on me."

Greg broke in. "And did you?"

"Did I what?"

Greg said, "And did you cross the line and pass on information to the Devils?" Paul simply shrugged his shoulders, stubbornly noncommittal.

Lloyd looked at Paul. "The leader of the WARLORDS is dead. He died of a heart attack. The new leader is already in place and living in the WARLORDS' den."

For a brief moment, Paul looked excited. "Hey, we'll all be okay then. The new boss won't know what any of us did."

Greg interrupted again, "I doubt that very much, Paul. This new guy was a cop, and he's as tough as they come."

Deflated, Paul said softly, "Oh!"

Lloyd calmly leaned back in his chair. "Brutus said that Lester Laboucan brought all of you here by himself. That means to me that everyone that is captive here is a member of either the East Van Devils or an errant member of the WARLORDS. Would you agree?"

Another noncommittal shrug.

"Now, Paul," Lloyd said in a most deadly tone, "I want to ask, and if you don't give me a truthful answer, I can guarantee you that I will leave you to suffer, WHY DID YOU LIE TO ME?"

Paul stared, wild-eyed, at Lloyd. Feigning ignorance, he managed to blurt out, "What do you mean, why did I lie to you? About what?"

Speaking through a clenched jaw, Lloyd said, in a deceivingly calm voice, "You know what I'm asking you. But if you insist, here's the question and don't you DARE play dumb with me after I ask it or so help me, I'll call the WARLORDS myself and wait with you until they get here, and I'll personally hand them your head on a platter. Now, I'm asking for the final time, and bear in mind I already have a pretty good idea of the answer, WHY DID YOU TELL ME OUR MOTHER WAS DEAD OF A DRUG OVERDOSE? YOU KNEW SHE WASN'T DEAD, YET YOU TOLD ME SHE WAS!"

Greg placed a warning hand on Lloyd's shoulder before he looked over at Paul and said, "Answer Lloyd's question, Paul."

Paul looked appalled. "Who told you that, Lloyd? Anna isn't —"

Lloyd cut him off, "I TOLD YOU, DON'T PLAY DUMB; DO NOT LIE! You have 10 seconds before I pick up my phone and call the WARLORDS' new boss. Make no mistake about it; I will spill the beans. Working with you, I know a lot of your dirty little secrets, so you better start talking!"

"Have you seen her, son?" Paul asked. "Have you seen that pathetic, brainless excuse for a person? She is so addicted that she can't even remember her own name. I kicked her out of my office when she came begging for money, when she was so desperate for a fix that she was willing to do absolutely anything I asked her to do. My skin still crawls when I think of what she offered to do to me! When I kicked her out that day, I was done with her. She was dead to me. I don't consider telling you she died of a drug overdose to be a lie. Like I said, she was dead to me."

"You bastard," Lloyd said softly, his voice muffled. Tears streamed copiously down his face, dropping on to the floor when Lloyd bent over, his head in his hands. "I'll never forgive you for that, ever. I wish you were the dead one. You heartless, selfish bastard. 'You' are dead to 'me', but unlike you, I have no intention of lying about what you did. I hope you rot in hell. I hope you kill yourself. I hope I never see you or hear about you ever again." Lloyd got up from his chair, nodded at Greg, and left the room.

Greg looked at Paul. "You are a gigantic piece of shit, Paul Martin Jordan. I hope you suffer a million times over for what you did to your kids. When you go back to prison, I intend to spread the word that you abandoned your children, left them to fend for themselves at the tender ages of 9 and 13. Prisoners don't like child abusers, and that is what you were, Paul. Better say your prayers, because once you are in the pen, you won't have much time left to live."

Too disgusted to say anything further, Greg left the room, slamming the door behind him. Before he left, though, he taped Paul's mouth shut once again, even tighter than before.

"Lloyd, just check the remaining rooms on your side. Don't speak to anyone. Just make sure they are still breathing. Once everyone on our list has been accounted for, we will go back to the parking lot and wait and see what's next."

Paul lay still in his bed, unable to speak through the tape, unable to move because of the restraints. His mind was spinning; his eyes reflected nothing to indicate that he was sorry for anything he had done. They only reflected a scheming mind, already trying to find a way to weasel his way out of the sorry mess he had created for himself. Of course, it was not his fault that he was in this situation; it never was his fault. Right? Feeling mighty sorry for himself, Paul Martin Jordan could do nothing except lay in his bed and wait.

Chapter 12
Fredrich Gablehaus

Parked on the side of the street that faced the 'CAST ONLY' parking lot, the man in the expensive black car sat still, calmly waiting for something to happen.

Mindlessly, he lit another cigarette, forgetting that he had quit smoking several months ago. Despite an outwardly calm exterior, the man's guts were roiling and his temper was within a couple degrees of bursting the banks of the dam.

His eyes were on the fourth-floor windows. He knew, by looking at the chart in his hands, which window was the room that Anna Marie Jordan was in – Room #12 was the last window to the right on the street side of Building #4, Riverview Hospital. He wasn't too worried about Mrs Jordan at the moment. His thoughts and plans involved her husband, Paul Martin Jordan, Room #5, directly across the hallway from the third window to the right – Room #6.

Paul Martin Jordan, the man thought, *accountant for the East Van Devils. Arrested and thrown in cells this very night, charged with numerous, serious offences. Paul Martin Jordan, the biggest threat to me, Fredrich Gablehaus, new leader of the* WARLORDS. Fred laughed hollowly as he recalled how he had sent one of his gangsters to the gaol with bail money; how his flunky had waited for Mr Jordan to be released, and then brought him right back to this deserted building and plopped him right back into his bed in Room #5, chained him back to the bed, and gagged him tightly once again.

Fred had already scoped out the two vehicles parked near the entrance to the parking lot. The vehicle closest to the exit was a large, dark, multi-passenger van. Peering through his binoculars, he counted six officers waiting quietly in the lot. Each officer was wearing a Kevlar vest and appeared to be armed. Well maintained, the vehicle was running but quietly and with no lights.

The second vehicle was parked immediately behind the van. Fred Gablehaus could see no one inside. He recognised the vehicle for what it was, a ghost car. The unmarked police car was not running.

The new 'Big Chief' of the WARLORDS knew exactly what he had to do. He had appointed a less senior gang member to examine the area earlier in the evening. Confident that he would be able to gain entry into the building undetected, Fred Gablehaus stealthily exited his vehicle. He had earlier had one of the gang's mechanics make some changes to his car so that nothing, not the interior light, the dashboard lights, or any exterior light would illuminate when he opened or closed the car doors. A single button was now attached to the dash, just below the steering wheel. One press and voila! Total darkness. Press the same button once again and all the lights worked normally. Clad all in black, he was able to back up and wind his way to the back of Building #4 and go around the far side of the building, undetected by the team of bored-looking officers in the parking lot.

Finding the hidden opening to access the building proved a touch more difficult, but after a half-dozen swipes, he found it. The 'cop-turned-rogue' squeezed himself through the narrowest of openings, praying that no one noticed the pinpoint flashlight beam before he was in and had shut the door.

As silent as a cat, Fred ran up the stairs to the fourth floor. He opened the door just a sliver and listened intently for any sounds. Finally, hearing voices at the far end of the hall, he hurriedly raced to Paul Jordan's Room #5. Praying that the door was unlocked, he tried the knob. His heartbeats slowed to normal as he felt the doorknob turn easily in his hand.

With a now clear head and steady hands, he approached the bed where Paul Martin Jordan lay.

Seeing only a man dressed in black approaching his bed, Paul's eyes nearly bugged out of their sockets. He didn't recognise the man in the darkness of the room, but he clearly saw a knife in the man's left hand. Tossing his head frantically from side to side, Paul tried to holler, but because the tape was on so tight, not even a guttural grunt came out of his mouth. Restrained so tightly to the guardrails, he couldn't even wriggle his body an inch. All he could do was watch with dread as the man and the knife came closer and closer. The stranger bent his head down next to Paul's ear and whispered, "I'm going to take the tape off your mouth now, Paul Martin Jordan, and if you so much as whimper, and I hear you, I will slice your stomach open and leave you bleeding, for the flies to eat. Understand? If you do, blink twice." Blink. Blink.

"Good," Fred said, "you understand. Now lay still and keep your mouth shut!" He grabbed a corner of the tape with his right hand and ruthlessly ripped the tape off. By this time, Paul's forehead was pouring sweat, and he was shaking uncontrollably, but no sound escaped through his clenched teeth.

"Now, open your mouth, Paul Jordan."

"Why?" whispered Paul.

"Just – do – it!" Fred ordered, speaking succinctly through his gritted teeth. "And be quick about it." Recalling a childish game his mother had played with him when he was a little boy in order to get him to eat his vegetables, he recited to Paul, "Open your mouth and close your eyes, and I will give you a big surprise!"

Paul squeezed his eyelids shut, placed both hands over his eyes and opened his mouth. Before he could even begin to comprehend what was about to happen, Fred grabbed Paul's tongue with his rubber-gloved right hand. In the blink of an eye, his left hand, gripping the razor-sharp knife, came down like a bolt of lightning and cut off the front quarter of his tongue and the outer edge of his bottom lip!

Fred stood still, watching. "Now, Mr Paul Martin Jordan, let this be a lesson to you. You do not rat on any gang member, EVER! As you have just found out, there are consequences when you do. Let this be a deterrence. If I have to discipline you again, you won't survive because I'll cut out your heart."

Fred watched Paul watching him. "Now," Fred said, "I'm leaving. I suggest you give me time to get out of here and then you holler for Greg and Lloyd to come and help you before you bleed to death. So long, buddy; I suspect you will make a better gang member now that you know what's good for you!"

He turned away from the bed and silently slipped out of the room, down the stairs at the end of the hallway, out the hidden entry door and back to his vehicle. He got in just as the ambulance raced into the parking lot, the paramedics on their way to take Anna to the hospital.

Fred sat calmly, chuckling to himself. *I guess they will have room to take Paul with them. I can hear Paul hollering from here, so they certainly won't miss him.*

Starting his car, Fred figured he would have time to bail Lester out of gaol before Greg got back to the detachment.

All in all, an eventful first full day, Fred thought. *I'm pretty sure I'm going to love this job.*

He reached into his wallet to make sure he was carrying enough cash to bail Lester out and to 'pay' the justice to ensure that there would be no difficulty with Lester's release. That left him enough cash for his lawyer, Paulo Santonio, to give to the crown prosecutor so that a suitable deal could be made wherein guilty pleas to lesser charges could be entered, and every gang member who had been arrested in the last day would walk away with only small fines and no gaol time, other than time served while awaiting bail hearings.

Fred quickly jotted down the names of the remaining detainees. Earl Turner, Mickey McGuire, Jose Sanchez, and Billy Gray. The new 'Big Boss' ordered his driver take pick up all of those men quickly, before the police got them first and take them to Oppenheimer Park, to leave them wander homeless through the park, to live their unproductive little lives. When his driver reminded him that neither Jose Sanchez nor Billy Gray was homeless, Fred just shrugged his shoulders. "Dump 'em off there anyway," he ordered. "Who cares what happens to them – not I. Just do as you're told."

As for Bernard (Brutus) Belcourt, Fred Gablehaus had big plans. Once he had checked with the courts and got rid of any outstanding criminal charges that might be hovering about, Fred intended to make Brutus his second-in-command. The man was bright but not overly so, and he would follow orders. Fred was comfortable with his choice; he truly believed that Brutus had all the qualifications necessary to be Fred Gablehaus' biggest asset.

Yuppers! Fred thought gleefully. *All in all, an eventful first full day. I'm going to love being the 'Big Boss' of the WARLORDS, I most certainly am!*

Chapter 13
Domingo Sanchez

Before leaving at the end of this traumatic day, Greg called his superintendent and requested a meeting. His superior officer was just going to leave for the day; however, he agreed to meet, so long as Greg came to head office immediately.

Lloyd had already left. He was going for a run and would meet Greg at home.

Greg reached Superintendent Julie McMaster's office, in the downtown headquarters of the Vancouver City Police, in less than 20 minutes. Superintendent McMaster rose and shook Greg's hand firmly.

"Please, Sergeant Gablehaus, have a seat. What can I do for you? You sounded pretty stressed when we spoke on the phone a little while ago."

"Thank you for agreeing to meet with me, Superintendent," Greg said. "I appreciate it."

Superintendent Julie McMaster listened intently as Greg filled her in on the recent happenings. Although she was already aware of everything Greg told her, she said nothing until he finally ceased to speak.

"Greg, thank you for coming to me. I appreciate the fact that you filled me in before the rumour mill reached my office."

"Sergeant Gablehaus, listen to me! You are an excellent policeman. I know that your brother's involvement with the WARLORDS is going to cause difficulties for you. I want to assure you that you have my support and that we will sort out any problems as they arise."

She stood up and held out her hand. Greg shook it gratefully.

"Now, young man," Superintendent McMaster said gently, "Go home! Get some rest so that you can continue to be the exemplary role model you have always been."

Driving home, Greg felt at least some of the tension between his shoulders easing. He knew that he had done the right thing by speaking to his superintendent in such a timely fashion. *At least I can cross that hurdle off my bucket list*, he thought as he pulled into his driveway.

. . . .

No one slept well in the home of Greg and Bethany Gablehaus. Greg couldn't sleep because of the lasting shock of finding out that his beloved brother, Fredrich, had been working for the WARLORDS for years, using his professional capacity as a policeman to enable him to win favour with each new 'Big Boss' that took over. It certainly explained why there was so much drug running activity in northern Alberta and why so few runners crossing the British Columbia-Alberta border were ever charged with any criminal offences. And it certainly explained how Domingo found out where Lloyd and Lacey were living and how Domingo showed up and ran them off the road during the moving expedition to the farm.

Greg had no doubt that Fred would avoid any consequences from the current hostage taking situation, serious or otherwise. The biggest plus he had going for him was that he was not in Vancouver at the time of the abductions. Fredrich Gablehaus had been back in Alberta. He had retired shortly before he officially accepted the offer from the WARLORDS to take over the leadership of the most powerful gang in the Province of British Columbia. He knew he was going to accept the challenge, and so he made sure that he retired before any rumours could surface about his change in 'careers'.

Although they were highly suspicious, the R.C.M.P. had no proof that Fred had been working for the gang and the police simultaneously. Consequently, he was able to retire with full pension before it was revealed that he was now the leader of the WARLORDS! Greg had never heard of any other police officer working for a gang and the police force at the same time and getting away with it. *Disgusting dirty cop!* he thought as he lay in bed, wide awake for hours, his mind turning dizzying summersaults in the darkness.

Greg agonised over the fact that he hadn't figured out that something was amiss. He ignored the fact that the two brothers lived in different provinces and worked for different police forces. He also was ignorant of the fact that his brother was so brilliant – evil but brilliant. Greg always knew that his brother was smart, but he sure had not realised the depth of Fred's ambition and his cold-blooded leadership abilities.

It was going to take a very long time for Greg to come to terms with the fact that he no longer (in his own mind) had a brother. He was pretty sure that some of his own city police brothers would be watching Greg closely, figuring the 'apple doesn't fall far from the tree'. That part Greg wasn't worried about. He knew he was an exemplary cop. They could surmise whatever they wanted about him; he was squeaky clean.

. . . .

Bethany Gablehaus couldn't sleep because she was so concerned about Greg's reaction to discovering that his brother was the leader of the most evil, notorious gang in British Columbia. She had no doubt that her husband had the strength of a lion when it came to enforcing his policing duties, but even Sampson lost his strength when they cut off his hair! Bethany lay in bed, agonising, trying unsuccessfully to predict if and when this family catastrophe would break him. Greg had always been close to his family, and this irrevocable split was bound to cause some very hard times for her husband.

As if reading her thoughts, Greg rolled away and softly uttered a most hearrending moan. Bethany snuggled close to his back, wrapped her arms around Greg, and squeezed with all her might, trying desperately to convey her love and support for her man.

. . . .

Lloyd couldn't sleep for a few reasons. The first was, he was homesick. He missed Susanna something awful, and he missed Lacey and Parker. This past week had been so full of all kinds of happenings that it was mind blowing.

The second reason he couldn't sleep was Domingo Sanchez. Domingo was required to show up in court for plea the next day. Lloyd fervently prayed for two things – #1, that Domingo would actually show up, and #2, that he would change his plea and be sentenced immediately. Why? Because, if Mona Grace had to appear at his trial as a witness, who knows what might happen. When it came to Mona Grace and Domingo, it was a crap shoot. It was almost as if he had cast a spell over her. If she didn't see him, she was fine; if he showed up, she lost her entire ability to reason and sort out the good from the bad! He worried that if she had to testify against Domingo, the end result would not be pretty. He was sure that should she support Domingo rather than help to put him away in prison for many years, and he was released, Mona Grace would take up with Domingo once again. Charley would disown her mother. That would be a tragedy for both of them.

Lloyd worried as well for his friend, Greg. Lloyd had believed for years that being deserted by his parents was the absolute worst thing that could happen to a kid; now, he wasn't so sure that it really was the worst! He couldn't imagine how he would feel in Greg's shoes – to go from having a brother you adored to having an evil brother who would stop at nothing to get what he wanted, no matter how wicked or evil, and to hell with the consequences? Unthinkable.

The last thought that entered Lloyd's head as he finally drifted off to a fitful sleep was about the tiny little person growing inside his wife, and the tiny little human being that grew inside his sister. Those little ones would have the best upbringing possible, the idyllic childhood that neither Lloyd nor Lacey had after being abandoned. Those two little cousins would even have each other to play with. Finally, a soft smile spread across his face, and Lloyd was able to doze.

. . . .

Charley couldn't sleep because she was worried sick about her mother. Nobody seemed to believe that Mona Grace was truly over her obsession with Domingo. Charley certainly did not believe it! She struggled between anger with her mother, so thick that she couldn't discuss anything civilly, and empathy, so emotion-plugging that she couldn't discuss anything with Mona Grace that might cause her even more emotional turmoil.

Charley had never had a serious relationship with anyone, man or woman. That made it even harder to understand her mother and Domingo's on again-off again love affair. Well, love on her mother's part anyway. Charley didn't believe for a single second that someone who was leading an evil gang was capable of love. Domingo was a user, a tormentor.

Charley was trying mightily to support Mona Grace, but it was definitely an uphill climb. She suspected that this was the beginning of many more sleepless nights before this 'Domingo thing' was truly complete.

. . . .

Mona Grace couldn't sleep for both physical and emotional reasons. Still not completely healed from the vicious beating inflicted by Domingo upon her, she got up and did some stretches, went into the bathroom to get a pain pill, being careful not to disturb Charley, who lay unmoving in the twin bed next to Mona Grace's, her back to that bed. Rather than try to crawl back into bed before the pain medication kicked in, she sat stiffly on the toilet lid, waiting and thinking about Domingo and his appearance in court the next morning. *Nobody understands our love for each other*, she thought as she sat in the dark. *Nobody knows the horrendous childhood he had; nobody knows the stress caused by running a gang. I consider myself so lucky to be his stress relief.*

Charley calls me his punching bag, but Charley has never even had a boyfriend; she doesn't understand that Domingo hits me, not because he hates me but because he loves me. If he didn't do what he does, he would explode. I'm the only one in the world, besides Domingo, who understands that!

. . . .

Everyone understood that nothing would happen in court on Tuesday morning other than a plea would be entered. If Domingo plead not guilty, a trial day would be set and the justice would either release him, with conditions, until the trial date, or remand him in custody until then. A guilty plea could go one of two ways; either the justice might sentence him right away, or he could adjourn the matter for sentencing at a later date. The latter scenario was the most likely disheartening as it would be to drag things out for an even longer time. If the justice ordered that Domingo be admitted to the psychiatric hospital for a psych report, then the delay would be even longer.

It was pretty quiet around the Greg and Bethany Gablehaus breakfast table. Each person was sunk into their own deep, dark thoughts. There wasn't one of them who was willing to miss this court date, short as it might be. The group headed out to the courthouse as soon as the breakfast dishes were cleared away. They took both Greg's car and his wife's and arrived with a half hour to spare.

Once they cleared the scanner, they waited outside the courtroom, waiting for the clerk to open the door. Greg kept looking at his watch and then over at Bethany. He then paced from one end of the hallway to the other. Lloyd just assumed that he had a lot on his mind and was trying to walk off some of his frustrations.

A tap on Lloyd's shoulder caused him to turn around. Without paying any attention to who had tapped him, he foggily asked, "What?" A soft giggle had him paying attention! Standing beside him was his beloved Susanna!

"Whatever are you doing here?" Lloyd asked as he lifted his wife into the air, putting her down with a loud sloppy kiss, for once oblivious to other people's reactions.

"Oh, I'm so happy to see you." Stopping abruptly, he gasped, "Is anything wrong? The baby?" Before he could work himself up into a full-blown panic attack, Susanna assured him that everything was just fine, that she simply couldn't wait any longer to see him and, with Greg's help, here she was! Before they could converse further, the court clerk opened the doors to the courtroom and the group quickly found seats together, close enough to the front that they would be able to see Domingo's face as he stood before the court.

Early, earlier in the morning – 3:30 am, in fact, Fredrich Gablehaus answered an urgent ringing of the doorbell on his front door. *Where the heck is everybody?* Fred thought as he fumbled for his robe and slippers. "Yeah, yeah, yeah," he bellowed, "hold your horses! I'm coming. This better be good!"

Just as he was reaching for the doorknob, the ringing changed to a furious pounding. When Fred opened the door, he came very close to getting his face punched, rather than the heavy door!

"This better be good!" he repeated, staring at Bill-Don Santos, the senior enforcer for the WARLORDS.

"Let me in quickly, Senor Boss," Bill-Don pleaded. "We cannot take any chances on someone seeing you and me together. Let me in."

Fred looked around and, seeing no one, stepped aside so his employee could enter. After closing and locking the door, he turned and said, "What can possibly be so urgent at 3:30 in the freaking morning that you have to disturb my sleep?"

"Senor Boss," Bill-Don said urgently, "I would not have come here if it was not necessary. You know that Domingo is scheduled for court this morning, right?"

Fred Gablehaus nodded, stood impatiently facing his enforcer with his arms folded across his chest. "So…?" he queried.

Bill-Don took one look at his boss's intolerant face and spoke more quickly. "Senor Boss, I have just heard that the prosecutors' office is going to ask for time served if Domingo will spill the beans about not only the activities at the East Van Devils' Clubhouse but the comings and goings of the WARLORDS. He must tell many stories to the prosecutor; otherwise, he will spend his life in prison for all his criminal activities. I thought, senor, that you would like to know this as soon as possible."

Fred stared at Bill-Don. "What do you propose should be done?" he asked.

Humbled but very nervous to be asked by the Big Boss for his opinion, Bill-Don Santos stumbled a little as he spoke one word. "Suicide?"

Fredrich Gablehaus, newly appointed crime boss for the WARLORDS, said calmly, "Bill-Don Santos, make it so."

. . . .

In the courtroom, at 10 am, just before the clerk was about to call the justice to say they were ready, she was approached by the prosecutor. He handed her a sheet of paper, folded in half. The clerk looked up questioningly at him. "Please give it to Justice Tanner, Madam Clerk, before court convenes. It is very important."

The clerk waved one of the police officers over and asked him to keep an eye on things while she was away from her desk. She was back within a couple of minutes, turned on her recorder, and announced, "Order in court, all rise!" As soon as the justice entered the courtroom, the clerk said, "Court is now in session. The Honourable Justice G.P. Tanner presiding. You may be seated."

Justice Tanner glanced down at the piece of paper in his hands, then scanned the courtroom briefly before he spoke. "In the matter of Domingo Sanchez, I have just been informed that Mr Sanchez, early this morning, committed suicide in his cell. Mr Prosecutor, do you wish to withdraw the charges against Domingo Sanchez?"

The prosecutor's voice was barely audible over the sound of a woman's scream. Mona Grace rose out of her chair, yelling, 'No! No! It's a lie!' before she crumpled to the floor in a dead faint.

Epilogue

Watch Your Back

Greg Gablehaus had his work cut out for him. Because the new leader of the WARLORDS was his brother, Fredrich Gablehaus, the chief of police wanted Greg to resign from the Vancouver City Police. Although Greg was a highly respected police officer, the chief couldn't see how there could not be a conflict between the present time and the time when either Fredrich Gablehaus would be convicted and behind bars, or a different WARLORDS leader was chosen or appointed. If previous leaders were any indication, that could be years in the future!

After several days of seriously thinking things through, Greg made an appointment to meet with the chief of police. Superintendent Julie McMaster accompanied him, together with a union representative. After a lengthy four-hour meeting, the chief finally agreed to let Greg stay, on the stipulation that at the first sign of even the slightest favouritism, Greg would be immediately dismissed from the Vancouver City Police, without a reference.

Greg had no problem with that harsh condition. As far as he was concerned, he no longer had a brother named Fred.

The chief of police stood up at the end of the meeting, shook Greg's hand, and said, firmly and succinctly, "Good luck, Greg. Remember this. You won't know WHERE, you won't know WHEN, you won't know IF, but you will be under scrutiny at all times while your brother is not only leader of the WARLORDS but a gang member of any rank. Watch your back."

. . . .

Visit to Coquitlam

Greg and Lloyd had their hands full with Mona Grace. With the assistance of a paramedic who happened to be in the courtroom at the time the announcement of Domingo's suicide was made by Justice Tanner, Mona Grace was revived from her fainting spell, and they took her back to Greg's house.

Mona Grace sat motionless on a chair in the living room, stared down at her hands as if they belonged to someone else. Silent tears rained down her cheeks and puddled on the floor. She appeared to see nothing, notice nothing, hear nothing, even though Charley sat beside her, holding her mother's hand, speaking softly and encouragingly. She didn't respond to questions, nor did she respond to someone touching her to try to get her attention. Finally, in desperation, Greg called his family physician, who came immediately to the Gablehaus home and examined poor Mona Grace. He could get no reaction from her. Even when he checked the bottom of her foot with a sharp object and gently hammered her knee to test her reflexes, there was no reaction. No part of her moved, not even her eyelids. She appeared to be in some sort of catatonic state.

The perspicacious doctor called the psychiatric hospital in Coquitlam and arranged for the unfortunate woman to be admitted forthwith. Hanging up, he then called for an ambulance, which arrived in surprisingly short order.

Once the EMTs had loaded Mona Grace into the ambulance and headed off to Coquitlam, the doctor turned to Greg, Lloyd, and Charley, and said, "I would like to suggest that you all stay here and perhaps come and see Mona Grace tomorrow. You have all had a shocking day, and to be honest, looking at each one of you, I must tell you that I don't have time to take all of you on as new patients today. I have other patients to see."

"Lie down. Even if you think you can't sleep, get some rest. If you rest up, when you go to see Mona Grace tomorrow, things will fall into place much more easily."

"Thanks, doc," Greg said and shook the doctor's hand warmly. "We'll try to do what you have suggested."

Once the physician had departed, Greg told everyone that they should all heed the good doctor's advice and get some rest. He and Bethany headed down the hallway to their bedroom. Charley appeared dazed. She slowly descended the stairs and went to her room to try and rest.

Patting Susanna on the shoulder, Lloyd said he would be down as soon as he called Lacey.

"I think Lacey needs to fly here as soon as she can get on a plane, Susanna. I'm not sure how to tell her why the urgency, but I just realised that our mother, as well as Evelyn Bronson and Mona Grace, are all residents of the Coquitlam psych hospital."

"I haven't even told Lacey that I have found our mother, let alone that Mum is a hopeless mental patient, thanks to our father, who made sure she had a continuous supply of illegal drugs and treated her in such a vile manner that she lost all confidence and respect. Lacey needs to come with me. She won't believe me until she sees for herself."

"Call her, Lloyd," Susanna said quietly. "See you in a bit."

Finding himself alone in the kitchen, Lloyd sat at the table, head in his hands, mustering up the courage to call Lacey with the news that their missing mother was missing no longer, if only in body and not in spirit.

He pulled his cell phone out of his pocket and hit the speed dial for Lacey and Parker's. As luck would have it, Parker answered the phone. Lloyd explained everything that had happened to date to Parker, including the fact that the man who had been Parker's best man at his and Lacey's wedding was the new Big Chief, Grand Pooh-Bah, Leader of the WARLORDS. Whatever you wanted to call him, he was it.

He explained to Parker that Anna Marie was a permanent resident of the psychiatric hospital, a victim of drug abuse and mental abuse, thanks to Paul Jordan. Bitterly, Lloyd told Parker about the tremendous lie that Paul had told Lloyd, telling him that his mother was dead of a drug overdose, when indeed she was not!

Parker asked Lloyd where his father was now. Lloyd bitterly replied that he neither knew nor cared. The only thing that Paul Martin Jordan was to Lloyd was a biological sperm donor. He had no father.

Sensing that Lloyd was about to break down, Parker assured him that he and Lacey would be on the first possible plane to Vancouver. He said he would call Lloyd back with their arrival time.

Lloyd assured Parker that he would pick them up at the airport and they would head straight to Coquitlam. He felt more than slightly guilty for leaving Parker to break all the bad news to Lacey, but he just didn't have the mental strength to do it over the telephone. With a deep sigh, Lloyd headed down the stairs towards the welcoming, comforting arms of his beloved wife.

By three o'clock the next afternoon, Lloyd and Susanna were waiting at the airport for Lacey and Parker to arrive. Too many emotions bubbled and broiled in Lloyd's brain for him to remain still. He paced up and down the lengthy hallway in the arrivals area, artfully dodging people as he navigated the crowded aisle.

Finally, he spotted his sister and brother-in-law. They stood with their arms around Susanna as they waited for Lloyd to return from his pacing. Muttering apologies as he bumped into people, Lloyd raced towards his family. Reaching Lacey first, he grabbed hold of her and swung her off her feet. She giggled loudly, then hollered, "Put me down, you fool! You're scrambling the baby! It's no longer an egg! Put me down!"

Lloyd acquiesced, then turned to Parker and gave him a manly hug. "Thanks, man," he whispered to his brother-in-law. "I owe you."

Once the luggage had been collected and stored in the back of Greg's jeep, which he had generously lent to Lloyd for the day, Lacey had a million questions. Susanna answered as many as she could as Lloyd was too busy trying to navigate through the dense airport traffic and get on the main road to Coquitlam.

"I think we should stop for a quick supper before we go to the hospital," Susanna suggested. "It's close to suppertime now, and besides, Lacey and I are each eating for two these days, and we're hungry, right, Lace?" Although terribly anxious to see her mother, Lacey agreed that they should probably eat first. Lloyd pulled over to the first decent-looking restaurant that he spotted, parked the jeep and they went in. As they sat waiting for their food, Lloyd tried to prepare Lacey for what she was about to see at the mental institution. Lacey kept insisting that everything would be okay, that when their mother saw Lacey, she would recognise her. Everything would be okay. Lloyd finally gave up. Lacey would have to see for herself. He switched the subject, asking about the farm and how Lacey was feeling. Still in early pregnancy, she assured her brother that she was feeling just fine; the farm was fine; Parker was fine too.

An hour later, all four young people were standing outside the door to Anna Marie's room. Taking a deep breath, Lloyd opened the door and walked over to her bed, reached for her hand. It lay motionless beneath Lloyd's. She gave no sign of recognition.

Lacey uttered a heartbroken gasp as she stared at the woman lying in the bed. Nothing Lloyd had told her had prepared her for her first look at the woman who had birthed her. She lay there, broken, an empty shell. Wherever her brain was, it was not within the skull of this tormented, demon-ridden creature.

Lacey leaned over and kissed her mother's cheek. She whispered, "Hi, Mama. It's me, Lacey. Don't you know me?" The skeleton of a woman lay there, unresponsive other than continually picking at the blanket that covered her and moaning continually.

Suddenly, an obnoxious odour permeated the noses of Lloyd, Lacey, Susanna, and Parker. Anna Marie had soiled the bed. She gave no sign of awareness.

Susanna quickly slipped out of the room, in search of a nurse. Returning with a kind and caring woman in a white uniform, the nurse asked that everyone leave the room while she made her patient more comfortable. She directed them to a waiting room at the end of the hall and told them the doctor would be with them shortly.

As they waited for the doctor's arrival, Lacey lay her head on Parker's shoulder, too distressed to speak. Finally, she lifted her head and told Lloyd she forgave him for not telling her sooner about Anna Marie. "I wouldn't have believed you, Lloyd," she said brokenly. "That's not our Mama lying there. She's gone." Salty tears, unbidden, slithered down Lacey's cheeks and into the creases of her neck. Lacey paid no attention and so Parker got a Kleenex and wiped his wife's throat and eyes.

Within minutes, the doctor approached the waiting area. He quickly filled them in on Anna Marie's condition. "Unfortunately," he said, "Mrs Jordan will not get any better. The drugs have taken a terrible toll on her physically as well as mentally. It is only a matter of time, very short time, before she will no longer be with us."

"Why don't you just say it, doc?" Lloyd responded dully. "You're saying she is going to die and very soon, right?" He waited for the doctor to confirm or deny his statement.

"Unfortunately, you are correct," he said. "I'm very sorry."

As he turned to walk away, Lacey stopped him. "Please, doctor, just a minute more of your time. You have two other patients here. They are Evelyn Bronson and Mona Grace Ford. We understand Evelyn has been here for quite some time already, but Mona Grace was with my brother yesterday when she had her breakdown. Are you able to tell us anything more?"

The doctor just shrugged his shoulders. "Too soon to say," he muttered and turned and walked away.

Lloyd quickly ran after the doctor, explained that Mona Grace was the girlfriend of one Domingo Sanchez, leader of the East Van Devils gang who committed suicide in his gaol cell the morning before. Did the doctor know if that's what caused her breakdown?

An ambiguous expression appeared in the eyes of the doctor. At the mention of Domingo and the East Van Devils, he looked very nervous and turned immediately and walked away without looking back.

Returning to where the others were waiting, Lloyd suggested that they drop in and see Mona Grace for a brief visit and then stop in and see Evelyn.

All three of the patients appeared to be heavily drugged and malnourished. They understood Mona Grace's weight loss. The mess she had involved herself in by getting involved with Domingo once more, caused her internal turmoil, lack of appetite and consequently, weight loss. It was obvious that Anna Marie and Evelyn were not being fed nutritiously. It was a worry, but other than voicing their concerns, they were at a loss to repair a process that appeared to be firmly in place.

With Domingo deceased, there was no reason for Lloyd to stay in Vancouver any longer. Their mother didn't recognise them and apparently would never again recognise her own children, so there was not much point in staying for her sake.

When Lloyd had explained to Lacey their father's part in everything, she agreed that he was dead to her as well. There was nothing they could do about Paul Jordan.

What Goes Around, Comes Around

They booked a flight back to Alberta for the following day. That evening, they had a lovely farewell meal prepared by Bethany. They tried to convince Charley to come and stay with them in Alberta while Mona Grace recovered, but Charley refused their kind offers. She felt she needed to be close to her mother, visiting her whenever she was not in class, working towards completing her university education. She did promise to keep in touch and to check in on Anna Marie whenever she went to visit Mona Grace.

Back home, Lloyd threw himself into his furniture-making business.

They had only been home for a few days when Lloyd got a frantic call from Parker. Lacey had experienced severe stomach pains and had begun to bleed heavily during the night. Parker had rushed her to the small but excellent hospital across from the detachment. Sadly, she miscarried because of an ectopic pregnancy, which is sometimes referred to as a 'tubal pregnancy'. The fertilised egg had been lodged in one of Lacey's fallopian tubes. The other fallopian tube, it was revealed, was severely infected. An emergency hysterectomy had to be performed. Parker said she was doing as well as could be expected but was, of course, having a hard time, dealing not only with the loss of the baby but the fact that she would be unable to conceive.

Heartsick, Susanna and Lloyd endlessly discussed how best to help Lacey. They both agreed to tell Lacey and Parker (who, of course, suffered also), that they were available day or night should they need anything or just need to talk.

Susanna's due date arrived. Two days later, a healthy, beautiful baby girl was born without incident. They named her Anna Marie, after Lloyd and Lacey's mother. As she lay in the hospital bed, Susanna and Lloyd worried over the best way to help Lacey through what would be undoubtedly a difficult meeting between Lacey and her new-born niece. While they were still pondering this dilemma, a timorous tap on the door of Susanna's private hospital room sounded. Lacey and Parker entered the room. Lacey rushed to Susanna, who had just finished nursing her tiny daughter. Lacey had looked longingly at the little pink bundle and asked if she could hold her. With a growing lump in her throat, Susanna passed little Anna over to her Auntie Lacey.

Several minutes later, Lacey looked over at her brother and sister-in-law. Lacey gushed, "She's beautiful guys! Any time you need a sitter, Uncle Parker and Auntie Lacey are here to provide!"

"Oh! Guess what?" Lacey could switch lanes faster than a winning NASCAR driver. "Parker and I have been talking, and we have made a huge, important decision." Lacey looked over at Lloyd. "You, Lloyd, will understand this as well as anyone. We are going to meet with Child Services and apply to be foster parents. With our first-hand knowledge of the foster care system, we figure we will be perfect foster parents! And, who knows, we might even get the chance to adopt somewhere along the way."

Lloyd stared at his sister in total amazement. "Wow, Lacey! You surprise me! I thought you would be in the depths of despair and yet here you are, fully loaded and ready for bear! I'm so proud of you."

Shyly, Lacey stared at her brother. "This isn't a snap decision, Lloyd. We had talked about becoming foster parents even though we were having our own child. When we lost our baby, our hearts were broken. But you know the old saying, 'When God closes a door, he opens a window.' You and I both know the desperate need there is for good foster parents. I think we will be perfect!" At this point, Parker leaned over and squeezed his wife, hard.

There wasn't a dry eye in the room.

Finale

Two men and two women stood at the edge of the water. The late morning sun glistened brightly on gently dancing waves of emerald green. Their crafts waited expectantly, tied to the jetty. The men helped both women settle comfortably in the canoes before they climbed in and picked up their paddles. They glided smoothly along on the cool water, headed for the small island that beckoned in the distance. Reaching the land, the men positioned their canoes alongside an old jetty. They held the canoes steady, and Lacey climbed out of the craft. She approached the other canoe and Susanna handed the squirming little girl to her. She then reached in and removed a wicker picnic basket. Parker removed four folding lawn chairs from his canoe. It was beautiful on the shore of the island. A cool autumn breeze heralded the coming winter, but today, the sun shone brilliantly and warmed their cheeks as they sat on the beach. The man pointed skyward. "Look," Parker softly said. "See them? There are only four. One parent must have lost its love. Trumpeters mate for life, just like you and me." His wife smiled and patted his hand. Some time passed. Little Anna Marie played happily in the sand, filling, dumping, and re-filling her little plastic pail with her little plastic shovel. Nearly four years old, she was a bright little girl. Soon she would have a little brother or sister to keep her company, although she told her daddy very solemnly that she would rather have a puppy!

After an enjoyable picnic lunch, they packed up both canoes and headed for the centre of Mountain Goat Lake. Reaching the centre of the small lake, the men stopped paddling. Susanna leaned back against Lloyd, and he put his arms around her. Riding in the other canoe with her Auntie Lacey and Uncle Parker, Anna Marie trailed her small hand in the cool water, watching the ripples grow larger until they disappeared. They all quietly watched in the distance as a young deer drank from the water's edge, in the same spot they had sat only a few minutes ago.

Utter silence. Not even a bird trilled. The four Trumpeter swans floated in place; their beauty reflected in the stillness of the water. Time stood still. Each lost in their own separate thoughts, they deeply appreciated the peace and the quiet. They fully realised that all too soon their busy lives would drown out their memory of this blissful silence.

After one last look at the island, with tears wetly rippling down her cheeks, Lacey reached to the bottom of the canoe and brought up a wooden container. She kissed the box and then gently placed two yellow roses on top. Before she lowered it over the side of the canoe, she kissed the box again.

"Good-bye, sweet Mama," Lloyd gently said.

"Good-bye, sweet Mama," Lacey echoed. After several minutes more, the men picked up their paddles and continued to paddle back from whence they had come.